The Crystal Ribbon

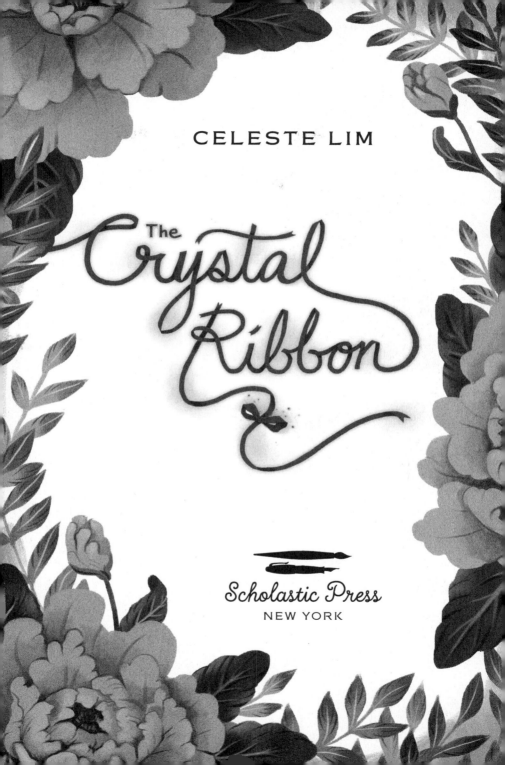

CELESTE LIM

The Crystal Ribbon

Scholastic Press
NEW YORK

Library of Congress Cataloging-in-Publication Data available

ISBN 978-0-545-76703-3

10 9 8 7 6 5 4 3 2 1   17 18 19 20 21

Printed in the U.S.A.   23

First edition, February 2017

Book design by Carol Ly

FOR ARTHUR AND CALVIN,
WHO BELIEVED IN ME
EVEN BEFORE I DID.
AND TO MUMMY, FOR ALL
THE *DATOU CAI* YOU MADE
ME EAT. I STILL PREFER
YOUR *YONG TOFU*.

■ 1 ■

AN UNUSUAL BIRTHDAY

If someone had told me two years ago that I would be married the year I turned eleven, I would've laughed at them and said, "But boys are filthy and stupid, like oxen! I shan't get married. Besides, my baba loves me more than any husband in the world could."

But that was before.

It was early spring, and for my eleventh birthday, Grandmama had agreed to slaughter a chicken—something more than our regular rice gruel, *mantou* buns, legumes, and bland corn broth. Just for me!

But when everyone sat down, the topic of marriage came to join us at our table. Aunt Mei was telling Baba about this maiden in the village who recently got engaged to a nice family, but Baba only nodded and gazed intently into his bowl as though trying to count the grains of rice in it.

I dared to interrupt. "What will happen to Lingling after she gets married, Baba?" I'd long ago learned that if I directed my questions or comments at Baba, I would be less likely to get reprimanded for interrupting a grown-up conversation. Baba never minded my questions, and would even laugh if my comments were witty.

But this time, Baba did not even look at me. Instead, he started chewing on the ends of his wooden chopsticks.

My heart plummeted faster than a rock down a ravine. I stopped eating. "Baba, what happens after someone gets married?"

Baba looked around at the other grown-ups, but when both Grandmama and Aunt Mei said nothing, he sighed and scratched at the stubble on his neck. "Well, Jing . . . when a girl gets married, she leaves her family and goes to live with another."

Immediately, Wei's hand clasped mine underneath the table. My little brother didn't like the idea any more than I did. Leave my family to live with someone else? I imagined waking up one day with a completely different family—voices I didn't know, faces I didn't recognize, people I didn't care about. I'd hate them. I'd be miserable.

I gave Baba what he usually called my I-know-better look. "Then I don't ever want to get married. I want to stay here forever."

"Don't be silly, child!" Aunt Mei cried, flourishing the sharp end of her chopsticks just inches from my nose. A single grain of rice spewed out of her mouth and landed on the plum-sauce-roasted chicken. "What a disgrace to the Li family you'll be if you don't get married," she continued. "When the time comes, you will wed."

To my surprise, even Grandmama nodded as she picked up a piece of pickled carrot. "We will have to start looking for a suitable family soon."

Aunt Mei probably needed a suitable family more than I did. But I knew better than to answer back, for it was seen as great disrespect for children to do so.

Aunt Mei was Baba's older sister, and had been married to Uncle Tai, a blacksmith in our village. Having no in-laws, she eventually came back to live with us after Uncle Tai died at war nine years ago. No one ever mentioned that Aunt Mei should remarry, but back when she was still alive, Mama had told me that men rarely considered widowed or divorced women as wives because they were thought to bring bad luck. One time I asked, "Why then do we keep Aunt Mei with us if she's bad luck?" and Mama had hitched on such a stern look that I never dared ask again.

▫ ▫ ▫

After breakfast, Wei and I kneeled in front of the small wooden altar on the ground beside our front door. On it were three tablets carved out of bamboo: two of them belonged to deities—Guan Yin, the goddess of mercy, and the Great Golden Huli Jing, the guardian fox *jing* of our village. The last one was Mama's mortuary tablet, and on it were the words, written in red: *Here be the place of early departed daughter-in-law of Li—Wu Caihua.*

I brought my hands together, holding a lit incense stick, and bowed thrice. I closed my eyes.

Mama, I don't want to go to another family. Please watch over me; don't let me leave you.

Finally, I stuck my incense into the incense holder, moved back, and touched my forehead to the ground in a kowtow.

Then Pan began to wail from his reed cradle, and from the fitful way he cried, I could tell he was uncomfortable from wetting himself. I hurried with a clean rag into the room Wei and I shared. At about twenty moons, Pan was still a wrinkly little thing. His nose turned slightly upward like a pig's snout, especially whenever he cried, which was why I called him Zhuzhu.

Ever since Mama left us after giving birth to Pan, I had been put in charge of caring for him. Wei and I had believed the reason we lost Mama was because of Pan. The midwife said that Mama had bled too much. But Grandmama did not take the responsibility away from me even though I hated it so much. I had sulked and cried and sulked. I hated the idea of Pan replacing Mama in our family, and Grandmama would often scold me for being neglectful in my babysitting. On my cruelest day, I even left Pan in the daisy field on purpose, thinking that wolves could have him.

But no one ever found out my horrid deed, because as I left, my heart started to feel as though someone was using a soy grinder on it.

Pan was only a baby. He never meant to cause Mama's death. He hadn't asked to be born. Mama had birthed him out of love, and here I was, trying to harm the son for whom she had given her life. Would I really dishonor my mother like that?

I had gone back for Pan. And from then on, I made a promise that I would love him as much as Mama would have if she were alive. I would be the mama Pan would never have, and in that way, I kept Mama alive in my heart.

"Zhuzhu, it's time for breakfast," I crooned as I nudged a spoon of rice gruel mixed with goat's milk to his mouth. Then Baba poked his head into the room. "Jing, come down to the farm later. It's time to dry out the tea leaves."

Wei let out a squeal and my heart missed a couple of beats. Was Baba finally allowing us to help with tea drying? But there was something else.

"Baba, are we going up to the Huli Jing shrine today?"

It was the first week of spring on the lunar calendar, which was when every family in the village prepared offerings from our harvests and produce to pay homage to the tutelary spirit of Huanan village—a powerful five-tailed fox *jing* known as the Great Golden Huli Jing.

Sure enough, Baba nodded. "Yes, after noon. Aunt Mei is helping Grandmama prepare our offerings, so I'll need your help on the farm. Don't be too long."

There was a knowing grin on Baba's face as he left, and I couldn't wait for tea-drying time. After Zhuzhu finished his food, I placed him in his wooden playpen, where Grandmama could watch him from the kitchen, and I dashed out the front door with Wei behind me.

Our village was small, with only two streets—a wider one that led to the village square, where there was a cluster of hawker stalls, and a smaller dirt path that went an entire circle around the village, leading to the wooden huts of twenty-nine families. I always thought this made a shape like a copper coin—a circle with a square in the center. Wei and I weaved in and out among the stalls on the bustling street. I barely dodged Peng's flower cart, heaped with early violet columbines.

Huanan village was settled halfway up the east side of a hill. Behind our house was higher ground, and a stream running from farther up the hill provided the irrigation our farmlands needed. Beyond the bamboo fences that surrounded our village were patches of carefully plowed land. Each family had their own plot, and in ours, Baba grew simple crops such as jujubes, prunes, tea leaves, and various legumes.

The farm was always busiest during the day. When we arrived, villagers already dotted the entire plot like sesame seeds on rice, wide-brimmed straw hats pulled over their heads to keep out the sun. We found Baba in our harvest shed, checking on the condition of the tea leaves we had picked a few days ago. The young flushes had been loosely scattered on straw-woven trays, and Baba had a small pinch of them under his nose. The room was airy and filled with the slightly stale scent of wilted tea leaves. I walked up to another tray and rolled a little pinch of leaves gently between my fingers.

Still slightly springy but dry around the edges . . . I could be wrong, but they should be ready for the wok.

Sure enough, Baba gave a satisfied grunt. "These will make a fine batch of black tea indeed. It's time to dry them out completely. Wei, go get our biggest wok."

Wei practically floated out of the shed, and I could see why. Black tea was popular and usually sold for a lot of money, especially in the colder seasons. Harvesting a good batch at this time of the year could easily mean a more comfortable winter.

By the time Wei came back with a metal wok as big as a cart wheel, Baba had already moved a few trays outside, and we were making heat from a pile of embers inside a stack of bricks.

"Baba, Grandmama says we need to head over to the shrine soon," Wei reported as I helped him set up the wok. "We won't have time to finish drying all of them."

Baba nodded, placing his bare hands on the wok to test the heat. After making sure the temperature was just right, he tossed in the first tray of leaves. "Well, we'll get at least a few trays done so some of them can be given to the shrine as part of our offering."

No.

Our family had hardly enough to feed ourselves as it was; couldn't Baba see that offering the tutelary spirit such good crops that would otherwise earn us money was a horrible waste? This was unfair. This was ridiculous. Couldn't the fox *jing* get food for itself? Why did it have to depend on our offerings? I couldn't help telling Baba exactly what I thought.

"Jing, you mustn't speak disrespectfully of the Great Golden Huli Jing."

Even when berating me, Baba managed to sound gentle. With his bare hands, he began to deftly toss and stir the black curly flushes in the wok. "The pact between Huanan village and its spirit guardian goes back more than thirty years. Our village owes the Golden Huli Jing a great debt."

"I know, I know," I cut Baba off and squatted to fan the embers underneath the wok with a straw fan. "If not for the Huli Jing, we wouldn't be here at all . . ." I'd heard the story so many times I could tell it backward. Every child in the village grew up listening to the tale about how the Great Golden Huli Jing saved Huanan from a fatal bandit raid some thirty years ago.

I wondered if Baba would berate me some more for interrupting, but he only nodded. "I understand why you do not feel the same way. But the grown-ups in Huanan view our guardian much in the same way as the people of Song view our Emperor Taizu, who ended the upheaval of the Ten Kingdoms and birthed our glorious Dynasty of Song. So, to Baba at least, that incident thirty years ago was truly something else . . . I was hardly older than you myself when it happened."

For Baba's benefit, I tried to imagine what it would've felt like to have seen the epic battle with my own eyes. In my mind, I was atop the village watchtower like Baba had been, just behind the outer fences, shielding my face against the howling storm as a line of burning torches encircled the village. The trepidation was real, just like the relief must've been, when in the nick of time, a giant five-tailed fox *jing* had appeared and fought off the ring of fifty bandits before they could raid and burn the entire village. Such a narrow escape from death would not have been forgotten easily.

Wei leaped off his perch on a wooden stool. "Baba, if I were you, I'd have jumped off that watch-tower like this and given those bandits a few good whacks with my shovel!" he exclaimed as he kicked and punched the air in front of him. "I wouldn't have needed any old *huli jing* to save me."

Baba only laughed as he tossed the tea leaves with his bare hands, not seeming to mind the heat from the wok at all. He was tough like that. People even called him The Man of the Iron Palm.

Thin wisps of steam from the drying flushes rose above the wok, carrying a fresh, woody aroma. I took a deep whiff. Did I still feel that the *huli jing* didn't deserve our expensive black tea? To be honest, I wasn't entirely sure I liked the idea much more than I had moments before, but at least now I understood that some promises, like the one our village chief made to the Great Golden Huli Jing about seasonal offerings, had to be kept. It was a question of honor.

Baba rose from his seat all of a sudden and gestured at me as he emptied the wok and tossed in a third tray of flushes. "Put on a pair of gloves. You're old enough to try this. And maybe we can offer yours to the shrine."

Wei squealed and jumped up and down as though Baba had spoken to him. "Can I try, too? Please, Baba?"

I couldn't help grinning when Baba shook his head. "You're only eight. Wait till you're a little older. Let's watch your *jiejie* and see how she does."

I leaned over to Wei when Baba wasn't looking. "I'll let you try once I get the hang of it." I winked.

Wei giggled and held out his right thumb. "Promise?"

I pressed mine to his and we slapped our palms thrice. It was a little thing we came up with called the Sibling Oath.

The thick fabric gloves felt prickly as I pulled them on, but before I could get to work, Aunt Mei appeared around the corner, and the eggplant look on her face as she approached us told me that I wasn't going to like what she had to say.

"Tao, surely you're not going to waste your time teaching her this?"

A frown formed between Baba's eyebrows. "I don't see why not."

Aunt Mei folded her arms and gave a laugh that sounded like a mating baboon. "Why? Because in a year or so, Jing will go to another family, and then what use will your lesson be? It's always more worthwhile to teach your sons; surely you know that?"

From his face, I really couldn't tell what Baba was thinking, but his next words put a big smile on my face.

"Wei and Pan are too young. And besides, I think my daughter can do just as good as any boy."

THE HULI JING SHRINE

A flight of steps made from horizontally placed logs led to the shrine farther up the mountain. Wei and I both knew there were eighty-nine of them, but we still liked to count with a beat as we skipped up each one. The grown-ups walked ahead of us, Zhuzhu sleeping soundly on Aunt Mei's back.

We wouldn't be the only family visiting the shrine today, so I wasn't surprised when we heard a sing-song taunt.

"Li Jing, Li Jing, Huli Jing!"

It was Lu Shang—someone I wished I could grind into soy milk. I turned around with a hand on my hip so it would look like I didn't care. Wei stuck out a tongue at him, but I kept my face straight and said, "I see your mother forgot to sew your mouth shut this morning."

Wei burst into laughter and the smirk disappeared from Lu Shang's face as he struggled to think of a comeback but, of course, couldn't. Boys loved making fun of my name, but most of them did not have very quick wits.

"You won't sound so cocky when I beat you at the tree-climbing match later, Huli Jing," Lu Shang said before shuffling off, tugging on the leash around the neck of a young goat.

"Bet you won't!" Wei stuck his tongue out after him. Now why do you suppose the Great Golden Huli Jing's name had to sound so much like mine? Couldn't Mama have thought of something else to call me? Li Jing and Huli Jing—with only one measly syllable of a difference, she was practically asking for kids to poke fun at her daughter.

"Why can't I have your name?" I grumbled at my brother and kicked a pebble in the general direction of the stream that flowed right by the shrine and down toward our village. Baba saw this and told Aunt Mei and Grandmama to go ahead of us. I crossed my arms and looked away. I wasn't about to be convinced.

Baba kneeled to my height and took my hand. "Jing, you should always be proud of your name. Your mother chose it with great care. A different word from the guardian's." Baba picked up a twig and told Wei to write two words on the ground:

晶　精

Then he tapped on the left character. "This is you, and it has a completely different meaning."

I kept my arms crossed. "I know, Baba, but it doesn't stop monkeys like Lu Shang from calling me names."

Baba got up with a smile and hurried us on. "I won't try to convince you any further, but I hope someday you will change your mind. Because regardless of whether you like it, it is still a part of you."

A brass gong hung near the entrance of the shrine, and worshippers rang it with a soft mallet before entering. Mama used to say that it was supposed to alert the deity residing within that someone had come to pray. My hands itched. Wei and I loved taking turns doing that, often more than once, and often until Yue Shenpo, our village shamaness, came out yelling at us. But today was different.

Today I was eleven. And I had my own tea leaves to offer the guardian. I shouldn't act childishly.

Wei dashed up the last few steps to reach the gong, and I called out, "Only once, Wei."

He turned to look at me, his left brow twitching a little. "Why? You love doing it yourself."

Now what could I do to deter him? I slid my shoulders back a little more so I looked taller. "I'm not doing it anymore. I don't want Shenpopo to come at me with her walking stick. I heard from Lu Shang when he'd stolen peaches from the shrine that it hurts really bad . . ."

Wei gulped and sullenly rang the gong just once. It produced a deep, reverberating chime. *Great Golden Huli Jing, here we come.*

We stepped into the front yard where the stone well stood in the center. Wei and I reached into the bucket beside the well and tossed prayer coins into it. When mine made a little splash, I brought my hands together. I probably should have wished to never be married, considering our family's unpleasant conversation earlier, but all I remembered was:

I wish I had a prettier name that no one could make fun of.

Then we headed into the shrine after the grownups, kicking off our fabric shoes before stepping onto the veranda. I followed the crowd toward the right side of the entrance hall, where the offerings were left so that Yue Shenpo could bless them later. I placed my box of tea leaves next to our family's offerings. The air was thick with the rich smell of sandalwood from the incense that was burning.

On the lacquered altar, behind rows of red candles and positioned between two giant sticks of incense thicker than my arm, was the statue of the Great Golden Huli Jing. It reached all the way up to the ceiling and looked old. Baba said that was because it was made of bronze, but that wasn't the most peculiar thing about it. The statue had the head of a fox, set on the shoulders of a man clad in warrior's armor, with five fox tails behind it. The sculptor must've been drunk while working on our statue, because it looked nothing like how Baba described the guardian, who looked like an actual fox, but stood as tall as a farming horse, with a snowy-white chest, a coat of brilliant golden fur, piercing emerald-green eyes, and five majestic white-tipped tails that fanned out behind it like a halo.

Yue Shenpo was sitting at her desk next to the altar with a thick fortune-telling manual. People formed a line to have their fortunes told—something the grown-ups seemed to love. Wei and I never understood enough to care for that, but Yue Shenpo was a very important person in the village, second only to the chief. Baba said she was like a mix of priestess, healer, exorcist, and fortune-teller. But in her black shaman robe with her hair pulled into a dull gray bun, she looked more like a mix of cider, pickles, soy sauce, and sun-dried prunes.

Someone behind Yue Shenpo waved at me, and when I stood on my toes, I saw Lian. She had been standing next to the doorway that led to the back of the shrine, handing out amulets. I turned to Wei.

"Stay in line for the prayer mats." I ignored his protest and darted over to Lian. She looked lovely today in a red apprentice *hanfu* dress, with her hair in two little buns on either side of her head.

"You have to come down to the village this evening," I said. Yi Lian was only twelve but had no family, so she had been taken in by Yue Shenpo and raised as her apprentice. I grabbed her hand that had several colorful amulets dangling from it. "Lu Shang says we're having a tree-climbing match later. You have to come watch me beat that son of a hopping zombie," I said. But Lian lowered her gaze.

"The shrine is really busy today, I don't know if Shenpopo will let me . . . ," she murmured.

Lian fidgeted with the amulets. She really wanted to come. And why shouldn't she if she managed to finish her chores? "I'll help you. Come, let's ask

Shenpopo." I pulled her over to where Yue Shenpo was waiting for the next villager.

"Shenpopo, *nin hao*." I bowed and greeted in my sweetest I-need-something-from-a-grown-up voice.

Yue Shenpo looked up from her manual and gave us one of those smiles that always reached her gray eyes. "*Ni hao*, dear child. Have you presented your offerings?"

I beamed. "I brought tea leaves that I dried myself."

It was nice to see Yue Shenpo nodding with approval.

"That is very good indeed. The Great Golden Huli Jing will grant your family a bountiful harvest this year," she promised, then opened up her thick manual and motioned for me to sit down. "Come."

I fidgeted with the green sash around my waist. Yue Shenpo was looking at me very closely. Could she really tell my future just by looking? If it was that easy, I could probably tell hers.

When she reached out and swept aside the hair over my forehead, I knew she was looking for the little red mole that nestled right in between my eyebrows. "A divine symbol of purity, this little thing," she said as her finger brushed over it. "But for you, Jing, it is a bringer of change."

Of course, the most obvious question to ask was, *What kind of change?* but before I could, Yue Shenpo had found the page she was looking for in her manual. She spun it around to face me. "You've never had your fortune told, so let's start with the basics. Which character belongs to you?"

I scanned the whole list of words that were all supposed to read *jing.* I had never been to school and might not recognize most of the characters, but I knew which one belonged to me. I found it near the bottom of the second column and pointed at the one that meant *crystal.*

Yue Shenpo peered closely at the inscriptions under my name. "You were aptly named, child. And you should know that a good name holds great power and often carries with it its owner's destiny."

Grrr. I had had about enough of grown-ups telling me to like my name.

As though she'd read my mind, Yue Shenpo smiled. "Lian often complains about how they tease you. But I can say this: It wasn't by chance that you were named thus." She took my hand and patted it. "Fate is *yuan,* and *yuan* is fate. It is like a ribbon that binds things together. And you, child, happen to share a lot of *yuan* with our guardian *huli jing.* This ribbon of Yuan that binds you together suggests an intertwined destiny."

"What kind of destiny, Shenpopo?" It was difficult to imagine that my fate could be in any way bound to something I had never even seen, but Shenpopo seemed determined to be what most grown-ups loved to be—overly mysterious.

"We shall know as life unfolds," she said as she turned the pages of her manual. "But you can be assured that because of *yuan*, the guardian will watch over you closely. And I believe you are going to need it, because it seems you have a rare calling." Yue Shenpo stopped at a particular page, and continued. "A calling that will lead you to many places, and bring good to those around you . . . anyone but yourself."

What kind of calling was that? It didn't sound nice at all. Would it be rude to tell a shamaness that you didn't quite appreciate the fortune she told?

Probably reading my thoughts again, Shenpopo said, "I know this sounds horrid, but dear child, no matter what happens in our lives, if we seek the home where our spirit belongs, we will always find refuge. And it's no use asking me where you'll find it, because not only is it different for everyone, it is one of those things you will have to figure out for yourself."

I didn't quite know what else to say other than the obvious "Thank you, Shenpopo." So this was why only grown-ups consulted the oracle—it was simply too difficult to understand! But now that this was over and done with . . .

"Shenpopo, I was wondering whether you could allow Lian to come play this evening. I know the shrine is busy, but if I stayed and helped Lian finish her chores before sunset, could she please come?"

Shenpopo waved her hand dismissively for the next villager in line. "I can handle a few dozen visitors without my apprentice. Just place the amulets in the basket by the main entrance and run along with Jing after she's done with prayers," she said to Lian, then added, "Be home before dark."

As we went back to the doorway, Lian's face brightened so much I could almost see drops of sunshine squeezing out of her eyes. "Thank you, Jing!" she said.

"I want you to come as much as you do," I said. When I turned to go, Lian tugged on my sleeve.

She held up the little fabric amulet bags in her hands. "Here, take an amulet for blessing," she said, then added with a wink, "Or two, since it's your birthday. But don't tell Shenpopo."

I picked out one of the red ones with pink plum blossoms embroidered on it. "What's this one for?" My guess would be love or something.

"That one's for romance and marriage," said Lian, making a face. "You don't want that. There are also amulets for health, studies, wealth, and protection," she said, holding up the other colors.

Marriage, hmm . . . I stroked my chin. Only boys went to school, so getting the amulet for studying was silly. I took one of the bright yellow amulets with Chinese gold ingots embroidered on it. "I'll take the one for wealth," I said, then stuck out my tongue as I took a red one as well. "And a red one, only because it's my favorite color."

"Liar!" Lian laughed as I ran back to where Wei was.

I stuffed the amulets under my waistband. I didn't care if I got teased; maybe this amulet could protect me from having to get married before I was ready. When it was our turn to pray, I lit my incense and kneeled on one of the moth-eaten cushions in front of the altar. I held up my three incenses—one for the body, one for the mind, and one for the spirit.

I closed my eyes.

Great Golden Huli Jing, I am sorry for the way I have been disrespectful toward you before today. I will continue to bring my own offerings to you from now on, and will try not to hate my name if you make Lu Shang stop teasing me about it. I suggest visiting him during the night and giving him a good scare. And if we really do share a lot of yuan, *please let me stay with my family forever. And help Wei and me win the tree-climbing match later. The prize is a big, fat, juicy peach.*

Ai, ma! What did I just see? I rubbed my eyes and looked again. The statue couldn't have grinned, could it?

Wei was still praying. I scrabbled onto my tip-toes. The statue had a long snout and a mouth that pulled all the way back. But there were no teeth, and never had been. So had I imagined that big toothy grin a moment ago?

Shenpopo said that like most *jing* in general, the fox *jing* was an elusive creature. Since its glorious deed thirty years ago, the Great Golden Huli Jing had only shown itself again once when the village was attacked by a pack of wolf *jing* during the Ghost Festival fifteen years back. So, like most of the other kids, I had never seen our guardian in the flesh.

But now I had! Or at least a hint of it. Maybe what Shenpopo said was true; perhaps the ribbon of Yuan did connect us. Wait till I told everyone! But would they believe me? Wei might, if I could make the statue move again. Perhaps if I concentrated hard enough . . .

I gazed so intensely at the statue I must've looked as though I was glaring at it. Didn't work. Was there something I wasn't doing right? But before I could try anything else, Wei tugged on my sleeve.

"Jie! What're you doing? Tree. Match. Peach. Now!" he cried and dashed out of the shrine with me and Lian after him. Mr. Huli Jing would have to wait for another day.

- 3 -

A TRIP TO XIAWAN

I never did get a chance to solve my little mystery of the grinning statue. Compared to things like the Lunar New Year, harvest season, and Wei's birthday, it wasn't very high on my priority list, *yuan* or no *yuan*. And so, spring came and went, bringing with it fair amounts of rainfall, and when the time for harvest came, Aunt Mei returned from town one fine day with the most exciting news I had ever heard from her.

"I'll be heading up to Xiawan early tomorrow."

"Xiawan?" Grandmama murmured, fanning off the afternoon heat with her straw fan. "It's that big city beyond the next mountain. It's a good place." She nodded approvingly.

"Yes," said Aunt Mei, then jabbed her chin in my direction. "Jing could come along with me if she'd like to."

I almost dropped Pan. Oh, would I love to! I wouldn't give this up for the emperor. "Yes!" must've been written all over my face, because Aunt Mei said, "You'll like it; it's a lot bigger than Baihe town at the foot of the hill."

At this, Wei jumped up. "I want to go, too! Please, Aunt Mei?"

"Certainly not. You have school, and you are not about to miss classes for something like this," Aunt Mei scolded.

"Well . . . can't we all go during the weekend?" I asked, keeping my voice tiny so Aunt Mei wouldn't think I was challenging her. I'd love for Wei to join us, but I didn't want to jeopardize my own chances of going.

"*Ai tian!*" Aunt Mei threw her hands up in the air. "This isn't a vacation, child. We'll be running errands for your baba, and that cannot wait," she said, giving Baba a nudge. "Isn't that right?"

Baba gave a tiny nod, but when Aunt Mei nudged him again, he said, "Be good, and listen to your aunt." He did not look at me when he said this, but at that time, I only vaguely wondered why.

▪ ▪ ▪

It was hardly past the hour of the ox when Aunt Mei shook me awake. The sun wouldn't even rise for ages. But today was special, and the earlier it started the better! I hopped out of the bed I shared with Wei, who was still snoring underneath the goatskin rugs.

I clawed at the itchy spots on my back that came from sleeping on a straw bed, then threw on a white linen robe. The autumn breeze attacked me as soon as I stepped out into the darkness. I wrapped my braid around my neck like a scarf and sprinted for the nearest public well. Unlike the nice prayer well at the shrine, this was just a hole in the ground built up with a couple of wooden beams. The flat wooden surface next to the well was where people showered and did their laundry, and a drain led the water out to the farmlands.

I grabbed one of the buckets on the side and lowered it into the well. When I emptied half its content over my head, I braced myself.

"*Ai, ma!*" I gasped. The water felt like a sheet of ice daggers. And my bathrobe now stuck to me like a second layer of skin. I scrubbed myself with a rag and as much haste as I could before emptying the rest of the bucket onto myself.

When I arrived back in our hut, Aunt Mei already had a fire going in the stone hearth and was making congee.

"*Zao an*, Aunt Mei," I greeted her before darting into my room.

"Put on your *hanfu*," Aunt Mei said. "We're getting a new one for you this year, so we'll need your measurements."

Did Aunt Mei really say *new hanfu*? I bundled up my robe and squealed into it. *Hanfu* were fancy, semiformal clothing that men and women wore during major festivals, and the ones sold in bigger towns were expensive. The only one I had was one Grandmama had made me for my eighth birthday. It had a white, cross-lapelled top and a pale orange full skirt with motifs of pink and purple peonies above a white underlayer. The skirt had a *yaoqun* that went around the waist like a thick band and was secured in place with a pale green sash.

It'd be nice to do a simple little *faji* to match my dress, so I grabbed a couple of ribbons and began to braid the topmost portion of my hair. It occurred to me as I brushed the rest that eleven was beginning to feel like an age of breakthroughs—tea-drying for the first time, my first offering to the guardian, visiting a new city, getting a new *hanfu* . . . new adventure, new experiences!

I had no idea then how true my thoughts were to become.

▪ ▪ ▪

Aunt Mei and I set out downhill for Baihe town before sunrise. We spent almost an entire day on a horse carriage that went straight to Xiawan. By the time our vehicle passed through the towering stone-carved gates of the city, my behind already felt like it could use a trip to the acupuncturist. I couldn't bear to sit on it a moment longer. Besides, there was too much to see out the window. Xiawan was so huge and vibrant. Baihe town, where our family sold our produce every weekend, wasn't even half the size of this one.

"Aunt Mei, look! There's a man doing kung fu on the streets."

I shifted onto my knees in my seat and turned to look behind our carriage as we passed a crowd gathered around a burly, half-naked man who was flourishing a Chinese broadsword. "Look at that huge weapon he's wielding! Aren't *yamen* officials the only ones who are allowed to carry swords and spears? Isn't it illegal?"

Aunt Mei gave my already sore behind a sharp slap. "Sit down, child!" she scolded. "You make yourself out to be silly and unrefined when you prattle on like that. Sit properly. It is very rude to climb up on your seat."

I sulked and slid back down into my seat. My behind didn't need any more abusing. But I still kept my eyes peeled. Wei would love to hear stories when we returned home.

Unlike Huanan, most of the buildings in Xiawan were big, grand, and at least two levels high. The main street was paved neatly with stones all the same size, and instead of stalls of food flanking it, there were rows of restaurants with people flooding in and out of them like waves. There was an open theater farther down the road, where it seemed like hundreds of people were watching a *zaju* performed by actors with the most bizarre face paintings.

People covered the streets like ants on an anthill. I had fun trying to tell the different classes of people apart through their outfits. There were those who dressed in plain robes with unattractive braids and buns, much like the people in our village, but I imagined the people in thick, colorful *hanfu* with the most elaborate headgears and hairstyles to be from rich and distinguished families. We even saw *yamen* officials who worked for the local magistrate patrolling the streets in their red-and-black uniforms, their handsome swords hanging from their waistbands.

As our driver hollered out for pedestrians to make way, the cart trundled past an enormous temple that honored the local guardian *jing* of Xiawan. If I could read, I'd be able to tell from the bloodred sign over the entrance arch what kind of *jing* the city worshipped. Would it be something stronger than the Great Golden Huli Jing of Huanan? Unlike our cozy village shrine, this temple was entirely whitewashed, and at least ten times bigger, so most likely Xiawan had a more powerful *jing* . . . but I didn't like the idea of any other *jing* being stronger than our guardian.

"I wonder who the tutelary spirit of this place is," I asked, but directed the question at no one in particular so Aunt Mei could ignore me if she chose to. To my surprise, our driver spoke.

"Young lady, Xiawan worships one of the most powerful and menacing *jing* in the region—the White Lady Baigu."

A *baigu jing*. I'd heard of those. Baba said they

were also known as *jing* of white bones, risen from . . . "So that means she's one of those *jing* that rose from human bones?"

The driver nodded. "Though nobody I know has ever seen the guardian in the flesh, excuse the pun." He laughed at his own joke before continuing. "You'd do well not to speak ill of her. No one knows what she's capable of, but none of us are eager to find out, either."

As we went farther into the city, the streets grew narrower. Here, smaller shops and private homes lined the sides in neat rows, and down one of these roads, our cart stopped in front of a shop that sold fabrics. Then Aunt Mei grabbed the sides of my shoulders and shook them.

"Now, you be on your best behavior. Don't speak unless spoken to." She was clearly unhappy with my behavior on the carriage. Although uncertain why this was necessary for a mere visit to the dressmaker, I lowered my gaze and nodded.

I stepped into the shop and thought we had been swallowed by a rainbow. The walls of the shop were lined with rolls upon rolls of beautiful fabric of every shade, texture, and material. Some had multiple tones of colors, others had intricate brocades or smooth surfaces with sleek sheens; some were gauzy and translucent, and some even had beads that sparkled like stars sewn onto them. I sighed. How lovely it would be to have a dress made from any of these fabrics.

Aunt Mei greeted the old shopkeeper and was led toward the back of the shop, disappearing behind a veil of bead curtains.

I inhaled deeply. The smell of freshly dyed and pressed fabric was unfamiliar—rich, and a little sour. I ran my fingers over the surface of a piece of white silk. It felt so soft under my skin that it could've been woven from fluffy clouds. Dared I ask Aunt Mei if I could have this cloth for my new *hanfu*? I loved white, for it reminded me of beautiful things like snow and fields of cotton, but Grandmama always said no because black and white were colors for the dead.

I was just admiring the intricate beadwork on the next roll of fabric, when someone called my name. I whirled around and stood at attention, facing Aunt Mei as she reappeared from behind the curtains with another woman by her side. Casting a warning glance in my direction, Aunt Mei turned to the woman and spoke in the nicest tone I had ever heard from her.

"Mrs. Guo, may I present to you my niece, Li Jing."

"*Nin hao*, Mrs. Guo." I did a traditional curtsy, then kept my head bowed and eyes averted, for it was considered rude for children to lift their heads and look into the eyes of respectable adults.

Then I heard footsteps, and very soon, a pair of red shoes embroidered with golden threads appeared in my line of vision. My chin was lifted up, and when I beheld what stood in front of me, I almost had to bite my tongue to keep from gasping.

Mrs. Guo had a face practically caked in makeup—pearly white skin that had been powdered down to the neck, upward-slanting eyes enlarged in a ring of black, penciled on with an ash stick, thin lips drawn and colored in bright red, and—one could not help noticing most of all from my angle—a double chin, and hairy nostrils that flared every time she spoke.

Mrs. Guo turned my face this way and that, her small eyes lingering on the red mole between my eyebrows. I had an incredible urge to fidget. Why in all of China was this dressmaker lady looking so closely at me? My face didn't have anything to do with a new *hanfu*, did it? She had this look that made me feel like if my face was served to her on a platter she would lap it all up.

When, finally, she straightened up to her full height, the numerous hair ornaments wedged in her elaborate *faji* tinkled sharply. Swathed in the multiple layers of her flowing *hanfu*, which was different shades of pink, Mrs. Guo looked like an empress. Or a fat, overripe peach.

"Hmm, rather scrawny, I'd say," the empressy peach concluded in a baritone almost too deep for a woman. "But quite a pretty thing, especially with that mole on her forehead. It's a mark of beauty and prosperity." She spoke as though she were commenting on the condition of livestock.

Prosperity, indeed. Although Baba had always said that the little mole made me look pretty, I wasn't so sure about it being a bringer of prosperity, for if it was, certainly it would've done something for our family before now.

Then Aunt Mei spoke. "Yes, and it signifies intelligence as well." She sounded suspiciously like an eager saleslady. "Jing has always been a smart girl, very quick to learn."

Mrs. Guo waved one of her hands dismissively. "I have little use for her intelligence. We're not producing scholars," she sneered. "Bring the scales."

Well then! I might not have liked what Mrs.

We're-Not-Producing-Scholars said, but I knew where that came from, because there was this silly Chinese proverb that said, "Blessed is the woman who is talentless and uneducated." But really, it didn't matter how true the saying might be, because I always felt proud whenever Baba told me how smart I was.

The old shopkeeper brought in a large weighing scale, and the grown-ups steered me through one procedure after another that seemed to have little or nothing to do with dressmaking. Aunt Mei produced samples of my needlework and answered numerous questions about me, ranging from family background to temperament and even household abilities. I chewed on the insides of my cheek. This wasn't a measurement session; this was an interview of some sort.

"Good, and her lunar birth date, if you please. We'll see if they are compatible," said Mrs. Guo.

Compatible? Who was the other person being referred to here?

While both women pored over a thick fortune-telling almanac, Aunt Mei ordered me to sit in a corner, where I was free to fidget with my sash all I wanted. I craned my neck and saw the women lifting their heads. Then Mrs. Guo uttered one word along with a series of tinkles from her *faji*.

"Five."

And one of the brightest smiles I had ever seen on Aunt Mei's face appeared as she nodded. It sounded as though a deal had been struck, and at the same time, my innards shuddered, as though someone had also struck a gong inside my stomach.

· 4 ·

FOR FIVE SILVER PIECES

I stared at my father in disbelief. "Why? Why, Baba? Why are you sending me away? What have I done wrong?"

I had not uttered a single word on the way back from Xiawan. I wanted to save all my questions for Baba. I didn't dare to believe what I thought might be coming, and I did not trust Aunt Mei. I only wanted to know one thing: Did my baba know about this?

He did.

I was to be wed in a week.

In a week, I'd be going away. I'd have a new family. Begin a new life. Elsewhere.

The woman we'd met today was indeed a dress-maker, but she was also my prospective mother-in-law. And what had taken place in Xiawan was, in fact, a bridal inspection. And I had passed, with flying colors, Aunt Mei said, fetching a bride price of five silver pieces. For once in her life, she sounded proud of me.

Oh, why didn't I misbehave at the shop? Why do you have to be so hopelessly obedient all the time, Jing? Really, you'd throw yourself under the wheel of a horse cart if a grown-up told you to. But what was the use of lamenting at this point?

I couldn't even bear to look at her—the woman who had sold me. My own aunt. But what hurt so much more was the look of sorrow and defeat on Baba's face as he tried to explain his part in this awful affair.

"It's not like that, Jing . . ." Baba scratched his chin vigorously as he cast a desperate glance in Grandmama's direction.

My fate lay in the hands of the senior women in the family, because men were not supposed to concern themselves with petty household affairs. I knew Baba wouldn't, and couldn't, save me. But I was still disappointed, not just at Baba. At everyone.

"Jing," Grandmama began in her raspy voice. "I'm sure you'll be happy there. The Guo family is respectable and wealthy. They will feed and clothe you well."

As though I cared! I burst into loud, cracking sobs. "I don't care if they're rich or if they'll feed me well! I don't care if they treat me like a princess! I don't want to marry someone I've never seen and live with people I never knew!"

At the sudden sharp pain on my left cheek, I realized my aunt had slapped me across the face.

"How dare you speak to your grandmama in that manner?" Aunt Mei shrieked, pointing a quivering finger at me as though she could not believe her niece's impudence. "No family would ever tolerate such disrespect from a daughter-in-law!" she yelled, and with every word, spit spewed from her mouth onto my face.

This was real. This nightmare. Would I ever wake up from this?

Wei ran over and threw his arms around my neck. "Aunt M-Mei . . . p-please . . . don't send Jie away."

"You hold your tongue when a grown-up is talking, boy!" Aunt Mei tried to shove Wei aside, but he did not budge. She continued yelling at us.

"We didn't bring you up to be such an ungrateful and dishonorable child! What is wrong with living with the Guo family? They are nice and generous people! They offered five silver pieces for you!"

Suddenly, she reached out and yanked on my left ear. I whimpered as she twisted it at a horrible angle. "Five! Enough to buy two strong bulls! Do you understand how much that is? Surely this is the least you can do for your baba and our family for raising you all these years?"

When she finally released me, I recoiled on the floor, Wei sobbing in my arms. Pan, too, was bawling from his cradle. I swallowed my own sobs in case we agitated her more. And then, finally, Baba stepped in and put a hand on Aunt Mei's shoulder. "Jie, that's enough. I think she understands . . ."

But Aunt Mei whirled around, brushing his hand off her. "No, she doesn't! Look at her!" she snapped, jabbing at my forehead. "Tao, you've spoiled this girl, and now look at the trouble she's giving us over such a simple matter! Why, did you see me making such a fuss over my wedding?"

"That's because you were married to someone you knew. Jie, try to understand, Jing is just afraid—"

"What is there to be afraid of? It's something every girl goes through!" Aunt Mei screeched. "If you're so against this whole affair, then maybe we should just forget about the wedding and the five silver pieces!"

Silence.

Say yes. Say it, Baba. Save me. Please, tell her I can stay, that your daughter is worth more than five miserable pieces of silver! Worth more than two stupid bulls. Mama would've said the same.

"That's not what I meant."

"Baba, no! How could you!" Wei began to wail.

A peculiar kind of humming began in my ears. Did Baba really say that? My chest felt like it was splitting open and bleeding all over the floor.

Didn't Baba love me anymore? Didn't I belong here? If Mama had still been alive, she wouldn't have stood for this to happen. She would've gathered me into her arms and told Aunt Sadist to stick her nose into business where it belonged.

But Mama wasn't here. Not anymore. And Aunt Mei was in charge of my life and my future. And somehow, all the grown-ups were agreeing with her.

She straightened up like a cobra about to strike, and spoke to Baba. "Well, if that's not your intention, then you'll excuse me if I take things into my own hands." She turned and grabbed my upper arm, lifting it so high that it hurt, then tore Wei away from me and shoved me backward into the bedroom. "In here is where you will stay until you've managed to see reason!"

I landed heavily on the earthen ground. The door slammed shut and the bolt slid from the outside. "No one is to let her out until I say so. Is that clear?"

Baba spoke again, and I couldn't help holding my breath. "Jie, perhaps this could still wait a year or two. I don't think Jing is ready . . ."

But Aunt Mei cut him off again. "Tao! Do not be foolish! The Guo family is wealthy. We are lucky they're even considering a farmer's daughter for an in-law! Such good fortune will not come easily a second time, if at all."

Then even Grandmama spoke. "Jing will be ready when we say she is, not when she feels she is," she sighed. "Li Tao, my son, I'm not trying to send her away. But when there's a chance for Jing to enter a good family, we must take it. Besides, eleven is as good an age to marry as twelve or thirteen. Why, I myself was married to your father when I was barely twelve!"

I wasn't sure how much breaking my heart could take, but it couldn't be a lot more. Baba went silent. He stopped fighting for me. Why wouldn't he fight harder to save me?

"Do not worry, Tao," Grandmama continued. "We still have a week. I believe she'll come around by then."

"Never!" I screamed my loudest and highest. I screamed till my voice cracked. I had never raised my voice at grown-ups before, but I did it again. "Never!" Yes, I would never change my mind. Not if the sun rose from the west. Not if fire fell from the sky. Not even if my own mother came back from the dead!

I huddled in a corner, crying into my sleeves. I couldn't think, and over and over in my mind, the same questions kept repeating themselves like mantras: Was this really happening? Was Baba really giving me up? Couldn't all this be just a bad, horrible nightmare?

I stayed up the entire night, listening to little Zhuzhu's restless wails in the next room. Wails that told me he hadn't been tucked in properly.

▫ ▫ ▫

The following days, I wasn't allowed to leave the room at all. Not even for the bathroom—Aunt Mei gave me Pan's urine pot. When I finally came to accept that no amount of screaming, crying, or begging was going to do the slightest good, I stopped speaking, ate very little, and slept even less.

No one was allowed in except Grandmama, who brought my meals twice a day and would sit on my bed, teaching me the ways of a proper daughter-in-law.

Leave me alone.

"Believe me, Jing, I promise you will be happy there."

I jumped when a hand touched my head and cowered further against the wall. Even its coldness felt better than the warmth of Grandmama's hand. I continued pulling at a loose straw in the bed mat.

"You are pretty and smart, and if you are good, I'm certain your in-laws will love you as much as we do."

I pulled at a second straw, twisting it around my finger like how a snake circled around its prey. The straw came off with a yank.

"Love is not something the poor can afford to indulge in, Jing. This is what people of our upbringing deserve. Sometimes, we are not meant to marry for love."

I looked away when she began to stroke my hair. *Stop trying to touch me.*

"Forgive me, child. When you grow older, you will understand why Grandmama chose this path for you."

I pulled at two pieces of straw at once. The twines cut into my fingers. Grandmama got up, leaving a bowl of congee beside me.

"You need to eat more."

The door closed and the bolt outside slid home.

My fingers stopped. I had made a hole in the mat.

▪ ▪ ▪

It was on the final night that a voice came to me in one of my restless dreams. It was female, achingly familiar, and spoke in a tone that reminded me of the first gentle breeze of spring.

"Jing, dear one," it said. "Your desperation has called upon me."

Who was this? I tried to look but couldn't see past the shroud around me.

"Take heart, dearest." The voice rippled like the sound of a running stream. "And follow the path set before you. It is not an easy one, but walk it with courage, faith, and strength. Persevere, for better times will come."

When I opened my eyes, I sat up and glanced around the empty, windowless room. The voice had been so real, but whatever it was, this was all it could do for me.

I touched my tear-soaked rug, stained from another night of crying.

Silly Huli Jing, your situation is not going to change just because you lie here feeling sorry for yourself. You have to be strong. Because no one else is going to do it for you.

That was the hard, cold truth.

▪ ▪ ▪

On the day of the wedding, I got up before the rooster even crowed so I could pay my final respects to Mama as a daughter. My eyes blurred as I reached out to feel the surface of Mama's tablet, running my fingertips over the natural bumps of the bamboo.

I guess . . . this is goodbye, Mama.

Aunt Mei came out from her room, gave an impatient click, and slapped my hand away. "Stop wasting time and head up to the shrine. We've got a lot to do before the bridal procession arrives," she said before heading out of the hut.

I glared after her. If this was the last time I could do this for Mama, I would take as long as I pleased. I sucked in the mucus in my nose and wiped away my tears. I offered incense, then moved back and touched my forehead to the ground. Once, twice, thrice.

May what I do always bring you honor, Mama. Farewell.

I looked up and saw Wei.

"Jie . . ." He dashed into my arms. I kissed his forehead, feeling his wispy hair tickle my lips. I hadn't seen him in a week. I hugged back so hard that it was difficult to make out his next words.

"You could run away, you know. And come back when they've changed their minds. I will help you!"

Run away? That was unthinkable! I broke our embrace and gazed at him, and Wei revealed the little bag he'd been holding. "See? I raided the kitchen. There's food, clothes, and . . . money!"

I gasped and snatched up the copper pieces. "Where did you get these?"

"I stole them from Baba and Aunt Mei."

Wei . . . what have you done? I pulled him fiercely into my arms. "You are so stupid! Stupid, stupid, stupid!" I sobbed. "Do you know how hard they're going to beat you for this?" That was a silly question. Of course he knew.

"It'll only hurt for a little bit . . . but if you leave, it's going to hurt a lot longer."

My sleeves were completely wet from his tears. "Stop. You know I cannot do this. When I'm gone, it'll hurt, but it will go away, all right?" I stroked his hair. "Didn't it hurt when Mama left us? But we're fine now."

"I don't want to go through that again . . ."

No. I didn't want Wei to go through that again, either. I pulled back and cupped his face in my hands. "When you grow up, come to Xiawan. Find me." I gazed straight into his puffy eyes. "I promise, if I'm not happy, we'll run away together."

He looked at me for a long while, then raised his hand.

We pressed our thumbs together and slapped our palms thrice.

A WEDDING WITHOUT GOODBYES

Later that morning, I headed up to the shrine to pay my final homage to the guardian and pray for a fruitful marriage. I didn't care about any of those things—what I really wanted was to say goodbye to Lian. And sure enough, she was there waiting with Yue Shenpo.

"Fret not, dear child. The ribbon that binds you to the guardian will protect you," said Shenpopo. "Find the home of your spirit. It will be your final refuge, for its doors will always be open even when all others are closed."

I thought I knew what Shenpopo meant then. No matter where I went, I would never forget my home in Huanan. Lian pressed a yellow amulet into my hands. She held on longer when she felt how cold my hands were, and then began to cry.

"This is for luck and protection. I embroidered the sachet myself."

I pulled her into a hug because I couldn't find anything else to say that wouldn't make me burst into sobs. I wished her a life of more freedom than my own.

Before leaving, I turned around to look at the statue of the Great Golden Huli Jing one last time. I remembered the other day when I thought it had grinned at me while I prayed. It didn't do anything today.

Goodbye, Golden Huli Jing. I may never get to visit your shrine again, but if we truly are connected by the ribbon of Yuan, maybe it doesn't really matter how far I travel, for you will still watch over me, won't you? But no matter what happens, I will always remember you.

▪ ▪ ▪

At home, I was surrounded and fussed over by a dozen village women as they readied me for the ceremony. Grandmama held up my bridal gown proudly. The red silken robe, covered in elaborate embroidery showing a phoenix rising into the clouds, was the most exquisite thing I had ever seen. And I was sorry I could only imagine the satisfaction of shredding such an expensive thing with a pair of scissors.

"This is what the Guo family has sent over as part of your dowry. See how generous they are? You'll be happy with them, you'll see."

I would've gladly given up a golden throne if it meant I could stay here.

One of the women smeared some kind of white, doughy clay all over my face. My hair was roughly pulled, twisted, and braided in small locks and tied into an elaborate bridal *faji*. From what they were doing to my hair in the bronze mirror, I was beginning to look as though I had a tiny model of the imperial palace on my head.

"Do not move!" barked Mrs. Lin, one of our neighbors, who was trying to give my lips a pouty, blossom-like shape with tint that was a deep red.

Was there a way to tell her without sounding rude that it was all that brutal yanking on my hair that was making me move? Ornaments of all sorts were being piled onto my head, each mercilessly scraping the skin on my scalp—ribbons, clips, floral pins—and by the time they finished, my scalp felt raw and my head heavier than two buckets of water.

Mrs. Lin finished the pattern she was drawing on my forehead to enhance the beauty of my red mole, and stepped back. I almost cringed as the women sighed with pleasure and pride. "Oh, what a pretty bride she makes!" they gushed.

A pretty unhappy bride was a more fitting description.

I looked away. Then Grandmama took my hands in hers. "Jing, from today, you belong to the Guo family. Honor us well by being an obedient daughter-in-law."

I was expected to nod, so I did without looking at them. Grandmama produced a black bangle, sliding it into my left hand. "This is our family heirloom—a bangle made of black jade. It is very rare. Your mother wore it in her time."

The bangle felt cool against my skin, and was a little too big for my wrist. I touched it with my other hand. This was a piece of Mama I could bring along with me. But what did accepting this gift mean? Perhaps even my own mother had meant for me to one day leave this family, just like Baba expected me to. For why else wouldn't Mama save me even after I prayed so hard to her?

A shout came from outside the hut. "The *xi niang* is here! The bridal procession has arrived!"

"Quick, the *xipa* and the jujube!" Aunt Mei ordered, and everybody jumped into action.

A large piece of red cloth was draped over my head and a big jujube pressed into my hands. The fruit was so big that it was almost the size of my fist, and like everything else, it was red. Redder than the blood running under my skin.

"This is for prosperity. Hold it tight, and for Buddha's sake, don't drop it," came Aunt Mei's stern voice. "And don't let your *xipa* fall from your head. No one is supposed to see your face, understand?"

Then why did they bother with all that makeup? I nodded nonetheless and was pulled to my feet.

"The auspicious moment has come!" the *xi niang* screeched as she entered. "Ready the bride!"

Aunt Mei whispered in my ear. "The *xi niang* is your bridal matron; listen to whatever she says and you'll be fine."

The *xipa* was a silk cloth that kept me from seeing anything not directly at my feet, so I had to be led to where Baba and Grandmama were sitting for the tea ceremony wherein the bride would pay her respects to her elders by presenting them with small cups of tea containing two lotus seeds.

After accepting my cup, Baba suddenly stood up and hugged me. This wasn't part of the ceremony at all . . . was I allowed to cry? Not sure. I managed to choke back a sob, but that didn't stop the tears.

Baba, I'm going to miss you . . . I still don't want to go, but would it displease you if I stayed? Would you stop loving me if I stayed? Does it hurt you at all to have to give me away? There was so much more I wanted to say, but a bride, the *xi niang* had warned me, was not allowed to speak on her wedding day.

I couldn't see Baba's face, but his shoulders shuddered under my chin. I clutched at the cotton fabric of his *shenyi*, his only presentable outfit. Then something was pressed into my hands, something long, thin, and cylindrical. I looked down and saw a *dizi*—Baba's Chinese transverse flute, made from cured violet bamboo that produced the most eloquent warbling sounds. I gazed at it, remembering how much I loved listening to my baba play.

"It sounds just like birds singing, Baba!" I had exclaimed the first time I heard it. "Like nightingales!"

Suddenly, the *dizi* was swiped out of my hands.

"The bride is not allowed to hold anything other than the Jujube of Prosperity," the *xi niang* barked. "I will get someone to place this in the carriage."

I let out a sob. I wanted to throw the jujube onto the floor and stomp on it so hard all its juices spurted out. I wanted to hold Baba's flute, not this stupid fruit! But Baba's hands on the sides of my arms held me still. I wasn't allowed to do that; I wasn't allowed to do anything! Why? Why did I have to go like this? Was this what all brides had to go through? Did Mama or Aunt Mei or even Grandmama have to go through such unbearable torture on their wedding day? No! They didn't! Weddings were supposed to be happy occasions. Feng got married last year to her neighbor and everyone was happy. Baoying looked happy at her wedding the year before, too. Baba and Mama must've been happy when they got married, so why did my wedding feel like a dreadful curse? Why was this happening to me?

"Farewell, my daughter."

And that was all I had time to hear from my father before the *xi niang* took me by my arm and led me toward the bridal sedan that waited for us outside the hut.

"Jie . . ."

I froze. It was Wei. I had the stupid red *xipa* hanging over my head, so I couldn't see him. I hated everything red around me—the jujube in my hands, the tinkling jewelry in my hair, the stupid, awkward gown with all its shiny embroidery that probably cost more than our entire farm—but more than anything, I hated the piece of red cloth over my head.

"Jie!"

Wei sounded like he was crying. I clutched the jujube, my fingernails digging into its rosy skin. The hand on my arm propelled me forward. It took all my self-restraint to climb into the bridal carriage without acknowledging Wei.

Be strong, little brother. May our promise carry you through.

Then the high-pitched *suona* trumpet sounded, accompanied by gongs, cymbals, and Chinese drums, and the procession began its descent toward Baihe town, where we would catch horse-drawn carts straight to Xiawan.

The bridal carriage was a small wooden coach, enclosed on all sides, draped with red cloth, and carried by two men—one in front and one at the back. I had to keep my balance as the thing jolted and jerked left, right, back, and forward. My *xipa* fell and landed on my lap.

"Stay there," I said. Now I had time to nurse that heaviness in my chest, thicker and colder than the blankets of snow in midwinter.

My husband-to-be, from what I was told, was the youngest and only son of the Guo family. And he was three.

Three! Hardly older than my own baby brother. Although I had no idea what it was like being a wife to another, at least I knew I could never see a mere three-year-old baby the way my mother used to see my father. Baba and Mama were perfect for each other; they were husband and wife. I didn't want to get married, but even if I did, I wouldn't want to marry a boy hardly older than Zhuzhu.

Grandmama said that I was what people called a *tongyang xi*—a wife and nursemaid to an infant husband.

This sounded about as appealing as Aunt Mei on any given day. Why did Baba agree to give me away to be someone's *tongyang xi*? My dowry was worth more than two strong bulls, probably enough for a couple of good years, but was I worth only that? A few years of comfort? Would Baba have refused to let me go if the Guos had offered any less?

I bit down on my lip and tasted the sour red tint. My chest felt like a wok bubbling over with boiling-hot oil. So was all love measured in terms of money? Perhaps it was I who had misunderstood the meaning of family. Perhaps family members didn't necessarily belong with one another. Perhaps I never truly belonged, not to the Li family, not to Huanan. For two strong bulls, a daughter could be traded like a sack of rice.

I suppose it was why Shenpopo told me to find my spirit's home—the place where I truly belonged.

Stop, Jing. Think of happier things. You don't want to keep crying and feeling sorry for yourself.

According to Grandmama, Mrs. Guo also had two older daughters—Yunli and Yunmin, who were fourteen and thirteen. Surely that was something one could be happy about? I'd never known what it was like to have elder sisters, but now it certainly sounded like a nice idea. And that, at least, was something I could look forward to. Maybe.

▪ ▪ ▪

With the *xipa* over my head, the rest of my wedding day passed by in a blur. I couldn't see anything, didn't know anyone, and no one other than the *xi niang* ever spoke directly to me.

"Congratulations, Mrs. Guo! You've picked such an auspicious day for the wedding!"

"I heard the girl has babysitting experience. You don't suppose . . ."

"*Ai, ma!* Of course not, she's only eleven. Do you think we'd consider her if she'd been married before? She has a baby brother, it seems. Jun'an will be in good hands."

"Five silvers, did you say? *Tian, ah,* these farmers' daughters do come in cheap nowadays."

Cheap. I cost them five silvers. They cost me my family, my life, my freedom, and my future.

I was gripping my robe so tightly the seams were in danger of coming apart. The *xi niang* pushed me from behind when I stopped walking, and that was when I realized I needed to tune out those voices in order to get through the day.

There was an endless array of proceedings and rituals—lots of kowtowing, incense burning, prayers, and a long, dreary tea ceremony. By the time I was allowed to turn in for the evening, I was so weary I could hardly drag my feet to bed. I had been given a small, windowless room at the back of the house, which doubled as a storage room. Grandmama had said that I would not have to share a room with my husband, which had something to do with what they called a bridal chamber. Whatever that was, they said we did not need it because we were too young to be a real husband or wife to each other.

As I lay on the thin layer of mattress on my wooden bed, which was actually an improvement from the straw-strewn one I'd had, I fingered Mama's bangle on my wrist. How was a real wife different from what I was now? No one had told me what would be different after I became real. Grandmama said I would know when the time came, and I hadn't cared enough to ask further. Could it be that I wasn't really married until then?

6

THE GUO FAMILY

Tired as I had been the day before, I woke up at dawn purely out of habit. I lit the oil lamp on the crate next to my bed and looked around. Brooms and mops were propped up in a corner just an arm's reach away, crates of various sizes piled on top of one another along the walls and a bunch of worn-out shoes heaped in another corner, which I suspected gave the room its musty smell.

I changed into a simple blue cotton *hanfu* they had given me for everyday wear and did my hair up before heading down the first corridor. My porcelain lamp gave me so little light that I couldn't find the bathroom. The house was that huge. Eventually, I wandered into what appeared to be the kitchen.

It was bigger than our entire house in Huanan. Lining the walls were larders and racks filled with crockery and cooking utensils, and built into the wall was a large stone tank of water with the cooking hearth right beside it.

I didn't want to continue wandering around this place until I had my bearings, so I scooped water from the tank for my face. Then I started a fire for hot water and breakfast. Mama's bangle on my wrist was too big and kept knocking things over. I didn't want to scratch or break it, so I slid it farther up my forearm until it fit snugly at a spot above my elbow. While working the bamboo pipe to strengthen the fire, I heard heavy footsteps.

I got up and bowed to a woman around Baba's age. She was built heavily, with arms that looked as though they could single-handedly tame a bull, but I liked her immediately because of her smile—the exact same kind that Shenpopo had.

"*Zao an*," I greeted her.

"*Zao*, my child. You wouldn't recognize me, since you had that little head of yours hidden under that *xipa* all of yesterday. I'm the cook. You may call me Auntie San," she said, placing a hand on my head. If I closed my eyes, I could almost imagine it was Baba's.

No, stop. I turned back to the hearth and continued working the fire.

"It's mighty early for you to be up," she continued and started bustling about. "I just cleaned out the incense clock, and it's barely past the hour of the tiger."

"I'm used to it, Auntie San." I heard a disdainful scoff. Did I say something impolite?

"You wouldn't believe that an earthquake couldn't wake this family till the sun's so high up in the sky." Auntie San indicated a height with one hand while the other punched at a hunk of dough that was to be made into dumpling skin. "Come help me with this while I prepare the fish cakes. Then you can go ahead and make tea. The mistress likes her oolong nice and bitter when it's served."

"Yes, ma'am." I washed my hands, eager to obey Auntie San. She let me watch her work on the dough, breaking off small pieces and rolling them out into flat circles, then sprinkling flour over them. She watched me for a bit after I took over, then said, "You're a good girl." And patted my head again.

And I didn't even mind the bit of flour that came off on my hair.

▪ ▪ ▪

When I was finally summoned to the living hall, it was already the hour of the dragon. Back in Huanan,

I would've been done with farm work by this time. I stepped over the raised threshold with care, balancing a tray of strong oolong in my hands. Mr. and Mrs. Guo sat in two lacquered wooden chairs with a square table between them, going through sheaves of papers while waiting for their morning tea. Behind them, I saw a huge altar that honored a few deities, the Guo ancestors, and White Lady Baigu—the guardian *jing* of Xiawan. I shuddered as I remembered what the cart driver had told me about the guardian, and hoped it was as elusive as our Huli Jing.

Mrs. Guo was dressed as usual in her full regalia— doughy makeup, elaborate *faji*, and a *hanfu* in beautiful autumnal shades of brown and red. Beside her, the small man that was Mr. Guo looked almost poor in comparison. But although he was dressed only in a simple *shenyi* robe of dark gray, he was undeniably handsome and had the sharp features of a shrewd businessman, especially with the long goatee under his chin. They made a most peculiar- looking couple indeed. If they were vegetables, they'd be a tiny bean sprout and a big, fat pumpkin.

After pouring them each a cup of tea, I curtsied and greeted them in polite speech. "Jing wishes Gonggong and Popo *zao an*."

Mrs. Guo cleared her throat after taking a sip. "You will address us as Master and Mistress from now on."

I frowned. What an odd request. Didn't all daughters-in-law address their in-laws this way? Maybe it had something to do with being a *tong-yang xi*. I inclined my head.

"Yes, Master and Mistress."

Mrs. Guo took another sip of tea. "Where is Jun'an? I told Liu to get him ages ago." She replaced her cup none too gently.

Presently, a man who must be Liu, the house butler, hurried into the hall, ushering a little boy only as tall as my waist, hobbling and still rubbing the sleep from his eyes.

Guo Jun'an had to be the most beautiful child I had ever seen. Unlike the small children in our village, who were dark, unkempt, and scrawnier than tofu skins, Jun'an was fair and well-groomed, his baby fat showing in his rosy cheeks and plump little fingers.

"Baba, Mama, *zao*," he said and went over to hug his parents. As Mrs. Guo started to fuss over her son, Mr. Guo got up and left to check on the fabric factories out of town.

"Now, Jun'an," began Mrs. Guo, turning her son to face me. "This is Jing, and she is your wife." Then she looked at me. "You will address him as Master Jun'an."

I nodded and bent over. "I'm happy to meet you, Master Jun'an. I do think we'll become the best of friends," I promised him and myself.

Jun'an obviously liked the idea, because he chuckled shyly and dimples appeared on both of his cheeks. But Mrs. Guo cleared her throat sharply, a gesture that I would soon learn indicated she wasn't happy with something.

"Do not confuse your place in this household, Jing," she said. "A friend would have the same status as the master of the house, but a wife doesn't. And especially not a *tongyang xi*."

Before I could decide how much I disliked her statement, two girls came sauntering into the hall. I didn't need anyone to tell me they were Guo Yunli and Guo Yunmin, my sisters-in-law. The girls were both wearing exquisitely beautiful *hanfu*—one in silken sky blue covered in glossy lavender brocades and swirly motifs, and the other in a gauzy, powdery pink material with elaborate embroideries of peach and plum blossoms. Typically, only the very rich could afford such *hanfu* for everyday wear, but were the Guos truly rich, or just pretentious? It was, after all, easy to own a lot of *hanfu* when you were in the dressmaking business.

"Jing, you will call Yunli, Da Jie," instructed Mrs. Guo, and turned to her other daughter. "And Yunmin, Er Jie."

Those meant "eldest sister" and "second eldest sister" respectively. I liked the sound of these better than Master and Mistress, so I inclined my head with a smile. "*Zao an*, Da Jie, Er Jie." When my gaze met Yunli's, I almost blushed.

She was a rare, exotic beauty. I couldn't help but notice her resemblance to Mr. Guo. Those sharp, catlike eyes and slender nose especially stood out from her perfectly sculpted features.

Unfortunately however, Yunmin was as plain as her sister was beautiful. She was slightly bucktoothed, had a face as round as a prune, and eyes that took after her mother's tiny ones. Even the sweet, pink hue of her lovely dress failed to conceal how unattractive she was, whereas Yunli could have looked breathtaking even in a farmer's tunic.

She was smiling at me, which made her look even more stunning than she already was. But it was the kind of smile that rang alarm gongs in my head. She looked like a cat that had found an interesting new toy.

"So . . ." She circled around me. "Is this the little *huli jing* we picked up from the dump?"

I almost sighed out loud. Would I never be rid of this name? Behind me, Yunmin chuckled and pretended to hold her nose. "The dump! Oh, no wonder she smells like garbage."

I had figured out by now the sisters probably liked me as much as the dandruff in their hair, so I needn't waste effort on first impressions. I'd love a good comeback, but it wouldn't be wise to show off too much on my first day here.

I inclined my head slightly. "I beg your pardon, Da Jie, Er Jie, but I am not from Xiawan. I came from Huanan village."

To my amusement, only Yunli seemed to have gotten my ingeniously subtle jab. Compared to the slightly bemused looks on her mother's and sister's faces, she looked as though I had just emptied a bottle of calligraphy ink over her head.

▪ ▪ ▪

My new life was drastically different from the one I'd had, but at least I was familiar with all the expected chores. After my briefing with the stone-faced butler, I managed to gather that my standing in this house probably ranked a little higher than rice weevils. Definitely lower than Mr. Guo's pet nightingale, Koko, for at least the bird got to sit on its perch all day and sing.

Also, I had one daily mission that was as vital as any other, and that was staying out of Yunli's way. Though it wasn't an easy task when she was set on making my life miserable.

One thing that came as a pleasant surprise was my little husband. Three years old and extremely eager to please, Jun'an turned out to be a delightful child, and babysitting him became my pleasure as much as his. We did almost everything together, and I grew to love him as dearly as I did Wei and Zhuzhu. He became one of my few sources of solace in my new home. And yet, perhaps *home* wasn't the most appropriate word, for even with all its luxury and comfort, I was never allowed to feel like I belonged, which was why this was the year I spent my first Mid-Autumn Festival alone.

As I sat on the wooden landing that opened into the garden, gazing at the full moon, I could see myself and Wei and the village children, playing all day in our *hanfu* after a visit to the Huli Jing shrine. We made colorful paper lanterns and showed them off in the evening. I saw Pan, and remembered how he loved to watch the burning candles that flickered like fireflies.

I remembered the mooncakes Grandmama made—fragrant baked crusts stuffed on the inside with sweet lotus-seed paste and salted egg yolks. And then there was always chicken for dinner. Although the food was nowhere as good as what I now had every day, at least everyone ate together as a family.

Here, I was not included at the dining table. I had my meals in the scullery, and sometimes, as I picked at the leftovers from dinner, tasting as well the saltiness from my tears, I couldn't help but wonder: Did my family know, before sending me away, the kind of life that awaited me in Xiawan?

7

THE GHOST FESTIVAL

The Mid-Autumn Festival wasn't the only time that made me especially miss home. My first Ghost Festival away from Huanan had to be the scariest I had ever experienced in my life and was also the first time I actually saw *jing* with my own eyes.

The annual Ghost Festival was a day in the seventh lunar moon when Guimen Guan, the gates of hell, would open so that the souls of the deceased could surface to the realm of the living for one night. People set up altars and prepared offerings of sanctified food, incense, and joss paper to appease the wandering spirits and to receive their blessing. This was perhaps one of the quietest days on the entire lunar calendar, because everyone stayed indoors to avoid running into evil wandering souls or any malevolent *jing* that might be lurking around.

Well, almost everyone.

Just before midnight, the mistress had me set up an elaborate altar just outside the front gate, piled high with offerings—sweet *mantou* buns, mandarins, hard-boiled eggs, and even a roasted piglet. But the real surprise came after that.

"You stay out here and keep a good lookout. Be sure to replenish the candles and incense. Keep the food coming for the spirits and *jing*; that way we'll receive more blessings than anyone in town," said Mrs. Guo.

I glared at her back as she retreated indoors.

Nonsense *hulu*-sticks! Never had I heard of such a ridiculous thing. Back home, Baba always made sure everyone stayed strictly indoors after setting up our altar. All night, we would hear sounds from outside, but we wouldn't even be allowed to look out. And by morning the next day, the candles and incense would've burned out and all the food would be gone. Some said that they were *jing*, some said they were wandering souls, but no one really wanted to find out firsthand, because if you encountered a nether-world being, it could latch on to you and follow you home, where it would haunt.

Underneath the altar, I wrapped a blanket around myself and curled up into the tiniest ball I could manage. My blanket and the yellow tablecloth on the altar were the only things between me and whatever lay outside.

Would the *jing* decide I made a better feast? Would I see a headless ghost or a hopping zombie? What if something evil possessed me?

There was no sound at all. I could not even hear the wind, and it made me feel as though I couldn't breathe. It was so quiet. I dared to lift a corner of the tablecloth and poke half of my head out.

There was the slightest breeze in the air. All along the sides of the street we lived on, each family had set up an altar. The white candles that burned on the tables made the street brighter than it was on normal nights. But they were like beacons, calling out to the spirits. *Come one, come all, dinner is served.*

My heart almost stopped when the ring of the time keeper's gong signified that midnight—the darkest hour of the rat—had come. I had to hide. I had to go back under the table. But as the reverberating ring of the gong receded, I couldn't move. The breeze had disappeared, and the silence took on a sort of thickness that made it almost tangible, pressing against my sweaty forehead.

Something moved out of the darkness farther down the road.

It was a person.

Two.

No, three.

And more were appearing out of the dark. Through walls. From the ground. Out of thin air.

And they had no feet.

My breath caught. I couldn't even scream. I scooted back under the table and pulled my blanket over my head. My heart beat so hard that even my ears throbbed. And for the longest time, I stayed where I was. I could hear munching sounds and the occasional jolt of the table right over my head, but I could only stuff my mouth full of fabric so I didn't whimper out loud.

Goddess of mercy, Great Golden Huli Jing, help me!

At one point, I thought I did hear a whimper. But it didn't come from me. I strained my ears. The other sounds had stopped, which probably meant the feast above was over for the night, or at least until I gathered enough courage to go out and refill Mrs. Guo's stupid altar.

There was the whimpering again. Something was out there. Something that actually sounded more like a small animal than some hungry ghost waiting to pounce on an innocent girl under an altar. I lifted the edge of the tablecloth. As I had suspected, sitting in front of the altar, gazing at me with a set of curious green eyes, was a most adorable golden puppy, no bigger than a cat.

With its pointy ears and bushy, white-tipped golden tail, it actually looked more like a fox cub. It had such a familiar gaze, as though it knew me, that I couldn't help picking it up. It did not struggle or try to lick me, and I buried my face in its warm, prickly fur. My chest heaved. It reminded me of home, this little creature. Of my guardian, the Great Golden Huli Jing.

"What brings you out on this horrid night?" I took a few deep breaths and straightened up. "Did our Golden Huli Jing send you, perhaps?" My answer was only another oblivious whimper.

Oh, it must be hungry! I reached into my bag and brought out a steamy meat bun. The puppy wasted no time and the food soon disappeared between two rows of little teeth. My own stomach grumbled, so I divided a few more buns between us. When we had had our fill, it was time for work.

Somehow, with the company of my new friend, being outside felt less frightening than it had been. The street was empty, and Mrs. Guo's altar looked as though a typhoon had swept through it—dishes were overturned, the incense holder upset, all the food gone. Even the food spilled all over the tablecloth had been eaten clean, leaving only stains behind. I worked as quickly as I could, removing the candle stumps from the holders and replacing them with new ones. After lighting them, I straightened up the table and refilled the dishes and incense holder.

Then it was time to burn joss paper. A small fire was burning on coal inside a metal bin just beside the altar. I reached into my bag and pulled out a piece of yellowish rice paper with a silver-colored center. The joss paper had been folded into a shape similar to a Chinese gold ingot called the *yuanbao*. When burned, they were supposed to turn into a kind of hell currency that the spirits and deities could use. Mama used to call it "ghost money."

I squatted in front of the metal bin and tossed the joss paper into the fire. It caught immediately, starting from the edges, then burning to a crisp.

"This is for you, Mama," I whispered. I didn't know whether she would receive this, or if there was a chance I would meet her tonight. But I wouldn't be scared if I did. I would have so much to tell her . . .

I felt a heaviness on my lap and looked down to see the puppy settling itself on my crossed legs. That was when something else occurred to me.

"This one is for my spirit guardian," I said, and tossed in another piece of ghost money. I scratched the puppy behind its pointy ears. "Did you know? My baba said that the Great Golden Huli Jing of Huanan is a handsome fox *jing* with green eyes and a coat of golden fur, just like you."

The little thing puffed up its snowy chest, looking almost proud of itself. I would've laughed out loud if the atmosphere hadn't abruptly changed. The air around us felt like fog . . . I knew they were coming. And also what they were coming for.

I gathered the puppy into my arms. The spirits were again emerging out of the gloom, growing more solid as they neared, but never growing any feet. That was how one could tell apart spirits and *jing*.

I tried to swallow but couldn't. I needed to hide, but my legs wouldn't move. But for some reason, my puppy friend did not seem perturbed by the newcomers at all. It sat sedately in my lap, gazing at the apparitions as they drifted past. And somehow, borrowing courage from my new friend, I was able to stay where I was. I kept my eyes firmly on the ground and continued to burn offerings.

Nothing bad seemed to be happening to me. My heartbeat went back to normal, and eventually,

I could keep my hands from shaking. Perhaps the Ghost Festival wasn't as dangerous as people made it out to be after all. I dared to look up and saw three apparitions drift past, none of them paying us any attention. Could they actually see us? One paused in front of our altar—an old woman with such a wizened face that she must've died of old age. She gazed blankly at the offerings as though pondering what to do with them, then drifted right through the entire table and disappeared.

That night, I learned a little-known truth about the Ghost Festival: that the true things consuming the offerings were not spirits, but something else.

Every now and then, the puppy would become alert, and I would hear something slinking along the shadows in the street. And when it came close enough, I would see an animal emerging warily out of the darkness, sniffing out the food on the altar. The first one we saw was a weasel *jing*, who regarded us with a wary eye before deciding that a girl and a puppy were no threat, then leaped onto the altar to begin its feast. Then came two raccoon *jing*, side by side, and a raven.

From the outside, they looked no different from

normal animals. The differences they possessed, should they choose to reveal them, were humanlike intelligence, the ability to speak, and, sometimes, great power.

Therefore, I shouldn't have been able to tell whether these animals were *jing*, but something else happened to affirm my suspicion.

A woman ambled down the street toward us. Her skin was paler even than the moon in the sky, but her features completely blew me away. It would take a hundred Yunlis to compare with her beauty. But that wasn't the most intriguing part about her, for she had a mop of long, flowing hair that could've been spun out of the purest silver. Dressed in a simple *hanfu* of white, the woman could've passed as a ghost herself if not for the sound of light footsteps that came from her feet treading softly on the gravel path.

Like the rest of the *jing*, the lady paid me no heed as she approached the altar, but when the other animals saw her, they bowed, then hastily leaped off the table to give her passage.

As though they're afraid of her.

My mouth felt abnormally dry, and I couldn't look away.

Stopping in front of the altar, the woman slowly reached out for the food, and what slid from within the long silken sleeves nearly made me scream.

Bones.

The skeleton of a human hand.

I stumbled backward, holding the puppy close as I realized whom, or more accurately, what I was beholding.

This was a *jing* of white bones—a *baigu jing*, but not just any one. This was the White Lady—the tutelary spirit of Xiawan.

All of a sudden, the *baigu jing* turned around and fixed a pair of cold gray eyes in our direction. Then a thin smile crept across her red lips as she spoke in such a sweet voice that it could've dripped with honey.

"Fancy seeing you here, darling."

My mouth opened and closed a few times. I tried to inhale but the atmosphere felt like it had been drained of air. It took me a few moments to realize that the *baigu jing* did not seem to be talking to me, for she was looking directly at the puppy in my arms.

"And in such an adorable form," said the *jing* as she brushed away a stray lock of her snowy hair and leaned closer. The silver-rimmed lapel of her *hanfu* slid dangerously low on her shoulders, revealing her pearly white skin. The skeleton of her hand slid out again from underneath her sleeves, reaching slowly toward us. The remains of a hand that was once human.

My puppy friend was no longer calm and quiet. A low growl was rumbling deep in its throat, and its hackles were rippling. Not impressed, but looking as though she got the idea that she wasn't welcome, the White Lady pressed her lips together and straightened up.

"Well, if you are too petulant as usual to exchange pleasantries." She turned the other way, taking a large pear from the altar.

When the *baigu jing* had completely disappeared, I looked down at the puppy in my arms.

"Are you a *jing*?" I whispered.

It could be a dog *jing*, or maybe even a young *huli jing*. And if it were, it should be able to speak. But the puppy did nothing I expected. It literally did nothing besides gaze at me solemnly, wag its bushy tail, and lick my hands, as though telling me: "Do not be disappointed that I am not what you think I am!"

I chuckled and stroked its fur. "I shall call you Saffron."

I had been convinced then that I was being over-imaginative, for Saffron had done nothing out of the ordinary. But I was no longer so sure in the morning when I woke up underneath the altar and found him gone. And the peculiar thing was, even after days of searching the town, I could not find a single trace of him.

8

SAVING SPIDERS

The Ghost Festival wasn't the only time that I
had encountered those normally elusive *jing*.
One afternoon very early in spring, I was passing by
the sisters' bedroom when I heard squeals and a loud
crash.

"Heeeeeeelp!" Yunli was screaming.

If she hadn't sounded like she might be in mortal
danger, I would have walked right past their door.
They gave me enough trouble without me asking
for it.

I pushed the doors open and found the room in a
huge mess—several porcelain items broken, chairs
overturned, dressers emptied, and *hanfu* strewn
across the floor. For once, the sisters looked happy
to see me.

"Th—There's a spider *jing* in our bedroom!" Yunli cried.

"A what?" I frowned. "You mean you saw a spider."

"No, tofu brain! I meant I saw a *jing.*" Yunli stomped her feet. "I know it is. It made a human sound."

"You have to help us find it! Or I won't sleep in this room tonight," Yunmin cried with a shudder.

"Don't be stupid. This isn't a regular spider; if we can't find it, Mama will have to call in the exorcist. Only they know how to get rid of pesky household *jing.*"

I tried not to roll my eyes. "Well, Da Jie, if it really was a *jing*, it should be smart enough not to let us find it now that you've made your threat so clear."

But I started rummaging around the room anyway, putting away clothes and clearing up the mess while hunting for the rumored spider. Not all *jing* were welcomed or worshipped by humans; therefore they generally kept to their own kind. But when situations like this arose, people sought help from exorcists, normally a shaman or monk from the local shrine. However, *jing* were usually intelligent enough to hide or escape before they got caught, and sure enough, we could no longer find any trace of a spider in the room.

"It might've run away already." I shrugged.

But Yunli wouldn't have any of it. The monk from the temple agreed to come in first thing the next day to perform a cleansing ritual. And that night, I laid out extra mattresses in the master bedroom so the entire family could sleep together and keep one another company, which, of course, did not include the *tongyang xi*.

It was not as though I cared, because I was used to this treatment by then. Besides, after my last encounter with *jing*, I wasn't particularly afraid of them anymore.

I settled into a comfortable sleeping position in my own room. Even back in Huanan, Shenpopo often told us that malevolent *jing* liked to disguise themselves as people or other things and live among humans to absorb life force that turned into negative *chi*. Therefore, if this spider *jing* had really meant us harm, we would've experienced misfortune of some form before now. If it was a *jing* at all.

I opened my eyes when I heard a tiny clicking sound, then something that was too soft at first to hear.

"Little girl, little girl, please wake up!"

I gasped and sat up. Upon lighting the oil lamp on the wooden box beside my bed, I found, sitting primly next to the lamp, a spider as big as my palm, waving one of its spindly front legs at me.

It couldn't have just spoken. Because if it had, then this was . . .

"Y-You're that spider *jing*! What are you doing here?"

Why was it still lingering in our house when its life was in danger? The exorcist would surely kill it!

There was a little sniffle, and then the spider spoke.

"Please, little girl, I need your help. I have lived in this house for a long time. When the weather is warm, I make my burrow in the garden outside, and during the white season, I retreat underneath the house and keep still for many moons. I am a very young *jing*, for I had just elevated from a regular spider after surviving my hundredth winter last year. The weather is just getting warm, so I decided that today would be a good day to return to the garden. But alas, I startled your sister when I crawled out from underneath her dresser, and she dropped a jar of face powder right beside me, and . . ." The spider looked down, twiddling her furry pincers hesitantly. "It was my fault, because I sneezed and she heard me. While she was squealing in panic, I scuttled underneath her bed and hid in between the wooden frames until all of you gave up searching the room."

"But I looked everywhere. Even under the beds!"

The spider seemed to chuckle as she gestured at me with a front leg. "Come, take a closer look at me." I held out my hands and the spider crawled sedately onto them. Her furry legs tickled and I couldn't help giggling. Then she made a proud little twirl. "Look at my outer shell. You wouldn't have been able to find me easily in the shadows under the bed."

I took a closer look at the creature in my hands. She was a beautiful Qifang spider—golden brown all over, with glossy black patterns on her legs and abdomen.

"You are very pretty."

"Thank you, little girl," the spider said. "So about tomorrow . . ."

I nodded. "Of course I will help you, but why can't you escape now? Or rather, why haven't you escaped already?"

The spider sighed. "I would, if I hadn't my egg sac with me. I cannot leave my children to their deaths." She spun a little handkerchief right from her abdomen and blew into it. "I didn't know what else to do and was crying beside my burrow. And that was when the nightingale who lives in the garden told me to come to you for help."

A nightingale? The spider must be talking about Mr. Guo's pet. But if the spider actually talked to Koko . . .

"You spoke to Koko? Is he a *jing*, too?"

The spider *jing* took a while to consider before speaking. "Well, I'll explain it this way: We animals have a way of communicating with each other that doesn't make sense to human ears. It's difficult to explain . . ." She drifted off enigmatically, and then continued. "Koko said that you're a nice girl who treats him like a friend and takes good care of him. He also assured me that you'd help if I asked nicely."

I nodded so hard my neck was in danger of snapping. "Of course I would. Let's not waste any more time. I will move you and your children to a safe place."

In my hands, the spider was shuddering. I thought she had caught a cold, but she sniffled and said, "You must be the most wonderful human child in the world."

The spider led us to a tiny burrow just underneath the peach tree in the garden. Even with an oil lamp, I could hardly spot the entrance. It was long past the hour of the boar, and the sky was pitch black except for a little patch of gray clouds that the moon was hiding behind.

"Over here." The spider lowered herself onto the ground and pushed aside a few blades of long grass, revealing a hidey-hole.

"How are we going to get it out?" My hand wasn't going to fit in the entrance, and if I dug at the hole, I might hurt the egg sac if the burrow caved in.

"Don't worry. I will go in and cut off the binding threads, then roll the sac out," said the spider and disappeared promptly into the hole. In a few moments, a pale little ball the size of an egg appeared at the entrance. The spider was pushing at it from behind. I held the sac as carefully as I could in my hands. It felt as soft as freshly picked cotton, and I couldn't help telling the spider so.

"Even softer." The spider *jing* waggled her spinnerets with pride. "It is made from the best silk in my body."

I wrapped the sac in a piece of cloth and placed it in an empty leather bag. Thousands of baby spider lives depended on me now. With the spider clinging on to my shoulder, I left my lamp on the ground and hoisted myself onto the lowest branch of the peach tree.

"Where are you taking us?" the spider asked, clicking her pincers with curiosity.

"The branches of this peach tree intertwine with the maple that grows in our neighbor's garden," I explained as I reached for the second branch. "See where the branches grow right across the walls into the next garden? I can just climb over."

I picked my branches carefully, testing the strength of each one before trusting my entire weight on it, and very soon, we arrived at the point right in between the two trees. I reached for a branch on the maple tree that seemed the sturdiest.

"Be careful, oh be careful!" the spider squealed. "Can't we just find a field or meadow somewhere instead of doing something so dangerous? I don't want you to get hurt."

"Xiawan is a big, ugly city. There is no field or loose soil except in these private gardens. Don't worry, I've climbed more trees than anyone I know. I'll be fine." I sat down on my branch and reached over to the other with my foot as far as I dared to test its strength.

It was wobbly. I retracted my leg. "That one's not good. The strongest branch I can see is the one below us. We will have to drop down on it. Hang on tight."

And before the spider could protest, I slid off my branch, holding on to it with my hands. Even dangling like this, my feet were still a couple of inches above the maple branch. I should move farther out so I could drop on a stronger part. I started monkey-swinging my way across.

"Please be careful; I shan't forgive myself if you get hurt."

I couldn't answer. I was holding my breath for the drop. If I went any farther, the branch I was clinging on to might snap. I forced myself to look down as I let go. My right foot slipped from under me when I landed, and the spider squealed. But I had managed to land directly on top of the maple. For a few moments, I kept hugging the branch until I stopped shaking.

The rest of the climb was easier. We were on a low branch now, and all I had to do was slide toward the trunk and scamper down the rest of the way. The bark of the old maple tree was rough and bumpy, so there were many foot- and handholds. Soon we were back on solid ground.

The spider crawled onto my palms and paced anxiously. "How will you get back home? You cannot possibly climb back the way you have come."

I couldn't help being proud of my own foresight. "Getting back is easy. I will just climb that last maple branch out of the walls. It is close enough to the ground for me to drop safely onto the street, and from there, I can sneak back into the house through the back door that I left open."

Without a lamp, the darkness made it difficult to see much, but in the moonlight, we managed to find a cozy, secluded spot under some bushes.

"This is a nice place; you will be safe here. And now we shall be neighbors," I said as I lowered the spider and her egg sac to the ground. She turned around to face me.

"Kind human child, I can't stay in Xiawan for much longer. Now that I have turned into a *jing*, it becomes dangerous for me to live alongside humans. So after my babies have hatched this spring, I shall move deep into the forest."

I looked away and tugged at a blade of grass. Why did she have to leave when she didn't want to? This was her home. My chest hurt, and I felt like crying. "Haven't you lived here most your life? Aren't you sad . . . having to leave your home?"

The spider crawled onto my lap and patted my hand gently. "No, dear child. I shan't be sad, because home is what I carry with me." She waggled her little silk-filled abdomen. "It is inside me, see? And it will be where I choose to make my new burrow. So I am not sad at all."

I stopped abusing the poor grass. She was right; how nice to be able to carry your home wherever you went. If I could do that myself, then maybe . . . maybe I would feel at home no matter where I was. Because then everywhere could be home, and I wouldn't even need a place to feel as though I belonged. All of a sudden, a spider's life sounded much more fulfilling than a human being's.

"I owe you a great debt, human child," the spider *jing* continued. "You saved my life and my children's. And for that, I would like to leave you with a parting gift." As she spoke, the spider began to weave very rapidly with her spinnerets, and something long and silvery appeared at the end of her abdomen. Holy Huli Jing—after a few moments, the spider placed a pair of the prettiest ribbons I had ever seen into my hand. They were translucent white, edged with elegant silver trimmings, and ever so soft. They glinted in the moonlight, as though they were spun from crystals.

"These are made out of every kind of silk in my body," said the spider. "Keep them as a memento, and if you should ever need my help one day, burn one and scatter its ashes into the ground, for then I shall know and will come to your aid."

My mouth had to open and close a few times before I could speak. "This is absolutely the most beautiful thing I have ever received."

The spider seemed happy to hear this, for she twirled around on my lap before leaping back onto the ground. Then she asked, "Little girl, what is your name?"

"My name is Li Jing."

I could almost see the spider nod her tiny head. "Such a magical name . . . and how coincidental."

"But it's not the same character," I tried to explain, but the spider waved one of her front legs dismissively.

"Oh, I know that very well. No parent would ever name their child after us *jing*." Here she paused for a moment, then continued. "But your name might have a bigger role to play in your destiny than you might think."

I remembered Shenpopo's words. Why did people speak as though they knew my destiny? It wasn't fair that I seemed to know less about myself than they. "It's uncanny how you're not the first one to tell me this."

"And I am sure whoever told you that is a wise person. Take it from a spider *jing* who has lived a hundred years. Keep this knowledge close to your heart, and when the time comes, you will understand. But for now, dear crystal maiden, we must part."

When the spider turned to go, I stopped her. "Wait! I still don't know your name."

"The names of *jing* are not for human ears, my child. But if you fancy, you may give me a nickname."

I thought for a moment. "Can I call you Sisi? For the wonderful silk that you spin."

"It's a pretty name; I should like that very much," she said, and then waved her forelegs at me before disappearing into the burrow with her egg sac. Sisi never appeared in the Guos' home after that, but I wore the beautiful ribbons in my hair every day.

9

WEI'S LETTER

A very nice thing happened to me about half a year into my stay in Xiawan. One afternoon, I had been out in the courtyard feeding Koko the nightingale some sweet pear and coaxing him to sing when a knock came from the front gates. It was the shopkeeper from Mr. Guo's fabric shop. I had seen him a few times, but my first was on the day I was brought to Xiawan for my bridal inspection. The old man pressed something into my hands.

It was a small pile of letters. But at the very top of it was one that had a single character written over it in an untidy scrawl:

A tingle spread over my entire body. From head to toe. I couldn't stop staring at the single word. Could it be from my family? Perhaps they wanted me back? A hand landed on my shoulders. I looked up at the shopkeeper and saw the encouraging look on his creased face. I fell into the deepest bow.

"Thank you." I whispered my thanks over and over even long after the man had turned the corner. Clutching the letter to my chest, I placed the rest on the table in the living hall and scuttled to the back of the kitchen. My room would be too dark for me to read this. I'd have to light a lamp and I couldn't quite be bothered with it.

Soon, sitting on the open landing of the hallway that faced the garden, I glanced down once more at my letter. It was only a sheaf of papers, crinkled and yellowed, but neatly folded and tied together with a piece of straw-woven string. I traced the strokes of my name with my fingers. This was a letter to me. Written for me. From someone I knew. Whoever sent it wrote this thinking about me. Whoever wrote it still remembered me. And missed me.

I gasped as a drop of tear stained the paper. I dried it carefully with my sleeves.

It had to be Wei. Baba could not read or write, but Wei took simple classes from a teacher in the village, along with the other boys. What would Wei say in a letter to his faraway sister? I tugged gently at the string, and it was just about to come undone when the entire letter was abruptly swiped out of my hands.

I looked up. Yunli had my letter dangling in between her thumb and index finger.

"Ah . . . I was wondering about that stupid smile you had on your face," she said with an amused grin as she studied the letter. "Could this be . . . from a secret lover?"

My heart almost stopped. If Yunli convinced Mrs. Guo I had a secret lover, it was adultery. A serious crime. I would be drowned in a river as punishment. "No, it's a letter from my brother Wei." I kowtowed at Yunli's feet. "Please, return it to me, Da Jie."

If she had asked me for an arm and a leg, I might have given it to her. The letter was the only thing that still connected me to the life I had had with my family.

Yunli laughed. "But what's the use of you having it, Huli Jing? You aren't even literate! You can't read," she concluded triumphantly. "Here, let me be a nice Da Jie and read it to you," she offered in her kindest tone, and, to my horror, ripped the string right off and promptly unfolded the first page.

My hands balled into quivering fists. *Jing, you cannot snatch the papers from Yunli. If the letter is somehow torn in the struggle, you would never be able to read it. Keep calm.*

"Hmm . . ." Yunli spent a moment squinting at the paper, then rifled through the rest of the pages. "Why, I do believe your little brother is as illiterate as you!" she finally exclaimed, and burst into laughter. "He has drawn pictures instead of writing."

What?

But I understood almost immediately. Wei wasn't the one who was illiterate . . . I was. The letter was written for me, so I had to be able to read it. This was the only way I could understand his letter. Sweet, thoughtful Wei.

The look of surprise on my face must've been apparent, for Yunli smirked and handed me the page she'd just seen. "Here, you may see for yourself."

I grabbed the paper and gazed at the image on it. Sketched probably with a piece of ash was a drawing of two grinning boys dressed in *hanfu*, together with a bull in a vegetable garden. The picture spoke to me as clearly as any words would have:

Jie, after you've been gone, Baba bought a big strong bull with some of the money. Our crops are growing well because of all the new tools and things we can now afford. Life is good for the moment... and Pan and I even got new hanfu for the Lunar New Year.

I had to blink a few times, hard. It wouldn't do at all to have Yunli see me upset. I turned to her. "Da Jie, please . . . may I have the rest of the pages back?"

But Yunli only straightened up and pretended to consider. "Oh, I don't know . . ." Then she bent over so she was eye level with me. "Tell you what, Huli Jing; how about I let you read one page whenever you make me especially happy? That'll only be . . ." She counted the remaining papers in her hand. "Seven times. Not too many, isn't it?"

And at that moment, I wished so badly to set an entire pack of *huli jing* on her.

▪ ▪ ▪

I clutched the yellow amulet Lian had made for me that I always tucked under my waistband. Other than Wei's letter, Mama's bangle, and Baba's flute, it was the only other thing that reminded me that someone still cared. My fingers traced the embroidery of peonies and chrysanthemums.

I had to get that letter back.

Only when Jun'an's plump little hand touched my cheeks did I realize they were wet.

"Why crying, Jing? Don't cry . . . I'll be a good boy; no more crying, please?" he pleaded.

The angelic face of my little husband made me smile. It was already sundown, and they had just finished dinner. I hadn't noticed Jun'an coming to sit beside me on the open landing until just now.

I rubbed at my cheeks so hard they felt sore. *It's no use crying, silly Jing, it will only upset Jun'an.* Somehow, I'd get my letter back. I had all the time in the world. Yunli wouldn't get rid of the letter as long as she knew it gave her power over me.

"I'm not sad, young master," I said. When he didn't look convinced, Lian's amulet gave me an idea. "Would you like to hear another story about the Great Golden Huli Jing?"

Jun'an's eyes lit up. "Oh yes, Jing! Please, please!"

I tried to think of one he had never heard before. "All right. Have I ever told you about the time the Great Golden Huli Jing defeated a horrible man-eating tree *jing* called the Renmian Tree?"

Jun'an gasped like the excellent listener he was. "What is a Renmian Tree like?"

"My mama once told me that this evil *jing* can uproot itself whenever it pleases and travel to remote villages, where the Renmian Tree would slowly feed on the souls of people who eat its beautiful fruits . . ."

Jun'an looked positively horrified, and I was beginning to wonder whether I had picked the wrong story to tell when he said, "Huli Jing will save the day!" And then he seemed to remember something. "Jing, why do Da Jie and Er Jie call you Huli Jing?"

I huffed. "Not just your sisters; even the kids from my village used to call me that."

"But why?"

"Well, because . . ." I crossed my arms. "Because they're jealous," I said, nodding. "Because my name, Li Jing, sounds like the name of the Great Golden Huli Jing, and they're jealous because this means that one day, I'm destined to become as great as the

Golden Huli Jing and they're going to be nobodies."

"Ooh . . . ," said Jun'an, and he sounded so genuinely envious and full of awe that I almost blushed.

▪ ▪ ▪

I was never considered a weakling, even back in Huanan. However, here within the Guo household, my standing was entirely different. Outward defiance or impertinence would earn me more than a mere beating, but that didn't mean they had frightened me into total meekness. After Yunli confiscated my letter, I itched to pull a prank or two to get mine back. I wanted justice served. I wanted her to appease my anger. And my chance came two days later while I was straightening out their bedroom.

I came across Yunli's favorite lip tints on her makeup dresser—a few pieces of paper colored on both sides. I picked them up carefully, marveling at the exquisite shades.

Yunli liked using soft pastel colors, which brought out the fairness of her complexion, and these appeared to be the best hues this season—a pale peach color, a faint red that reminded me of Jun'an's cheeks, and another a beautiful shade of the pink peony that blooms in summer. Yunli must be saving these for autumn because they were still brand-new and unused.

That was when a ingenious idea came to me. I opened Yunli's jar of makeup liquid, which was essentially just water mixed in with moisturizing extracts of almond and cucumber. Although I had only ever used makeup on the day of my wedding, I remembered how it was done. I sat down in front of the bronze mirror on Yunli's desk and carefully wet my mouth with the liquid. Then I took the peony-colored paper, positioned it between my lips, and pursed them. When the moistened surface came into contact with the paper, the tint came off and stayed on my lips in a perfect shape.

I looked into the mirror with satisfaction and sat there for a moment. I didn't look bad at all—the color made me look sweet, feminine, and even a little alluring. But looking pretty wasn't on the agenda today. I made a pig face at the mirror, then wiped the tint off with the back of my hand. A sour taste spread across my tongue when some of it got inside my mouth. I ignored the distasteful tang and carefully repeated the same process a few more times on each of those colored papers, careful not to get any more of it in my mouth. And then, for the final step, I walked over to Yunmin's dresser and stashed the used papers in one of her drawers.

That evening, my sides were almost splitting open with stitches from trying not to laugh as the sisters fought and argued over the makeup. They even managed to go a whole week without talking to each other. And during that time, although both were in especially bad moods, they gave me a lot less trouble on the whole.

10

THE PRICE OF
TWO PAGES

My first chance to retrieve the next page of Wei's letter came just a few days later. I was feeding Mr. Guo's pet nightingale in the garden, whistling and talking to him as I slipped him seeds and slices of fruits through the teak bars of his cage.

"*Twittery tweet tweet!*" the bird warbled. Koko was a singing nightingale, one of Mr. Guo's prized possessions, for he had won many singing competitions at the marketplace. I often played Baba's *dizi* for him, and the clever bird had picked up a number of songs and would sometimes even save his best ones just to get an additional treat.

"There you go," I cooed as the bird pecked at the tiny slice of pear in my hand. Then he fluffed up his unattractive brown feathers and trilled at the top of his voice.

"Jing jing! Jiiiiiiing—"

I almost dropped the fruit. Had Koko just said my name? Could nightingales actually talk like parrots or mynahs did?

"Oh, Koko, you clever, clever bird! Say it again." I held out a slice of persimmon, close enough for Koko to see it, but not reach. He hopped closer, tilting his little head to one side and giving a small chirp, regarding me as if to say, "Why don't you try moving that little treat closer?"

"Such an intelligent look you have, Koko." I couldn't help admiring his unblinking black eyes. "Say 'Jing' again and you can have this. Go on."

"Who are you talking to?"

I gasped and turned around to find Yunli and Yunmin standing behind me. "I heard Koko say my name and was trying to get him to do it again."

The sisters looked at each other, and then Yunli burst into laughter, immediately followed by Yunmin. "My dear, ignorant, uneducated sister-in-law," Yunli said. She took out her folding fan and opened it, idly fanning herself. "Nightingales can't do anything but sing."

I shook my head. "But Koko can speak, really. He can say my name. He just did." Yunli rolled her eyes and started fanning herself rapidly, as though wondering why she was wasting time arguing with a melon head. Yunmin, however, had more to say.

"Well, if you're so sure, prove it! Make it say your name again."

I looked down at the oblivious little creature in his cage. Koko was hopping around on his perch, expecting another piece of fruit. I picked up a persimmon slice and dangled it just out of his reach. "Smart Koko, say 'Jing jing'?"

But this time, the little creature only tilted his head to one side and gazed at us with his beady eyes, blinking once, then twice, but never opening his beak. My heart sank.

"See? We knew you were just fibbing!" said Yunmin.

"Unless the bird's a *jing*, no one," said Yunli as she paused for dramatic effect, "can ever teach a nightingale to speak . . . Nightingales are not parrots. They. Don't. Speak."

I knew what I'd heard. I didn't need their little lesson. I sat down and continued to feed Koko. But somehow, I must've touched a nerve, because part of Yunli's face literally twitched, horribly distorting her features before she flew into a fine rage.

"How dare you give me that attitude? Do you think you know more than me? You can't even write your own name, Huli Jing! Look at me when I'm talking to you!" And with that, she reached out a hand and smacked the cage aside, upsetting it completely. It fell off the stone bench and crashed to the ground.

Stunned, all of us froze for hardly more than a blink, but that was all the time it took for Koko to notice the broken cage and fly out. I screamed and lurched forward, trying to catch him. But the bird soared just barely out of reach, and instead of catching him, I tripped and fell forward onto the ground, knocking all the wind from my chest.

"Koko, nooo! Come back!" I wailed after the nightingale, but the little bird twittered a joyful tune, circled above us once, twice, and then flew out of sight.

"Oh no . . ." Yunmin moaned, covering her face. "Baba will kill us!"

But instead of falling into despair like her sister, Yunli simpered. "No, he will not," she said as she approached me and held up two fingers.

"Two pages," she said. "If you take the blame for this."

▪ ▪ ▪

I was beaten with a cane for losing Koko.

Mr. Guo rarely lost his temper, but whenever he did, no one wanted to be on the receiving end.

"How—dare—you—lose—my—bird? You stupid, careless, incompetent little idiot!" the man bellowed, and with every word, the bamboo cane rained on my arms, legs, back—anywhere that could be hit, for in his blinding rage, Mr. Guo did not seem to care which part of me he struck at all.

"Master, please . . . ! I'm sorry, I'm really sorry! Please, stop!" I screamed, holding my arms up to shield my face and jumping to avoid the cane.

But Mr. Guo did not look like he wanted to stop until he had completely appeased his anger, and my punishment continued until Jun'an lunged forward and hugged his father's legs. The cane froze in midair.

"Baba, stop! Please don't hurt Jing anymore, please!" Jun'an sobbed through the tears and gooey mucus on his face. "No more caning, please!"

Mr. Guo cast the stick upon the floor. "She will not get any food tonight!" he barked at his wife. Immediately, my little hero stumbled over and hugged me, crying as though he were the one who had been hurt. But his mother promptly removed him.

Still hiccuping, and despite the stinging pain all over my body, I crawled into a kneeling position and kowtowed.

"Thank you, Master! Thank you, Mistress! Thank you, Master . . ." And with every thanks, my head made a loud thud as it came into contact with the floor.

Only stopping after the grown-ups had left the room, I lifted my head to see Yunli walking up to me. "Well, at least you have this." Smiling to herself, she dropped two folded pieces of paper in front of me, and immediately, my tears made two droplets of stains on the parchment.

▪ ▪ ▪

Later that same evening, in the light of the flickering oil lamp in my room, I applied the healing balm Auntie San had given me on the angry red welts on my arms, legs, and anywhere else I couldn't see but hurt. I was not unfamiliar with the bamboo cane, because even Baba used it when we misbehaved. But it was different to be punished for something you did not do, and with every bit of pain that stung me, I yearned for Yunli to feel what I was going through in her place.

This pain belonged to her. These wounds belonged to her. And these tears should've been coming out of her eyes. I flung the healing balm across the room. I hated her! I slapped the stone wall until my palms throbbed, redder than the welts on my arms.

I didn't stop. I imagined Yunli's face as I continued to abuse the wall.

I wailed and wore myself out. And what had I achieved?

Enough crying, Jing! What about Wei's letter?

Yes, Wei's letter. Hadn't I been dying to read the next pages for such a long time?

I reached into my waistband and pulled out two pieces of rice paper, somewhat crinkled around the edges. I smoothed them out and gazed at the drawing on the first page. It showed a boy, beaming and carrying a toddler on his back as he walked through a meadow of daisies. I did not miss a single detail, not even the tiny drop of sweat drawn over the boy's forehead. A dull sort of feeling crept across my chest, as though someone was using a soy grinder on my heart . . .

Jie, guess what? Now I'm in charge of caring for Pan. I try to do everything you did, so I carry him everywhere I go, just like you used to. And we would often go to the daisy field. Remember? You used to bring us there all the time. Though it's not an easy job, babysitting Pan makes me think of you, just like how you often thought of Mama when you were responsible for Pan.

The next page showed the faces of a man, a boy, and a toddler, and although they were smiling, there was a tear beneath each of their eyes. An image over their heads showed a girl in a nice *hanfu*, happily laughing, with a little boy and two adults behind her.

Baba, Pan, and I miss you very, very much...
we think about you every day. But we know
that you must be happy and living a comfortable life with your new family. And whenever
we think of that, we feel happy for you,
because we love you very much.

I choked trying to hold back screams and sobs.
I tore at my blanket and my sheets. I kicked at the
stone walls around me until my heels felt sorer than
my wounds.

How? How could they even begin to compre-
hend the kind of life they had sold me into? I hated
them! Hated them for acting as though they still
cared after showing that they didn't, for how could
a father care for a daughter whom he would sell for
five miserable silvers?

Even more, I hated myself for still missing them.

I tried hugging myself, but my nails ended up
digging into my skin. I muffled my cries with a rug,
because even in such grief, I could not afford to be
heard. The pain felt like a relief, somehow. And that
night, I dreamed of returning home, riding on the
back of the Great Golden Huli Jing. I saw Wei, and
in my dream, Zhuzhu had grown into a toddler as
beautiful as Jun'an, and the three of us were back in

the daisy field, climbing trees and chasing one another. And at the edge of the field stood my baba, with a smile on his face brighter even than the sun in the sky.

I awoke in tears the next day, my chest heaving as though I had been up running all night. If I no longer belonged to Baba and his family, why did I have to miss them so much?

11

YUNLI'S PRANK

Thankfully, not all my attempts at retrieving Wei's letter were painful.

One chilly fall day when the sisters had just returned from classes, I had been heading to the scullery carrying a basin of warm water when I heard them coming down the corridor. Out of survival instincts, I ducked behind the doors to the living hall before they could see me.

"Ugh, that Lin Ran makes me want to tear out all her hair!"

Yunli did not sound as though she was in one of her best moods—all the more reason to keep out of sight. As usual, Yunmin echoed immediately.

"Yes, I never liked her. Such a show-off in front of Shifu."

Shifu was a respectful address form for a teacher, so they must be talking about another girl in class.

" 'Shifu' this and 'Shifu' that," Yunli mocked in an annoying higher octave. "What I can't stand is that stupid look on her face whenever Shifu praises her calligraphy and poetry."

"Yes, she's so full of herself . . ."

"But she's not going to be for long." Yunli suddenly sounded excited. "Come, I'll show you something really interesting!"

I shifted on my feet. When were they going to leave? I peeked through a crack. No . . . Yunli was pulling her sister into the hall. Now I was stuck. *Tian, ah*, why couldn't they just go to their room? Now I'd have to wait in hiding . . . and this would've been easier if I wasn't carrying a basin full of water.

"Look what I got!" Yunli pulled out from her sleeve a rectangular bar as black as soot, no bigger than the palm of her hand. It was an ink stick— solidified ink made from soot and glue that one ground against an inkstone with a little water to produce calligraphy ink, and this one had intricate carvings of lotus flowers on it.

Nonplussed, Yunmin's eyebrows knitted together. "But it's just an ink stick."

"Not just *any* ink stick; smell it!" Yunli thrust it under Yunmin's nose, and she obediently took a deep whiff.

Her tiny eyes lit up. "It's scented!"

"With sandalwood," Yunli finished for her in a triumphant tone. "The exact same kind that Miss Show-Off uses in class and that she boasted about last moon."

"Yes, I remember her saying that her father had brought it home from the imperial city of Dongjing. She even said you wouldn't find it anywhere in our province! How in Guan Yin's name did you manage to come by it?"

"Well, it is true that you can't get it anywhere here." Yunli nodded. "But your brilliant sister had already planned this a while back. With a little extra money, I ordered it sent specially from Dongjing to our local store."

"Oh, I can't wait to bring it to school!" Yunmin squealed as she held the precious ink stick in her hands. "And to see the look on Miss Show-Off's face when she finds out she's no longer the only girl in class with special scented ink!"

But Yunli gave an impatient snort. "We're not going to use it in class, stupid! Sometimes I don't understand how I came to have such a dumb sister."

I rolled my eyes and wondered the same thing. When Yunmin fell silent, Yunli went on, a smug look on her face. "On the contrary, we must *never* let anyone know we have it, because we're going to use this to write something nasty to Shifu."

"But why would you want to . . . ohhhhhh . . ."

I rolled my eyes again.

Yunli sighed loudly. "Yes, dumb duck, we're going to get Miss Show-Off into so much trouble with Shifu that he's going to give her a million lines to write!"

"Oh, what a sweet, sweet idea!" Yunmin clapped her hands.

"I know. Now go get my inkstone, calligraphy brush, and grab some Xuan paper from father's study. And if you see Huli Jing, tell her to come here."

I gulped. *Mama, Guan Yin, Huli Jing, don't let me be discovered.*

Yunli paced the room idly, humming and occasionally mumbling something to herself. Then Yunmin returned, half panting from her errand.

"I didn't see Huli Jing anywhere," she reported.

"Never mind, that can wait. In the meantime, I've come up with the absolute perfect thing." She promptly sat down at the round marble table.

Yunmin poured a small amount of water onto the inkstone and started to grind the ink stick against its surface. As the ink stick came into contact with the water, it began to dissolve into watery black ink that smelled richly of sandalwood.

Yunli dipped her calligraphy brush into it, smoothed it a few times over the stone to get the bristles into shape, and began to write. A few moments later, with a last confident stroke, Yunli held up her finished work. "There! A masterpiece, if I do say so myself. Her handwriting is so tidy it's easy to imitate; Shifu won't be able to tell the difference!"

I squinted harder.

床前明月光，
老師頭更光！

"*Chuang qian ming yue guang* . . ." Yunmin slowly read the words out loud. "*Shi fu tou geng guang!* Oh, Yunli, it's perfect! Shifu will be so mad when he sees this!"

I hadn't known then, but the lines were actually a play on the first stanza of a poem called "Thoughts on a Still Night" by Li Bai of the Tang dynasty, and what Yunli had written roughly translated into "Before my bed the bright moon shines, but brighter still Shifu's bald head shines!" I didn't recognize the words on the paper, but from the picture and what Yunmin had read aloud, the note sounded nasty.

I shifted the basin in my hands. It was getting so heavy . . . when were they going to leave? My elbow nudged against the door and it gave a creak so loud I almost bit my tongue.

"Huli Jing, is that you?"

Wonderful.

I stepped out sheepishly from my hiding place, and Yunmin grabbed the lapels of my *hanfu*. "What do you think you were doing behind there, you little eavesdropper?"

"Oh, step aside, Yunmin. That's no way to treat our reliable messenger," Yunli interrupted with a smile.

I swallowed. I'd have much rather been abused by Yunmin.

Yunli took the basin from me and thrust it into her sister's hands. She then flourished her artwork in front of me. "How would you like to earn the next page of your brother's letter by helping me deliver this?"

I nodded without looking at her. It wasn't a difficult decision, especially if it involved Wei's letter, but I'd be helping them get some poor girl in trouble.

It's not your place to worry about her, I kept telling myself later as I hurried through the town square with the horrid note in hand.

It had rained only a while ago, but there were just as many people on the streets. The air was misty and still smelled of rain, and the uneven dirt roads were dotted with yellow puddles. On any day, I would've enjoyed a leisurely walk in weather like this, stopping by to watch the *zaju* performers, *jing* tamers, and even buy myself a *tang hulu* from the candy stalls while I ran errands.

I steadied my breathing. All I had to do was leave the note at the door and not get caught. And then I'd get to read Wei's letter . . .

I bumped into a dirty beggar, stumbled a step back, and bumped into a kid. I regained my balance and mumbled an apology to no one in particular.

"It's all right."

Wei?

I whirled around and only managed to catch the boy's back disappearing into the crowd. "Wei?" I tried to follow, but which way did he go?

"It can't be him, fool," I muttered. How could it?

I shook my head and continued toward the east side of town. The little private academy wasn't difficult to find, nor was it very far, and I was able to inconspicuously slip the note into the center crack of the entrance doors and dart off before anyone saw me.

▫ ▫ ▫

I never knew for certain whether that poor girl was punished for the nasty prank she did not pull, but since Yunli did not come home particularly happy the next day, I assumed she probably hadn't been, which was quite a relief on my conscience. But although her little trick might not have gotten her the results she wanted, Yunli did at least go by her promise and give me the next page of Wei's letter.

This page showed a boy working hard on a piece of horseshoe, and daydreaming, with a smile on his face, of a big vibrant city.

Jie, this winter, I begged Baba to bring me along to work at the blacksmith's. I have not forgotten our promise. I will find a useful trade I can learn so that someday I can become an apprentice and earn enough to travel to Xiawan.

One day, Jie, I will see you again. Wait for me.

I sighed. My heart felt so full. "Yes, Wei. One day," I whispered as I carefully folded up the letter and hugged it to my chest. Perhaps my little encounter with an "imaginary" Wei that morning was a sign that we really would meet again someday.

12

LUNAR NEW YEAR

The Lunar New Year fell in midwinter that year. It was one of the biggest annual celebrations on the lunar calendar, and I used to think it was the best part of every year, better even than my own birthday. For one thing, no one had to work. And for another, there were food, games, fire flowers, and loud crackers that were supposed to scare evil *jing* away. All the children got to wear their best *hanfu* and play all day. Celebrations went on for fourteen days. But that wasn't even the best part.

The best part was the *hongbao*.

During Lunar New Year, adults gave out little red envelopes called *hongbao* to children. And they contained not sweets, not toys, but money. Maybe just a small copper piece or two at most, but collecting about thirty of those around the village could buy a comfy new pair of shoes.

Yes, I used to look forward to each new year, but probably never again.

Several days before the celebration, all the servants in the household were worked to the point of death—lots of shopping and cooking on top of cleaning and decorating. Mrs. Guo made me set up the thanksgiving altar each day for the *jing* and deities that might bring luck and prosperity to the family.

The idea of family reunion was the highlight of the festival. Therefore, relatives from immediate and extended families would come over for a reunion dinner on the night of New Year's Eve and stay for a few days. As the number of people in the house grew from six, to ten, to twenty, I got busier and busier. Both Auntie San and Liu had already gone back to their homes for the celebration, so I had even more to do than usual.

I did not get to play with any of the children who visited. I was not offered any of the delicious food or snacks. I did not get to watch the lion dance or the beautiful fire flowers. I did not even receive a *hongbao*.

All day long, I cooked, served, replenished the incense on the altars, and waited on the guests. And while the other children had darting vessel matches, played with bamboo horses, and even flew paper birds in the garden, I stood among the mahjong tables and chatting adults in the living hall, waiting to refill empty cups with more oolong tea.

Jun'an was one of the very few who paid me any proper attention, and would beg me again and again to join them.

"It's really fun." He would hold my hand and beseech me with his huge eyes. "The big kids are letting you play. We're starting a bamboo-horse race. I told them how good you are at it!"

Oh, how I wanted to go. Back in Huanan, I used to be so good on a bamboo horse they called me the "Bamboo Knight." I could have easily won.

I pressed my lips together and ruffled Jun'an's hair. "It does look really fun, but I can't right now. I'm busy, but I promise once I've finished I'll come play, all right?" And that would satisfy him.

Yunli, as usual, was the center of everyone's attention. Clad in an exquisite red *hanfu* underneath a sheer layer of shimmering white chiffon with embroideries of cranes and lotus blossoms, she could have easily been mistaken for a deity who had descended from the heavens.

"My word, look at your daughter, Mrs. Guo!"

"Why, I do believe that Yunli has managed to grow even more beautiful than last year, don't you think?"

"If only I had a daughter half as pretty as yours, Mrs. Guo."

"And Yunmin, too, of course . . . ," said Mrs. Chen without actually looking at the subject of her sentence. "You must be so proud of them."

I tried not to laugh. Of course, people usually managed to slip in a polite compliment or two for the less attractive daughter, but all the same, Yunli continued to bask in the glory of everyone's attention. However, I noticed there was actually one person's she especially desired.

Among the numerous family relatives was a cousin named Chen Han. He was a year or two older than Yunli and a charming young man—tall, dashing, and friendly. Now I would have been perfectly honest if I were to claim that I had never seen Yunli treat anyone with anything that resembled niceness, but I was about to be surprised that year.

Yunli did not pour herself all over him. She was

too proud for that, but she allowed him to talk to her without cutting in with snide remarks. And in his presence—I wouldn't have believed this had I not seen it with my own eyes—Yunli's smile even lost its nasty edge and dissolved into something gentler and more radiant.

Could this be what they called love? It was hard to keep a straight face remembering it. If this was what a simple crush could do to her, I couldn't wait to see Yunli fall head over heels. But I would never wish Yunli on someone as nice as Chen Han, because he was the only person other than Jun'an who did not treat me like a common servant. One time, he even saved a *tang hulu* for me.

"Here, have this," he said, holding out a stick of sugar-coated hawthorn berries.

I almost forgot to breathe as I held the candy in my hand. Because right then, I saw again the village square of Huanan. Saw myself and Wei giggling and darting through the crowds, each with a *tang hulu* in hand. The haw-centered ones had always been our favorite, and just remembering its sweetness left a nasty, sour taste in my mouth. I swallowed.

Someone tapped my shoulder. "You might want to start on that sometime soon." Chen Han was grinning, and he patted the space next to where he was sitting on one of the stone benches in the garden. I sat.

"You've grown taller, haven't you now?" he said, estimating a length of about two inches with his thumb and index finger. "At least this much since I saw you last year."

I stopped working on my *tang hulu* and smiled my first big smile that year. My mouth was sticky from the melted sugar that coated the sun-dried hawthorn berries. To be honest, I hadn't noticed exactly how much I had grown, but I liked being told that I had.

"And if I'm not mistaken, you're getting prettier, too. Let me have a look." And Chen Han motioned for me to stand in front of him. I hopped off the bench, still sucking on my candy. At his instruction, I turned around a couple of times as he pretended to consider me. "Hmm, why yes, maybe even prettier than Yunli, I reckon."

I laughed out loud. Thank all the Buddhas in heaven and hell that Yunli wasn't anywhere near to hear that. "I could never be as pretty as Da Jie," I said, finishing the last of my *tang hulu*. I resumed my seat on the bench, dangling my legs over the edge.

Chen Han rubbed my head. "In some ways, I believe you already are."

However, I soon learned that, with all the unwitting attention Chen Han was giving me, he had as good as dropped a boulder down a well that I had already been drowning in.

▪ ▪ ▪

If how Yunli had been treating me up till now could be considered nasty, the kind of treatment I received after Lunar New Year would definitely border on vicious. The first thing she did was to threaten me with Wei's letter. Until then, I had managed to earn five pages, and in the last one, I learned that Pan had been taken very ill with a high fever. I had begged Yunli to return the remaining pages then, but she only hitched on that hateful smirk of hers.

"I'm sorry about the cliff-hanger, Huli Jing. I hate those, too. But just try harder; I'm sure you'll get to the end of the story someday."

But now she had threatened to burn the letter.

I turned in my bed. Might she have burned it already? I turned again and buried my face in the quilt so I wouldn't cry.

There was no other way. I had to get it back before she destroyed it. Otherwise I should never be at peace.

It must have been long past midnight, because the gong for the hour of the rat had rung a good while ago. There was no better time to act. I slipped out into the dark and crept slowly along the now-familiar corridors toward the eastern wing, avoiding by touch and memory the planks that creaked or groaned.

I pushed open the sisters' bedroom door and stepped over the threshold. I could see quite well from just the moonlight that seeped in through the paper screens of the paneled windows.

The room was big. The two four-poster beds were built into the walls on one side near the windows, both concealed by a thin veil of gauze hanging from the wooden bed frames. The darker part of the room was where all the drawers and closets were.

I folded my sleeves and slid Mama's bangle halfway up my forearm so I wouldn't accidentally knock anything over. My hands shook as I rummaged through the furniture, making only as much noise as I half dared and replacing everything exactly where it had been. But the letter was nowhere to be found. I wiped off the cold sweat on my neck.

Think, Jing. If you were an evil sister-in-law, where would you hide someone's letter?

There was only one place left. My feet dragged like an elderly person's as I moved closer to where the sisters were sleeping. There were empty spaces right underneath the wooden bed frames. Perhaps . . .

I slunk over to Yunli's bed and got down on my knees. At that point, I was so close that I could make out her silhouette through the veil and even hear her slow breathing. Hardly daring to breathe myself, I reached far into the space under the bed and slowly felt around for a box or some other object. But alas, there was none. Where else, then?

Just as I withdrew my hand, someone grabbed a handful of my hair.

I screamed and looked up.

Glaring at me in the moonlight, with her long hair in disarray from sleep, Yunli resembled a blood-thirsty, flesh-hungry, demonic *jing*.

"Looking for this?" She dangled Wei's letter in front of me. I knew then that she had already anticipated my attempt.

Yunmin lit an oil lamp and hobbled over, yawning. "What's all this noise in the middle of the night, Da Jie . . . ?"

"I found a naughty little girl snooping in our room. Looking for something she'll never find." On Yunli's face was the same smile she had the first time we met. "You're a very bad girl for trying to outsmart me, so this is punishment to remind you that it never pays to cross your Da Jie, all right?"

And with that, she thrust the letter into the lamp fire.

It caught instantly.

"Da Jie, no!" I shrieked, but the letter had already gone up in a ball of flames. It burned out even before its ashes reached the ground. My letter. I fell so heavily on my knees that they went numb.

Wei . . . I had failed him. I glared up at Yunli, but she suddenly drew her hand back and slapped me across the face.

"Thief! How dare you come in here to steal!"

Before anything else could happen, she dragged me, sobbing, out of the room toward the master chamber.

13

THE ZANZHI

By the time Yunli had woken the entire household, I knew I had never been in more trouble in my entire life. Mrs. Guo was in a foul mood from being woken up in the middle of the night. I had never seen her in such a state. Underneath all that makeup, the skin on her face was yellowish and saggy. Permanent dark circles framed her crusted, bloodshot eyes. Her breath smelled like rotten eggs marinated in horse pee, and with her hair in such a matted mess, she looked even more like a demon than Yunli had.

"Stealing?" she rasped. I was on my knees with my head lowered in the deepest kowtow. I could explain. I really could. But I wasn't allowed to speak until spoken to.

"Yes, Mama. Yunmin and I caught the little thief going through our jewelry in the middle of the night," said Yunli.

I screamed as my hair was jerked back. Mrs. Guo leaned in close. "I don't know or care why you did it, but I will not tolerate stealing in my house. Especially not from a *tongyang xi*, do you hear?"

"P-P-Please, Mistress . . . Truly and honestly, Jing did not steal any—"

"Mama, she is lying! We found this on her." Yunli held out a golden brooch.

Mrs. Guo's small eyes narrowed into slits. When she let go of my hair, I fell to the floor and curled into a ball. "Still unrepentant, are we? Then this might serve as a good warning for any more funny ideas in the future. Bring the *zanzhi*!"

I had no idea what a *zanzhi* was, but from the look of extreme delight on Yunli's face, it seemed like something I should be terrified of. Yunmin brought in a peculiar instrument . . . and I wondered how much it was going to hurt. It was a good thing I didn't know then.

The *zanzhi* was a row of ten wooden rods approximately six inches in length, all vertically strung together. Mrs. Guo grabbed my hands and rammed each of my eight fingers in between two rods.

The pain was instantaneous.

As the ropes that connected the rods were pulled away from the center, the instrument squeezed with immeasurable force, compressing my fingers. I screamed so sharply my throat might have torn apart. I began to squirm and struggle—anything. Anything to ease this pain. This unbearable pain.

"Someone hold the little devil still!" Mrs. Guo shrieked, and then my hair was yanked back again as Yunli pinned my head on the table.

My fingers.

My fingers.

"Mistress! Mistress please . . . !" I choked in between sobs. "Please stop! I beg of you, please! I did not steal anything . . . I am not a thief, I swear! I swear upon my dead mother's honor! I swear in the name of our goddess Guan Yin! Please, have mercy!"

But the pressure did not relent, and my fingers went from a deep, angry red to a frightening dark purple. I screamed and screamed. But nothing I did would stop the pain.

"Please, Mistress! Oh, please stop! I cannot take any more!"

"Really? Well, perhaps you should've thought about the consequences before doing something so stupid!" And, impossibly, the *zanzhi* tightened even more.

Blood. There was blood, trickling down the rods. My bones must be breaking. "I—I'm sorry! I'm sorry, Mistress! I won't ever do it again! I was wrong! Please, stop!"

As suddenly as it had struck, the pressure around my fingers gave out. I fell to the ground in a heap, drenched in my own sweat. I couldn't move, but I twitched. And then I must've lost consciousness, because I no longer felt my fingers.

◾ ◾ ◾

I woke up the next morning in the toolshed.

"Mama said you are to stay in there with no food for three days," Yunmin sang just outside the door. My voice was hoarse, but I still managed to laugh. With what they'd done to my fingers, I would not have been able to feed myself anyway. I couldn't even pick up something as light as a pair of chopsticks.

"She's gone crazy; let's go before we catch it." I heard Yunli, and then their receding footsteps.

My fingers were a ghastly sight. Would I ever be able to use them again?

The *zanzhi* had grated off almost all the skin on the sides, leaving the bloodied flesh exposed, and around the open wounds on each finger were deep bruises, from dark red to purple to black. Rather than fingers, they looked like fat, horribly disfigured worms. I struggled into a sitting position against the wall. The open wounds felt like the time when a few drops of boiling oil had splattered on my arm in the kitchen, except now the feeling was all over my hands.

Stop, please, stop hurting. I didn't deserve this. I did nothing so bad to deserve this! I forced my hands into hard fists.

"I said, stop hurting!" I pounded the ground after every word and felt all my wounds reopen, but I kept going.

I bled more. I cried more. I hurt more. I hated even more.

Yunli could burn on the eighteenth level of hell and be cast into the animal reincarnation cycle for eternity and it still wouldn't be punishment fitting enough for her! I wanted to put my hands around her neck and dig my thumbnails into her throat and watch blood and life seep out of her in front of my eyes. I wanted her beautiful eyes to widen in horror. I wanted her to sob like a baby and beg me for mercy, and I wanted the immense satisfaction of giving her none.

I screamed again and again.

Finally, I sank back against the wall and closed my eyes. Being awake was hard work. If there was any mercy left in this world, let me sleep. Let me sleep through the entire ordeal and only wake up when these wounds were healed.

Sometime later, the bolt on the door slid open, and Auntie San came in. She cleaned and treated my fingers as I clenched my teeth and squeezed my eyes shut. The kind lady, however, wept silently as she dressed my wounds. "Those beasts," she said. "To have used the *zanzhi* on such a young girl!"

I tried to smile, which probably looked more like a grimace. Then she left to get me some water and a blanket for the night.

It was a good thing Jun'an had slept through the entire incident, but as soon as the cook left, I heard him crying. I got up and went to sit behind the door. The crying stopped.

"Jing . . . ? That you, isn't it? Jing, when I grow up, I will protect you," he promised. "Then no one can hurt you anymore."

That was my brave and kind little husband. And for the next two days, Jun'an would come down and spend most of his time near the shed, playing around the area, chatting with me, and telling me the stories I had so often told him. He even made me a pretty bracelet, woven out of long blades of grass.

Auntie San brought me food in the evening before she went home. "I will lose my job before I'd stand by and watch those beasts starve you to death," she exclaimed indignantly as she brought out all my favorite dishes from a basket. "I can only come down here once a day, but you can eat all you want, child. And it won't be leftovers," she added with a huff.

I parted my flaking lips as my first meal of the day was spooned into my mouth. The warm fish broth tasted both painful and heavenly as it slid past my throat, and the steamed soy chicken as well, and the leek buns . . . and the dumplings . . . and the . . .

This was a little silver lining in one of my many clouds.

▪ ▪ ▪

Night was the most difficult part of the day to get through. The shed was too cold for just a rug or two, and I was alone with my own thoughts, which often wandered to places I didn't want to revisit, people I didn't want to think about.

Mama. If Mama was watching, and if she had known this was happening to her daughter, how sad would she be? Baba certainly wouldn't be—he was the one who didn't want me anymore. But Mama would've cried for me, surely?

And as though in answer, there came the sound of thunder, followed by the heavy pitter-patter of raindrops on the thin straw roof. Look. Even the sky was crying. Mama must be crying for me. At least someone still cared.

I chuckled, and somehow, that hurt even more than crying.

Wei. Baba didn't care, but Wei surely did. He'd even tried to help me run away.

Could I?

No.

A daughter-in-law running away was absolutely unheard of. And what about Jun'an then? What would happen to him if I ran away? Would he have to find a new wife? How would she treat him?

I must have drifted off at some point, because in between spells of wakefulness and dreams, that same voice came to me again. Although I'd only heard it once before, I remembered the feeling it gave me, like a warm caressing wind.

"You said that better times would come." I tried not to sound accusing.

"Yes, they will, dear one. But perseverance is key . . . ," it assured me gently.

"I cannot take it anymore. I want to go home."

Then I began to cry.

Stupid Jing, you forget that you no longer have a home outside the Guo family. My own family had not wanted me in the first place. Huanan was no longer home. "I have to find my spirit's home, Shenpopo said . . . that place where I truly belong. Where is it?"

"And you will find it, dearest, but now is not yet the time," the voice whispered wistfully. "But believe me when I assure you that it will come."

"Who are you?"

There was silence for a long moment, then: "For now, I am a force that's alive within yourself."

She might as well have kept quiet. Who could understand that?

"Are you me, then?" I tried again.

"You will know in due time."

When I tried to roll my eyes, I ended up opening them instead. I woke up, and couldn't help gazing, for a long moment, at my mother's black bangle that used to be too big, but now fit my left wrist perfectly.

Abruptly, a dull scratching sound came from the closed window. Someone, or something, was trying to get in. The window was made up of a few wooden boards nailed together, so I had to open it to see what was outside. Too late at night for it to be Jun'an or Auntie San. Was it a burglar, then? But that was silly; why would a burglar try to break into a tool shed?

The scratching was light and hesitant, as though whoever was outside wasn't sure whether to make himself known. I swallowed. "Who—who is there?" And that was when the scratching stopped, followed by a timid whine that I immediately recognized.

I scrambled to my feet and, as carefully as I could, climbed into a sitting position on a large wooden box just beside the window. I shouldn't be opening it—the night was cold, and once the window was ajar, I wouldn't be able to pull it closed with my hands. But I didn't care. With my elbow, I slowly pushed one side open, and there, waiting on the windowsill for me, was Saffron, the same golden puppy I had met during the Ghost Festival last year.

"Why, hello again," I cried as he leaped onto my lap. I circled my arms around him, careful to keep my hands out of the way. Saffron seemed to know I was hurt, for he did not wiggle or jump up, only sat there, wagging his bushy tail and gazing at me with adoring green eyes. I hugged him again. "I've missed you, too. Where have you been? And why are you here?"

The puppy slid off my lap and padded over to the corner farthest from the window. When I sat down, he rested his head on my lap. Oh, how I would've loved to pet him if doing so wouldn't hurt my fingers.

"You haven't grown much, have you?" Against my bare skin, Saffron's fur felt softer than silk and warmer than a quilt. "You always seem to appear whenever I need someone. Are you sure you're not a *jing*? Are you sure it wasn't the Great Golden Huli Jing who sent you?"

Saffron only lifted his head, twitched one of his pointy ears, and gazed at me solemnly. And then he started to lick at my fingers. I inhaled sharply, but I felt no more pain than if a feather had landed on my wounds. I no longer felt cold, for there was a strange warmth coming from my little friend that kept away the chill.

And finally, as Saffron licked gently and purposefully, I must have fallen asleep, because in my dreams, I saw my little friend transform into a handsome golden fox that had me enveloped in the warmth of its five woolly tails all night.

14

LOOMING CHANGES

Saffron visited me every night until I was let out of the shed. I wanted so much to keep him, but who was I to ask for a pet? I couldn't even protect myself, and Mrs. Guo would sooner cook the poor pup for dinner. No, my little friend could not stay. I waved my goodbye from the window.

Thank you, Great Golden Huli Jing, for giving me a friend when I needed one most.

I could no longer visit the shrine back home, so after my ordeal, I took to praying to Guan Yin, the goddess of mercy, for whom the Guos had set an altar in the main hall. The porcelain statue of Guan Yin stood in between Caishen, the god of wealth, and White Lady Baigu. It was said that Guan Yin had a thousand ears so she could hear the cries of the wretched and distressed. I wanted her to hear mine. And perhaps she did, for my fingers had healed after one moon, leaving no effects other than unattractive, reddish-brown scars.

But no matter how fervently the Guos prayed to their deities, the family business had started going downhill very steeply. Mr. Guo's mood grew darker by the day, and the mistress had been throwing more and more tantrums around the house, striking fear among all the servants. I was extra careful about making any muddles, but most of the time the person who suffered the brunt of her wrath was poor Liu, the house butler.

One day in late winter, I was hurrying along the hallway with a basket of laundry in my hands. But when a loud crash came from the living hall just a few feet away, I stopped. I really should've minded my own business, but when Yunli's shrill voice came resounding from the hall, I couldn't help tiptoeing closer and kneeling inconspicuously behind the entrance.

"I will not! I refuse! I will never marry the magistrate's son!" she screamed at her mother. "He may be rich, but he's fat, and ugly, and stupid! I won't marry a pig like him!"

I peeked just ever so slightly around the vertical beams and saw Yunli picking up a tea set and smashing it onto the ground. From the amount of shattered porcelain on the floor, it looked as though she had already gone through more than a vase or two, which translated into more work for me. Yunli was throwing a proper fit—a kind I had never seen before.

I saw it coming before she did and winced as the slap from Mrs. Guo landed on Yunli's face with a loud smack.

"Foolish child! How old do you think you want to be before you get married?" Mrs. Guo boomed in her guttural voice. "Do you think that someone would still want you in another year or so just because you're beautiful? Ha! They'd say, '*Ai, ma!* There must be something wrong with this girl if she still hasn't found a husband at this age!' That's what you'll hear!"

Her mama was right. Yunli should've calmed down at this point, but she held on to her painful cheek as she stamped her foot and began to bawl. "But the magistrate's son already has two wives! I shall die before I become a concubine to that worthless, melon-headed son of a hopping zombie!"

"Worthless? Worthless?" At this, Mrs. Guo seized Yunli's left ear and twisted it so much that I almost felt it myself. "Do you know how powerful the

magistrate is? He works directly under the high magistrate of the Taiyuan province! His son could take
five wives and still provide comfortably for them
should he so desire! You have no idea how fortunate
you are. He made an offer of twenty gold pieces for
your dowry, and that's not even half of what our
business needs to recover!"

Upon hearing that, Yunli backed away, her eyes
opened wide. "Y-You're making me marry that
pig . . . because Baba is losing money? Is that it?"

"You're the only one in the house who can fetch a
dowry that high. Do you think Yunmin can demand
even half of what you can?"

There was what seemed like a long silence, and
then Yunli threw her head back and started laughing.
It was laughter, but it was the most heartbreaking
sound I had ever heard.

In Yunli's eyes, I saw many things. In her laughter, I heard many emotions, all roiling. Was that
how I looked whenever I thought of my own family?
My chest heaved. I couldn't watch anymore. I picked
up the laundry basket and fled.

▪ ▪ ▪

It was only a few days later that I inadvertently
learned another piece of shocking news. I had been

escorting Jun'an back to his room for the night, the child happily holding a heart-shaped snowball we had just made.

"We'll be able to make something bigger, like a snow hut, if we get a few more snowfalls," I said.

"Oh, I want a snow hut! Could we live in it?"

I laughed. "Of course not, silly; unless you're a snow *jing*, you'll freeze to death. But we can most certainly play in it."

When we passed by the master chamber, we heard voices in the room. "It's Baba and Mama! Could we say good night?" I nodded, but as we neared the wooden double doors, it became apparent that they were arguing. I laid a hand on Jun'an's shoulder so he wouldn't push the doors open.

"We can't wait till she's ready!" Mr. Guo sounded frustrated. "We need the money soon."

It seemed as though we had come at a bad time, for they were still arguing over Yunli's marriage. I kneeled down to Jun'an's height and placed a finger over his mouth. Jun'an nodded obediently and pursed his lips. We listened to his mother's next words.

"But surely we can still wait a little more, until we're able to find one who can offer a higher price . . ."

There was a sharp sound of someone slapping a desk. "The suppliers are asking for payment by the next moon, for Buddha's sake! It's their final warning. If we drag this out any longer and word gets out to the magistrate that our business is facing such a crisis, even Yunli's going to have trouble with her engagement!"

I covered my mouth. So it wasn't Yunli they were talking about. Now it seemed as though they were going to marry Yunmin off as well. The business must've been doing even worse than any of us had imagined. I kept my arms around Jun'an as we continued to eavesdrop.

"We take the first offer that comes in. When is the earliest you can arrange for a *baomu* to come for inspection?"

What was a *baomu*? Perhaps an inspector of brides?

"There is one from a reasonably wealthy *chinglou* who expressed interest. She said she could come in the day after . . ."

And it was then that time stopped.

Chinglou.

A place that housed courtesans—entertainers of men. Of the wealthy and influential. There wasn't one in Huanan, but such places were common in cities like Xiawan. My vision began to swim. Mr. and Mrs. Guo were not talking about Yunli or Yunmin.

They were talking about me, and Mrs. Guo's next words confirmed it.

"Jun'an might get upset . . ."

"Well, he'll learn to deal with it like a man."

I dimly felt tugging at my sleeves.

"Jing, what is a *chinglou*?" Jun'an asked in the smallest whisper he could manage.

I needed time alone. I hastily ushered my little husband down the hallway. "Well, it's . . ." I faltered. "It's very late; I'll explain some other time, all right?"

And Jun'an was very good about it.

▪ ▪ ▪

Sacrificed again.

Given away for the benefit of others.

Another change.

No more belonging to the Guo family.

Never belonged in the first place.

I couldn't concentrate on a single thought. I had been tossing in my bed for hours. I covered my face and tried to breathe normally.

If I allowed things to unfold on their own, I would be free of the Guos but trapped in a worse place. No! Wei was right. This time, I wouldn't just sit around and let bad things happen to me. I wasn't the same Jing as I was a year ago. Aunt Mei could argue that I owed my father enough to marry into a horrid family, but nothing could convince me that I owed the Guos anything—certainly not to be sold to a *chinglou*.

I would not let them make money off me. They did not even deserve the clippings of my toenails.

I would run away.

I didn't need the voice in my dreams to tell me it was time to leave. If I allowed myself to be sold into a *chinglou*, not only would it be more difficult to run away, but my life would practically be over.

But where could I go?

Huanan? I couldn't help a chuckle that hurt my chest. Would my own family welcome me home? Aunt Mei would get really mad, but surely even she would understand if I told them what a horrid fate I was running away from? Wei would be happy— no, he would be thrilled. And Baba . . . would he stand for such a thing to happen to me?

This was my sign. My family might have given me away, but Huanan was the only place that had ever made me feel like I belonged—it was the home of my spirit. My roots.

Yes, I would go home.

But I mustn't be rash. I rubbed Mama's bangle. It felt cool and soothing. The journey home from Xiawan would take at least three to four days on foot. If I wanted to make it back home alive in this harsh weather, I would need careful planning, preparation, and probably even some help.

Judging from what I had just overheard, I had one day before someone came in for the inspection and probably take me away. Which meant I had little time.

Very little.

15

THE LADY WITH
YELLOW EYES

I felt a certain kind of tightness in my stomach the next day, as though I had eaten an entire basket of sour mandarins. It was probably due to anxiety, and the fact that I hadn't slept at all. I had spent the entire night working out a plan of escape, and finally came to the conclusion that I would need the help of two key people to facilitate my plan.

Jun'an and Auntie San.

The best time to take action was during the night, when everyone was fast asleep. Auntie San could help me obtain directions or a map to Huanan. I would walk. Horse carriage and other rides were out of the question because those only ran during the day, and I didn't have enough money anyway.

The moment Auntie San stepped into the kitchen, I dove into her arms and told her everything. As horrified at the Guos as any person should be, the kind cook immediately agreed to help. "You can count on your auntie San, my child. I'll never let anyone send you to such a place! To be an entertainer of men? The very idea! I will have everything you need by the time you're ready to leave."

Auntie San pretended to have caught a bad cold and took her leave from Liu. "You wouldn't want me to be working in the kitchen with this, would you?" She paused as she coughed dramatically. "I've already instructed Jing on what to do in the kitchen today. She'll manage fine, that lass." And with that, Auntie San hurried out of the door and disappeared around the bend.

▪ ▪ ▪

The *baomu* turned out to be an old, wizened lady who managed the *chinglou*. The first thing I noticed about her after entering the room was how yellow her eyes were where they should have been white. She attempted something that resembled a smile. I couldn't help noticing that her teeth were as yellow as her eyes.

The mistress told me that the *baomu* was a family doctor who was here for a simple health inspection. I sucked at the insides of my cheeks. Would I have been fooled by this lie if I hadn't already known the truth? Gazing at the frail, yellow lady, who looked as though she could drop dead at any moment, I decided I wouldn't have.

When Mrs. Guo closed the door behind us and ordered me to pay respects, I sank into a kowtow. "*Nin hao*, Doctor," I greeted her without looking up, and then was struck by an unsettling sense of déjà vu as my chin was lifted up. Those slightly sunken, yellow eyes ogled my face, stopping to gaze hungrily at the mole between my eyebrows.

"Hmm . . . this would do," the *baomu* muttered indistinctly to herself. "This would do very well indeed."

It was almost all I could do to refrain from grimacing as the lady's rancid tobacco breath overwhelmed my nostrils. Finally, the *baomu* let go of me.

"How old are you, girl?"

I bowed before answering. "I'll be turning thirteen in the middle of spring."

The old lady's twig-like fingers wiggled as she did a mental calculation. "Year of the golden ram . . . an intelligent girl, no doubt," she said, though it did not sound like she meant it as a compliment. "Stand up and turn around."

The *baomu* measured my height and weight, then barked at me to raise my hands as she measured my waist. And when the old lady delivered a hard pinch on my behind, I yelped.

"Firm and healthy muscles, that's what we like to see," she said. My hopes rose when she lifted my hands and frowned at my unsightly scars. Mrs. Guo shifted in her seat.

"These won't go away," I said, even though I hadn't been addressed.

The mistress almost glared a hole through my chest, and I had to hold back a smirk. Then the *baomu* let go of my hands and turned to Mrs. Guo. "The examination is done. She may be excused."

"Get out of here, Jing."

I got up hastily, but stayed right outside after I closed the doors.

"She's passed," said the *baomu*.

Passed. If only I knew how to disqualify myself. Perhaps if I marred my appearance in some irreparable way . . . ? I winced just at the thought. I had enough people abusing me without doing it to myself.

▪ ▪ ▪

"Listen, Jun'an. A *chinglou* . . . is . . . it's a bad place," I said as I kneeled with my hands on his shoulders. We were in my room, and it was late in the evening. Very late. I had checked the incense clock moments ago, making sure that it was in fact so late that everyone else in the house was sure to be asleep. I figured out that I'd be going to the *chinglou* the next morning when the mistress instructed me to visit the doctor's clinic to collect the prescribed medicinal herbs. That night was my final chance to escape. I had crept to the bedroom doors of each of the Guo family members in turn, just to be sure that everyone was fast asleep, before going to Jun'an's room.

"But why are they sending you there?" my little husband cried, horrified at the idea. "They can't send you to a bad place! What if something happens to you?"

I covered his mouth.

"Shh . . . Jun'an, let's try to be a little quieter, shall we?" I tried to explain in whispers. "Your father is having a . . . well, a problem, and he needs money to fix it. That is why I have to be sold, so that . . ." I swallowed. "So that your family will have money."

"They can't do that! I don't want money. I won't let them do that to you."

"Which is why I have to go away, and you have to help me. I can't go to that place . . ." I had tried to imagine life at the *chinglou*. None of the possibilities

I could think of had a bearable ending. I began to shake. "I—I might die."

"You won't die, Jing. I will help you. I won't let you die." As though it were contagious, my little husband began to cry as well, but instead of dabbing his own tears, his plump little hand reached out to wipe away mine.

And at that moment, I knew that if there was anything from my life here that I would miss, it would be Jun'an. I gathered his trembling body into my arms and held him tight. This was me and Wei all over again . . . Could I take this wonderful child with me? But I could never give Jun'an the kind of life his family did. And what right had I to expect Baba to take him in? I might not even be welcomed myself.

We made our way toward the wooden gates in the backyard. Jun'an's role in my plan was to shut and bolt the door after I left so that I would not be missed too soon. Before stepping over the threshold, I kneeled to his height.

He gazed at me with his lovely round eyes. "Will you ever come back?"

"I—I don't know . . ."

"I will miss you, Jing . . . I will really, really miss you! Will I never see you again?"

His trembling hands told me that Jun'an was trying his hardest not to make a fuss. To him, my happiness took precedence over his, and it broke my heart.

I pulled him into another hug. My tears felt hot against my cheeks. "Maybe by the time I return, you'll be all grown up, but Jun'an, I promise you that someday, we will meet again. You are my husband, and we share this thing called *yuan*, like a ribbon that ties us together. So don't forget me, all right?"

All this while, hope was what had carried me through my darkest times, and I couldn't bring myself to leave this young boy with none.

"I won't, ever ever ever," he said, hugging me back.

And it was with this hope in each other's hearts that we were finally able to break apart. I kissed Jun'an on his forehead and was just about to get up when we heard a deep, guttural voice.

"It's a little cold to be out for a midnight stroll, isn't it?"

I froze as I glanced up at the mistress's face, so twisted from fury that it stunned me like a spell.

"See, Mama? I told you I heard a sound from Jun'an's room," Yunli said.

Before I could run, my hair was grabbed by the handful and I was yanked back through the doors.

I whimpered from the searing pain in my scalp. Jun'an screamed.

"So you think you can just get up and walk out on this household whenever you please, hmm?" Mrs. Guo sneered in my face.

"Please, Mistress . . . ," I sobbed. "You can't send me to a *chinglou*. I'll go anywhere but there, please—"

"Mama, please don't send Jing to a bad place." Jun'an clung to his mother's arm as though his life depended on it. "Don't send her away, Mama. I love her!"

Mrs. Guo's tone immediately softened as she spoke to her son. "Now be good, my son. Jing was lying to you. Mama promises you that it isn't a bad place at all—"

I could not let them do this to me.

"No!" I began to struggle under the woman's grip. "No, it's an evil place! I shall die if I go there!"

Abruptly, my left ear hummed with the after-effect of a sharp, resounding slap.

"Why, you scheming, insolent little imp!" the mistress hissed in my ear. "How is it that you, a lowly *tongyang xi*, could consider yourself in any place to argue against my decisions? And do you think that getting my son on your side would make it harder for me to give you up?" Somehow, watching Jun'an crying so piteously, relentlessly begging her to release me, made Mrs. Guo even more furious. She yanked my head up close and snarled. "Seeing as how you will soon belong to that *chinglou*, I will spare you the *zanzhi* this time." She turned to her daughters. "Get Liu!"

At her command, Yunmin scuttled off and soon came back with the sleepy-eyed butler. Mrs. Guo shoved me at him and I felt grips tighter than vises clamp onto my upper arms.

"Take her to Yuegong Lou now," the mistress barked, embracing her son.

It was no use. I couldn't escape these strong hands. But still I struggled. I reached out for mercy, for anything that might save me.

"Please, Mistress; you pray to Guan Yin, don't you? For the goddess of mercy, for your own son, please do not send me there. I'll do anything . . ."

Liu started to steer me away, but Mrs. Guo held out her hand.

"Wait!"

There was an urgency in her voice that made my heart stop. Had I convinced her to change her mind?

She walked over and grabbed my left wrist. Mama's bangle reflected the moonlight, dark and beautiful.

No . . .

Mrs. Guo grinned. "I knew I forgot something." And with that, she began to twist the bangle off my wrist. "You won't be needing this at the *chinglou*; they will dress you up prettier than a flower."

"No! That's my mama's bangle—don't take it from me! It's my only memento of her!" I sobbed and struggled and pleaded as pain spread from where the woman was forcefully twisting and tugging at Mama's bangle.

"Shut up! Help me, girls!" She heaved and huffed.

Yunli rolled her eyes and disappeared into the kitchen, but Yunmin came over, pushing Jun'an aside, and began pinching my waist. "Give it up, you greedy little thing!"

But the bangle wouldn't come off. I was glad. I would bear any amount of pain to keep it. They would have to twist my hand off, and that wouldn't do if they wanted to sell me. Then Yunli appeared with a bowl.

"Move over, stupid," she snapped at Yunmin, and dumped its content over my wrist.

It was oil.

The bangle slipped right off.

"There," said Mrs. Guo, straightening up and studying the jewelry in her hand. "This might just fetch a decent price at the pawnshop."

Stop, Jing. Just stop. It will only add to their pleasure. The sisters were leering. I bit down on my tongue. I stopped struggling and concentrated on the pain in my mouth and the taste of my blood. I imagined it was theirs. If it delighted them to see me suffer, I wasn't going to put up an overly enjoyable show.

I lifted my chin and looked straight at the woman. "I knew you never liked me, Mrs. Guo, and I never liked you, either. Therefore, before I leave, I want you to know that I hope no good ever comes out of the things you reap at the expense of others. Karma will find you and make you pay tenfold for all the suffering that you have inflicted upon others." I did not blink once as I said this, and I could tell it unsettled her.

Jun'an's sobs were ceaseless, and he struggled wildly against his mother's arms as Liu firmly steered me away. "Jing! Nooo! Don't go . . . don't go! Oh, please, Mama, let me go! Jiiiiing!"

Before the doors closed behind me, I looked back, but I neither saw nor heard anyone but Jun'an.

Saw him kicking and struggling, heard him crying and howling like a wounded animal, his voice filled with so much grief that with every sob, it felt to me like a piece of flesh was being sliced off my living body.

16

THE DAUGHTERS OF YUEGONG LOU

Liu's grip on my forearm never loosened throughout our journey. He walked briskly, and a few times I almost tripped in the snow trying to keep up. His mouth was pressed into a hard, straight line. Liu had always been a stiff man of very few words, but tonight, even though he didn't have to, he took the time to tell me about this place to which I was going.

"The *baomu*, Madam Qia, is the owner of the *chinglou*. The mistress has been given a deposit, but the full amount will only be paid after Madam Qia has assessed your potential and decided to keep you. Whatever full amount you fetch will completely depend on the *baomu*'s evaluation of how much of an asset you could be to the *chinglou* . . ." The man drifted off, but his eyes continued to glower at the road straight ahead. "There is no way you can change or reverse what is about to happen, but the least you can do is behave. Then perhaps you may still be able to be of some help to Jun'an and his family."

I almost bit my tongue again trying to hold back from screaming that the last thing I wanted was to help that hateful woman and her daughters. But Liu had been tactful to mention my soft spot. Would I really go through with this for Jun'an's sake? What would happen to him if I didn't?

I glanced up. The hard lines between the man's eyebrows and the tightened veins down his neck made me wonder about the possibility of persuading him to let me go.

Silly Jing, in your dreams he would. Unlike Auntie San, Liu would never do anything to cross his employer. And could I really blame him? For after all, he was a man who had a family to feed. And if my own family in Huanan wouldn't protect me from such a fate, what could an outsider like him do?

The streets were dark except for the light that came from the lanterns hanging at the front doors of the houses we trudged past. The red and orange lights cast an ominous glow on the snow that made it look as though the ground was covered in blood. Somewhere on the next street, the time keeper rang his gong twice, signaling the hour of the ox. Other than a few *yamen* officials on night duty, there was not a soul on the streets. Although I was tempted to scream, I'd be foolish to do so—selling helpless and unwilling girls to the *chinglou* was not against the law.

When we arrived in the central area of town, Liu stopped in front of a huge four-level building that, even in the night, shone like a palace, with light pouring out from all its windows, doors, and balconies. I saw a red wooden signboard over the arch at the entrance, illuminated by two red lanterns hanging on each side. It had three characters written on it in big, confident strokes of gold:

樓宮月

Although I didn't recognize the words, I was quite certain they read *Yuegong Lou*.

After crossing the expansive garden and stepping into the reception hall, I was stunned like a freshly caught fish. Yuegong Lou was unlike any place I had ever been in. The circular brick entrance opened into a spacious reception hall with a ceiling crisscrossed with red wooden beams that reached as high as the top of the building. Bright red lacquered pillars rose from the foundations and supported the entire structure from inside. I could clearly see each of the three levels above us from the corridor landings that spanned across all four sides of the building. Under the archway of the entrance stood a huge bronze incense clock shaped like a phoenix.

I had never beheld such a grand and magnificent interior, and would never have imagined such a place could be the home of courtesans.

But as soon as the *baomu* appeared, I stumbled back. What now? What would happen? What was this woman going to make me do?

The old lady hobbled up to us, grunted with approval as she saw me, and turned to Liu. "I'm sure Mrs. Guo has her reasons for bringing the girl in earlier than expected," she muttered in an oily sort of voice. She handed Liu a stack of that hateful paper money, on which I dearly wished to spit, and said, "I'd like a word before you leave, Mr. Liu."

"Certainly, Madam Qia." Liu nodded.

Behind the *baomu* stood a cluster of women, and I couldn't help noticing how beautiful and elaborately dressed they were. As soon as Liu left my side, they completely surrounded me. The women touched my skin, face, hair, and turned me round and round while remarking on my appearance, chattering nineteen to the dozen like a cage full of mynahs.

"Oh, such smooth and delicate skin! I remember when mine used to feel like that," cooed one of them with a lovely but heavily made-up face.

"That must have been decades ago, Feier!" laughed another, who was dressed in a most gaudy lime-green *hanfu* with heavy silver brocades. I felt the bangs of hair that covered my forehead being swept up.

"Girls, we may have an intelligent one; look at the high forehead," said a voice that sounded less high-pitched. I dared a glance and saw a perfect heart-shaped face, framed by wisps of carefully curled locks on each side.

"Why, you're right, Qiu Xiang," agreed another woman, with a stunning *faji* adorned with numerous glittering hair ornaments. "After all, we do need a certain level of wit to keep patrons entertained. This little one will be good indeed, unlike Miao, so dull and difficult to teach." When she shook her head, the accessories in the woman's *faji* tinkled merrily.

"Oh my! And is that a beauty mole I see?" someone else cut in.

"Where? Where?"

"I don't see it, Honghe."

"Look, there, in between her eyebrows. And a stunning red one, too," exclaimed the one called Honghe. "Exactly like the one on the imperial consort Yang Guifei—one of the four legendary beauties of the Middle Kingdom!"

"Oh, and to think the rest of us have to deliberately dab a fake spot in between our brows as part of our makeup."

"And this girl has it all natural!"

"It seems Qia Mama made a good investment this time."

"You're right, Xuehuar. I can almost see her as a *mingji* when she grows up."

The rippling excitement was contagious, like a disease. Suddenly, everyone was clamoring to see the mole on my forehead.

Just then, the outer circle of the crowd parted as Madam Qia came back, without Liu. He had left.

I was completely alone, in a sea of people I didn't know. And I had absolutely no idea what was to become of me. I wanted to curl up in a corner and scream so that they'd think I was crazy and send me back. I wanted to shove everyone aside and run away. I wanted to—

A cold, bony hand wrapped itself firmly around my forearm. I jumped.

Calm down, Jing. None of those actions will help your cause in the least.

Yes. It would only earn me a beating or two. First and foremost, I had to stay calm and passive.

"Well, Jing," the *baomu* drawled, her croaky voice sounding like metals grating against each other. "Come along inside. We have much to talk about."

By my arm, I was led through a door behind the reception counter into what seemed like a study. Madam Qia went behind a wooden desk cluttered with account books, receipts, paperwork, and a huge golden abacus. She swept everything aside and took the abacus in her hands. I had seen Mrs. Guo use those before, but never one as big or half as magnificent as the one in Madam Qia's hand. The woman noticed my gaze and grinned, showing her top row of dark yellow teeth. "An exquisite thing, isn't it? A gift from a powerful magistrate of Dongjing to Yuegong Lou."

I nodded as meekly as I could.

"Now, I understand that you've just tried to run away from your in-laws," Madam Qia began, bringing her hands together under her chin and fixing her eyes on me. "The first thing you must know is that there will be none of that nonsense here. You will be watched closely."

Madam Qia paused in her speech as she waited for my response. I nodded again.

"As of today, you have been bought over by Yuegong Lou. You will do well to remember where and to whom you now belong and behave yourself accordingly. Or learn the hard way that this *chinglou* tolerates no misbehavior from its residents." At another nod from me, she rambled on. "For now, you will be put under a period of probation. You will have chores to complete during the day, and in the evenings, you will observe and learn from your older sisters as they entertain our patrons." As she spoke, her abacus started to make rapid, rhythmic clacking sounds as Madam Qia calculated.

"Once the *chinglou* has ascertained your value, I will put you through a series of lessons to shape you into a proper courtesan. You will be formally educated in all fields—politics, history, literature, calligraphy, fine art, music, dance . . . When we are done with you, you will have turned into a young woman more refined and educated than a magistrate's daughter. Great and influential men will grace you with their company and shower you with attention and gifts . . . of this nature." The old woman flaunted the golden abacus in her hand. "You will have the opportunity to live and socialize among the highest echelons of society, and possibly even entertain the emperor himself, if you are successful enough. Our emperor Huizong is known for his love of beauty and the arts."

I almost sneered. Baba always said that Huizong was the weakest emperor since Taizu of the Great Song, concerned only about silly things like art and pleasure.

"In this industry, popularity is everything," Madam Qia continued. "I have no doubt of your potential, girl, which is why I am prepared to invest a fair amount in you, but only if you prove yourself worth it. Now that you belong to the *chinglou*, there is nothing you can do that would change your fate. The only thing that is within your control is how successful you become . . ."

Other than the abacus in her hands, Madam Qia probably had another one inside her head. Because from the way the *baomu* was ogling me, it was as though she was calculating in her mind how much of a potential moneymaker I would turn out to be.

"I do not keep anyone who doesn't make money, and if I eventually find you a liability, I shall not hesitate to sell you off to a worse place."

Looking into Madam Qia's hungry eyes, I wondered again whether the old hag might possibly be an evil *jing* in an unconvincing disguise.

17

THE GODDESS OF
THE MOON

Given the nature of its business, the *chinglou*, of course, was most active at night. It closed around dawn and reopened the following evening at dusk.

It was already dawn when I was finally allowed out of the study. I dragged my feet up the stairs to the landing on the highest floor, where the main sleeping quarters were. The ten courtesans had four rooms in between them, and I was to share a small room at the end of the corridor with three other young girls who were also maidservants.

When I slipped into the room after washing and changing, the other girls were already getting ready for bed, and had even laid out an extra mattress on the wooden floorboards. There were two older girls and a sweet-looking one who looked hardly over ten. She patted the vacant mattress next to hers. "Over here, Jing. That's your name, isn't it?"

I nodded as I walked over.

"I'm Xiaoyi." The girl's big eyes narrowed into half-moons, and I couldn't help but return her smile, despite how rotten I was feeling inside.

"Qia Mama kept you in the study for an incredibly long time," said one of the older girls called Shuang as she smoothed out her braid.

Who?

She noticed my puzzlement. "I mean Madam Qia, but only outsiders call her that. All her daughters call her Qia Mama. It's a rule."

Another word caught me. "Daughters?"

Shuang shrugged. "We're not really her daughters, but all the courtesans under a *baomu*'s wing are called such."

I sighed. No, thank you. I didn't want a mother like that at all.

I looked around the room. It was spacious, big enough for more than four girls, and relatively bare save for three shelves against the wall on one side. There was a sliding door that led out onto a small balcony, and I couldn't resist going over and looking out. There was no wind, but the frosty temperature made me shiver. I glanced down and found that the balcony overlooked the back alleys. Was it possible . . . ?

"It's too high to escape from." Shuang spoke abruptly and made me jump.

I shut the door and turned to them. "Haven't any of you ever thought of running away?"

There was a sharp intake of breath among them. Xiaoyi covered her mouth and made a gesture that meant quite clearly that I wasn't supposed to speak of such things. The other girl, who looked about fourteen, tilted her head in a puzzled expression. "But why would we run away?"

I frowned. But before I could answer that peculiar question, Shuang waved impatiently. "Oh, Miao, be quiet." She came over and placed her hands on my shoulders. "Listen, Jing. If there's any idea left in that head of yours about running away, my sincerest advice is to get rid of it right now." She said this with such a solemn expression that I swallowed. "Not only is Yuegong Lou impossible to escape from, Qia Mama makes sure that all misbehavior is well and severely punished."

At that point, Xiaoyi, who was curled up in her bed beside us, winced distinctly, as if she were feeling the pain from some sort of punishment. I shuddered. Was it possible that there existed a torture device more agonizing than the one I had endured?

"We may call her Mama," Shuang continued, "but she is a cunning and ruthless businesswoman. All of us know that a worse fate awaits whomever Qia Mama deems a liability to her business. Those who were too foolish to learn it the easy way no longer live here. Thus, for your own good, you should accept the fact that, the moment you stepped into the *chinglou* tonight, your fate was sealed. You belong here now."

Belong.

I gritted my teeth. Belong here? I could laugh. I was no more a part of Yuegong Lou than I had been a part of the Guo family. And other than my own mother, I would never call anyone "Mama," especially that devil of a woman. It would be an insult to my real mama. But Shuang's tone and expression told me that she was earnest in her advice. I'd have to listen to her, for now at least. But as we settled into bed and I crawled under the thick covers, my eyes wouldn't close.

I saw Jun'an—his tears and screams as he watched me being dragged away. I saw Auntie San, who was now worried sick over why I had failed to show up and where I could possibly be. I thought about my family in Huanan, who knew nothing of what I was going through.

"Why are you crying?" a voice whispered beside me.

I turned on my headrest and saw the girl called Miao, lying in bed with her eyes wide open, regarding me with curiosity.

"Because." I wiped at my eyes. "Because I don't want to be here. I don't want to be a courtesan."

"You don't?" Miao asked as though she couldn't imagine how anyone wouldn't want to. "But it's a good life, Jing," she said. "Courtesans are beautiful, rich, and admired by so many. Men would give them anything they want. I want to be just like them someday . . ."

As Miao trailed off with a faraway look, I turned to face the ceiling. I wouldn't be a courtesan. Not if men threw every last copper piece they owned at my feet, not if the emperor named his dynasty after me, not even if—I blinked when I suddenly saw Miao's face hovering several inches above mine. The older girl had crawled off her mattress and was crouched beside me.

"Can I see it?" she asked.

"Um . . . see what?"

Miao indicated between her own eyebrows. "That mole. Your beauty mole that looks like the one on the royal consort Yang Guifei."

"Oh . . ." I brushed my fringe to the side.

Miao reached out a finger and touched the mole as though it were the emperor's seal. It wasn't nice to make a fuss over such a petty thing, but I didn't know where to look. Then Miao sat back and sighed. "I wish I had one, too. All the courtesans were talking about you."

"Oh . . . what did they say?" Not that I was interested, but it just felt like the thing to ask when Miao had paused for a response.

"They said you'll most certainly become a *mingji* someday if Qia Mama invests in you well."

"What's a *mingji*?"

"A *mingji* is a term for a famous and exceptionally popular courtesan. When a courtesan becomes a *mingji*, the price she commands for her company immediately goes up several times above the regular amount," Miao explained, hugging her knees. "Yuegong Lou has only one resident *mingji*, and that is Chang Er. She has the same name as the goddess of the moon."

"Chang Er . . . ?" I had heard quite a few names among the courtesans tonight, but I couldn't really remember anyone called Chang Er. All the women I had seen were equally beautiful, which made it rather difficult to tell which one among them was the *mingji* Miao was talking about.

"Yes." Miao nodded. "She isn't in the *chinglou* right now. In fact, she's hardly here. Because she is so popular, Chang Er entertains mostly the high court magistrates of the Taiyuan province and is often invited to parties and events outside of Yuegong Lou. She even travels to the capital sometimes."

That night, I also learned that the name of the *chinglou* didn't used to be Yuegong Lou, which meant "Palace of the Moon," but ever since Chang Er became a *mingji*, the *chinglou* grew famous and eventually changed its name in order to promote her further.

"They even say, and it's only a rumor . . ." Miao's voice dropped to a whisper. "That Chang Er might be a *jing* in disguise."

It wasn't unheard of for a powerful but evil *jing* to take on the form of a beautiful woman and seduce men in order to absorb their *chi*. But the mention of *jing* reminded me of my guardian, and that night, I prayed to it again. I brought my hands together under my covers, and as I closed my eyes, tears wet my headrest once more.

Great Golden Huli Jing, I want to go home . . .
Please help me. Save me from this wretched place and
bring me home . . . Didn't Shenpopo say that the rib-
bon of Yuan links us to each other? That you will watch
over me? I promise you that if I come home, I will for-
ever devote myself to you.

But Huanan was so far away. Would it hear my
cry for help? Would my prayer ever be answered? I
continued to pray as I cried myself to sleep.

▪   ▪   ▪

After all those warnings I received the day before,
I knew I had to wait for my chance before I could
escape. Not only were all the entrances locked every
night, but everyone in the *chinglou* kept a vigilant
eye on me, making it nearly impossible to attempt
anything even close to escaping, whatever time of
the day it happened to be. Which was why a period
of time must be spent throwing them off, during
which I must act as though I had accepted my fate.
Eventually, they would relax their guard. It was a
long endurance battle, but I was prepared to fight it.

Each day, before Yuegong Lou opened for business, the maidservants spent late mornings and
afternoons going about our chores. Although I
wasn't allowed to run outdoor errands, I cleaned,

cooked, and waited on the courtesans, basically at the disposal of everyone. I had been familiar with housework all my life, so this was nothing. The real challenge was the sleeping hours. The first few days were the worst. I felt like my world was turning topsy-turvy, as each night, everyone stayed up until near dawn and slept through till noon. Never in my life had I woken up later than the sun, so each morning, I would find myself wide awake in bed while the others still snored around me. Then I would begin to nod off around midnight, when the evening, to everyone else, was only just starting.

As dusk approached, we would help the courtesans dress up in elaborate *hanfu* for the night, and then, when the *chinglou* opened for business, we would put on a simple *hanfu* as well to wait on everyone.

Not all the courtesans entertained in the *chinglou*. Some of the more popular ones were occasionally invited to attend events outside, which was where the real money was, because it was more expensive to request a courtesan's company outside of her *chinglou*. But for patrons who frequented Yuegong Lou, it had a public hall where courtesans would sit at tables with their guests. And for those who were willing to pay more for privacy, there were ten other separate rooms of different sizes in the *chinglou* for private parties and smaller gatherings.

Through observing each night, we were expected to learn how to entertain, and I had to admit that what I learned was, in fact, quite different from what I had thought I knew about courtesans. Because not only were these women knowledgeable and well-versed in most topics of conversation, they were talented in numerous forms of art as well, and in more ways than one could imagine.

For example, Feier was widely known for her alluring Persian dances and could paint with her bare feet as she danced across a huge canvas on the floor. Qiu Xiang could play a Chinese zither called the *guzheng* so well that even the birds would fall silent to hear her play. And Xuehuar could write poetry with calligraphy brushes attached to the end of her long satin sleeves.

Another fascinating thing about the courtesans was their names, for they were the most peculiar names I had ever heard. Shuang explained that they had been given attractive pseudonyms to add to their appeal. Qiu Xiang meant "autumn fragrance," and she was known for her heady scent from the sachet of lavender and sandalwood she always carried with her.

Xiao Honghe, or "little red lotus," always dressed in some shade of red. Tian Tianr—"sweet sweetness"—was named that for her delightful voice.

I couldn't for the life of me remember all those fancy names. But it really didn't matter, because the maidservants were only supposed to call the courtesans "Jiejie." But although I might forget names, I labeled them in my head. For example, there was Smelly, Songbird, Chili, Big Hair . . . Strangely enough, the only name that stuck with me was Chang Er, although I hadn't had the chance to see the *mingji* in person yet. In just a few days, I came to understand how much in demand Chang Er was, for many wealthy businessmen and local magistrates came in each day asking for her company.

▪ ▪ ▪

It was only three days later that I finally had the chance to see Chang Er, who, according to the gossipy courtesans, had returned from a long trip to the capital, Dongjing. There, under a sky full of erupting fire flowers and along with other *mingji* from across China, she had performed at a major function held by an influential magistrate within Emperor Huizong's imperial court.

Early in the afternoon, after cleaning out the incense clock and replenishing the altars, I was busy scrubbing the floor of the main hall. I wrinkled my nose as I tried to get a particularly stubborn and smelly stain of vomit off the wooden boards. Then someone called out from a little way across the room.

I looked up, and immediately understood why Chang Er was named after the goddess of the moon. Her complexion made even Yunli's pale by far in comparison. As the courtesan made her way slowly down a flight of stairs, she moved with a languid grace that could only be seen in dancers. Slender brows, well trimmed, arched over a pair of watery eyes that were framed by thick lashes. Long, dark hair let down from a usual *faji* fell over her shoulders like a waterfall, contrasting against the translucent whiteness of the chiffon outer robe that clung to her shoulders like a second layer of skin, bringing out the fairness of her arms. And even as she gently rubbed her right temple from an apparent headache, a slight frown creasing her forehead, Chang Er still managed to look stunning.

It was obvious she had just woken up, and as she slowly descended the stairs and sat herself at the nearest table, I hurried over to wait on her.

"My girl, can you please pour me some hot tea?" she asked.

Her smile, though brief, was warm, and I couldn't help liking her. The rumors about Chang Er being a *jing* in disguise were just nonsense. Although such an occurrence wasn't unheard of, how could such a nice woman possibly be the manifestation of a malevolent *jing*?

When I came back with a pot of steaming tea on a tray, Chang Er was still rubbing the side of her head. I filled a white porcelain teacup with steaming jasmine tea.

"Your tea, Jiejie," I said with my head bowed as I handed Chang Er the cup with both my hands. Then I moved behind her and began to massage the back of her neck.

Chang Er took a small, tentative sip from the cup, testing its temperature. "Thank you," she sighed as I continued to rub and press on specific acupunctural points on her head, neck, and shoulders. I was good at it, for I had done it countless times for my own grandmama and then almost every week for Mrs. Guo. When Chang Er replaced the cup on the table, I moved to refill it, and it was only then that she took time to regard me closely.

"What is your name?"

"My name is Li Jing, Jiejie." I dropped my gaze when she spoke and fidgeted with the long blue sash of my *hanfu*. Chang Er had such a sweet and gentle voice. She must also be a songstress, on top of everything else.

"Well, Jing. Lift your chin so I can have a look at you."

I shifted on my feet, but obeyed. When the hair over my forehead was swept back and a cold finger landed between my brows, I thought the courtesan was going to comment on my mole as well, but Chang Er said nothing. She let her hands drop and reclaimed the cup of tea on the table.

"So what brought you here, Jing?" She took another sip.

I twirled the sash around my fingers. "I . . . I was sold to the *chinglou*."

"I see. And how have they been treating you? Are you coping well?"

No, Jing. Not the truth.

I stopped myself just in time. It was a question that sounded harmless enough, but answering it incorrectly would have direct consequences for my plans of running away. And with that in mind, I nodded. "Yes, Jiejie, I am coping very well indeed. I like it here. Everyone is very kind to me."

I watched as Chang Er gazed at me, then she let out a soft sigh and replaced a half-empty cup upon the table. What did that sigh mean? Was she relieved? Disappointed?

"I'm glad." Chang Er smiled, though this time it did not quite reach her eyes.

18

MR. YAO'S REQUEST

I did not see much of Chang Er after that day. What Miao had said was true, for almost every evening since her return, Yuegong Lou's resident *mingji* would be overwhelmed with invitations from one party to the next and could hardly be seen in the *chinglou* at all.

One evening, Xiaoyi and I were waiting on Smelly, Chili, and Big Hair as they entertained two men in one of the larger private rooms upstairs. It was an elaborately decorated room, with red pumpkin-shaped lanterns and strips of red, orange, and brown laces and ribbons hanging from the walls and ceiling. It was the room Chili usually entertained in, for the warm colors of the interior complemented the signature red garments she always wore, making her seem so much a part of the decor that she looked almost like an illusion. Now, as Smelly serenaded her with a *guzheng*, Chili danced with a red folding fan in each hand, looking more like a giant chili than ever with her skinny figure swathed in a bright red *hanfu*.

The older man of the two watched her, entranced by the performance. He looked to be in his late forties, dressed in thick satin robes, and kept an equally thick beard to probably cover up his double chin. The courtesans addressed him as Mr. Zhang, and from how familiar they were with him, he seemed to be a regular of the *chinglou*. Apparently, he ran a huge liquor-manufacturing business that supplied all over the province, including Yuegong Lou.

I stood on the side with a ceramic urn of white liquor in my hands. The silly man didn't seem to notice or care that his young friend appeared out of his element in this place. For almost two *zhuxiang*, which was the time it took to burn two whole incense sticks, Big Hair had been trying to engage him in conversation but could only elicit a few nods or monosyllabic answers. He sat there, rigid and silent, and whenever the courtesan laid a hand on his arm or leaned too close, he would inconspicuously move a little farther away. He fidgeted as well, giving the majority of his attention to the cup of alcohol in front of him. I almost laughed.

Why was he even here? He was so obviously uncomfortable with the entire place.

When the dance was over, Mr. Zhang rose promptly to his feet and clapped. "Wonderful, Honghe! Simply marvelous, don't you think, Yao?"

The man called Yao put down his cup and cleared his throat. "Indeed." He nodded curtly, and then cast a glance in my direction again.

Yes, again. It wasn't the first time he had done this.

I looked down quickly. His gaze seemed to carry something I couldn't quite read. I shifted my feet a few times and glanced up again. When the man wouldn't take his eyes off me, Big Hair spoke.

"Jing! Can't you see Mr. Yao's cup is empty?"

I jumped, nearly spilling the contents of the bottle, and hurried over to apologize and refill Mr. Yao's cup with the warm liquor. My ears felt as though someone had slapped them.

The courtesans continued to entertain the men with interesting conversations and various drinking games, most of which involved dice playing and a lot of body contact. More often than not, Mr. Zhang would sneak a hand over to one of the ladies under the table, or gently smack their behinds, which would elicit a playful squeal. I swallowed and looked over at Xiaoyi. She seemed indifferent, but I could never stand being touched in that manner, and if this was what courtesans had to do to make a living, I was not cut out to be one. All this time, the man called Yao remained stoic, as though determined not to fit in.

"Yao, you do not seem to be enjoying yourself tonight as much as I had hoped you would," Mr. Zhang finally pointed out. "Is there anything not to your satisfaction?"

There was a moment of silence as Mr. Yao replaced his cup on the table. "Well . . . as a matter of fact," he began, "I would've liked someone else—"

"Oh, Mr. Yao!" Big Hair feigned a look of shock. "Are you suggesting that Honghe, Qiu Xiang, and I are not entertaining enough for you?"

Mr. Yao shook his head in earnest. "No. It's just that I would much prefer the company of someone else."

Mr. Zhang let out a loud, appreciative guffaw, turning his face even redder than the liquor had already done. He seemed to be in a rather tipsy mood from all that drinking. "You're always so straightforward, Yao. Well, you heard the man. Call in the rest of your sisters so he can have his pick and we can continue the party!"

"That will not be necessary, Zhang. I already have someone in mind."

"Oh? And who might that be? Is it Feier, the Persian dancer? I heard she has been quite in demand lately."

But Mr. Yao shook his head. Although he was also relatively red in the face, he did not seem to be as drunk as Mr. Zhang. "No, I'd rather . . ."

"You'd rather Tian Tianr, then?"

"No, I—"

"Oh, come on, you can't be that picky!" Mr. Zhang rolled his bloodshot eyes. Then something seemed to occur to him. "Or maybe you fancy someone more popular? Just say her name, Yao. I can get you anyone in Yuegong Lou—even the *mingji*, Chang Er!"

Sure enough, the man fell silent for a moment, and then somewhat hesitantly nodded in a certain direction. There was a collective response of—

"What?"

No one in the room fully understood what he meant until Mr. Yao had his index finger pointing across the room directly at me.

This time, I really did spill the liquor.

I dropped the entire bottle and it crashed to the ground, but no one even flinched. This couldn't be true. Surely this man couldn't possibly expect me to entertain? What was he thinking?

For what seemed like the longest moment, there was complete silence, but it was Smelly who recovered first. She gave a nervous little laugh. "My word, Mr. Yao, you do know how to kid around! For a moment there, I believe you had all of us completely fooled!"

The other courtesans tactfully joined in with the laughter, but my heart felt as though it was about to hammer a hole in my chest, because the man did not look the least bit like he was kidding. He turned to Mr. Zhang. "I would be delighted if she should join us tonight," he said.

This time, the courtesans could no longer laugh it off. Xiaoyi suddenly seemed to jerk to life and jumped in front of me. "No, you can't have Jing! It's . . . it's not allowed!"

"Be quiet, Xiaoyi!" Smelly scolded, then hitched on a businesslike tone quite different from the flirtatious one she had been using all night. "Mr. Yao, you may not be aware since you are not a regular visitor of the *chinglou*, but unfortunately, our younger sisters are not available to entertain until they have officially been promoted into courtesans."

At this, the others promptly joined in. "Yes, for now, the girls are mere maidservants," Chili said.

"And you wouldn't want Jing, Mr. Yao. She only just arrived two weeks ago!" Big Hair put in.

"Yes, hardly any experience."

"No training at all—"

"—not even an apprentice yet."

"She'd bore you to death."

"Yes, and give the *chinglou* a bad name."

"Enough!" Mr. Zhang let out a bellow that instantly shut everyone up. He walked over to where the other man was standing. "Do not worry about what these women said, Yao." He draped an arm around his friend, and then looked hard at me. "I can see why you fancy her. She's a pretty thing, this lass. And *tian, ah*! Especially with that beauty mark between her brows. But she's still a little young, so." He pointed a finger at me. "You're sure this is the one you want?"

Mr. Yao's thin lips hardened into a straight line. No . . . his mind was set. I covered my mouth and shook my head. Oh, great Huli Jing, help me, I didn't want to be a courtesan! I couldn't even stand the way he looked at me, much less the thought of sitting right next to him! Just remembering how the men behaved with the courtesans made me sick.

Where were the doors? Perhaps I could . . . The doors abruptly opened, and Qia Mama came in, followed by a panting Xiaoyi, who had apparently sneaked out to get the *baomu* to come to my rescue!

"Ah, just the person I wanted to see!" Mr. Zhang's eyes lit up when he saw the old lady. "You came at the right time, Madam Qia. I was getting tired of the nonsense your daughters have been giving me over such a trivial matter."

"Qia Mama, we—" Smelly began, but Qia Mama held her hand up. She grinned thinly, thankfully not showing her teeth.

"Then I must first apologize on my daughters' behalf. I will have them make it up to you, Mr. Zhang," Qia Mama promised in her raspy voice. "Now, what seems to be the problem?"

"My friend would like to invite your little daughter over there, Jing—is that her name?—to join our party tonight. But it seems as though it is not allowed . . ." Mr. Zhang tactfully drifted off, casting an impatient glance at the rest of the courtesans. "Mr. Yao is an incredibly important client of mine—" he continued, but he was cut off by Qia Mama.

"My daughters are courtesans, Mr. Zhang. Not common whores," she reminded him firmly. "This girl is still new and therefore, I'm afraid, not available for service yet. But if your friend Mr. Yao pleases, I can offer—"

"Nonsense *hulu*-sticks!" Mr. Zhang slapped the surface of the lacquered wooden table. "Never in my life have I heard of such a thing! Is that the way your *chinglou* treats a paying customer, Madam Qia? After all the fine liquor I've supplied Yuegong Lou, and the amount of businesses I have brought you?"

"Please, Mr. Zhang. Let us not blow things out of proportion . . ." Qia Mama was starting to look slightly flustered, as though contemplating whether she should change her mind. I covered my eyes. She was giving in.

"If Mr. Yao insists, then perhaps—" she began, but another voice cut in.

"Then perhaps I can offer my company to this gentleman tonight."

Abruptly, the doors to the room opened for the second time as someone else stepped in, looking ethereal in a flowing periwinkle *hanfu* and a white outer robe edged with snow fox fur.

"Chang Er!" Nearly everyone in the room blurted it out at the same time. I could not believe my eyes.

From the pink flush in her cheeks and the bits of snow that still clung to her robe and her long dark hair, it was obvious that Chang Er had only just returned. Had she come solely to save me?

"Well, I'll be! If it isn't the famous *mingji* of Yuegong Lou." Mr. Zhang looked simply delighted. "Chang Er, you still look as gorgeous as ever."

"Why, thank you, Mr. Zhang." Chang Er curtsied as Mr. Zhang came over and snaked his arm around her waist.

He cooed into her ear. "I requested your company tonight, but as usual you're too busy outside of the *chinglou* to entertain insignificant guests like us."

"Nonsense, Mr. Zhang," Chang Er argued in her gentle, hypnotic voice. "There isn't a day that goes by without me thinking of you when I entertain, seeing as how you supply liquor to our *chinglou* practically free of charge." She laid a perfectly manicured hand on his chest. "I do apologize for having neglected such an important friend as you; therefore I'd be most honored if you'd allow me to make it up to your friend here."

As did every man, Mr. Zhang looked completely smitten with the *mingji* and seemed as though he would agree to anything she suggested. My mind felt like it was in a tug-of-war. I didn't want Chang

Er to have to sacrifice herself on my behalf, but I didn't want to be the one sacrificed, either!

Mr. Zhang, thankfully, seemed perfectly agreeable to the idea. He looked over at Mr. Yao. "Well, if it pleases the gentleman . . . ah, then I have no objections." But unbelievably, even in face of Chang Er's beauty, the stubborn man still shook his head.

"I do not fancy anyone else," he replied.

"But, Mr. Yao . . ." For the first time, even Chang Er seemed caught off guard. Clearly, she hadn't expected any man to be able to resist her offer, much less completely turn it down.

Mr. Zhang shrugged and drank the last of his liquor. "Well, you heard the man. So it looks like I'll have to ask for you another time, Chang Er."

I bit on my fists. *Please. Please fight for me.*

"But, Mr. Zhang, you don't understand. Jing cannot—" Chang Er began, but a sharp crash cut her off when Mr. Zhang furiously dashed his cup onto the floor.

"I've had enough of this monkey *zaju*!" he hollered, then jabbed a finger at Chang Er. "Who are you, a mere woman, to tell me what I do or do not understand? Are you people trying to make a fool out of me in front of my client? You can name whatever confounded price you want for one evening with that girl, and by the gods, I will pay it!" He whirled around to face Qia Mama and reached into his sleeves. "Madam Qia, if you are anything like the businesswoman I believe you to be, you will take this amount I'm offering you now and let the girl join us." He fished out a bag and cast it with a heavy thud onto the table in front of Qia Mama. When she opened up the bag and fished out a sheaf of paper money, the *baomu*'s eyes almost popped right out of their sockets.

As my fate was sealed by those crummy papers, I let out a sob. I knew the expression on Qia Mama's face all too well. I had seen that very same look on Aunt Mei when she had been offered five silver pieces for her own niece. I saw it on my mother-in-law on the day the *baomu* had come to inspect me. And now it was written all over this woman's face.

Greed.

Sure enough, an ugly grin appeared on Qia Mama's face as she nodded. "It would be rude of me to refuse such a sincere offer, Mr. Zhang."

And that was when I sank to the floor.

19

A WAY OUT

"Now you listen well, you little wretch."

It would've been easier to listen well if Qia Mama wasn't yanking on my ear so roughly. We were alone in the hallway outside the room where the party was just continuing.

"I don't know what you did to make those gentlemen desire your company so badly, but I assure you that if you should do anything to upset our most important guests, I will make you wish I had thrown you into a wok of oil," Qia Mama threatened with the fiercest glower she could muster. "If you don't know what to do, just follow your sisters' lead."

And with a shove, the old woman sent me reeling into the room, almost tripping over the new *hanfu* they had changed me into. "I bid you enjoy the rest of your evening, gentlemen," Qia Mama said.

As the door closed behind me, I stood there like a rock. Everyone was looking at me. Well, almost everyone. Mr. Yao, oddly, wasn't. He continued emptying his cup of liquor. Big Hair sighed in a motherly sort of way.

"Why, isn't that Xuehuar's *hanfu*? It looks better on you, Jing, I must say!"

This wasn't true. The *hanfu* was ill-fitting and cumbersome. The gossamer sleeves that were too long got in my way, and I kept stepping on the edges of the full, multilayered skirt. Furthermore, pink was never my color, especially such a gaudy shade.

Smelly patted the empty seat next to hers, and mercifully, it was the farthest from Mr. Zhang and Mr. Yao. The fragrance from the sachet of lavender and sandalwood she always carried smelled surprisingly soothing this evening.

"That's Qiu Xiang, always the responsible big sister," Chili teased. Then she picked up a mug containing five dice. "How about another round of Liar Dice? Jing doesn't know how to play, so she can just watch."

Thankfully, for the rest of the evening, the men in the room made no inappropriate advances toward me at all. The most Mr. Yao did was engage me in cordial conversation. Mr. Zhang hardly paid me any attention, being a lot more attracted to the older ladies. No one even offered me any of the liquor because Smelly had asked for a pot of hot chrysanthemum tea instead. When Smelly was invited again to play a famous piece of music on her zither, I became completely entranced by the beautiful melody. It made me long to play Baba's *dizi*. In fact, when it gradually became clear that nothing too bad was probably going to happen, I had begun to relax, and only stiffened when Mr. Yao rose from his seat and asked to be shown to the bathroom. Any one of the courtesans could have escorted him, but Mr. Yao was gazing intently at me.

No. Surely someone else could go in my place? I glanced at the other courtesans, trying to hold back tears. Smelly had stopped playing her zither.

"I would like Jing to escort me." Mr. Yao made it very clear.

I upset my cup.

Mr. Zhang, too drunk to notice what was happening, exclaimed, "What's going on? Qiu Xiang, don't stop playing now, we've just come to the crescendo!" Chili, sitting next to him, gave me a look and jabbed her chin toward the door. The message was clear: *Just go!*

Big Hair leaned in and whispered in my ear. "Nothing's going to happen. All you have to do is show him the way, wait outside, and bring him back."

I didn't believe her, but I had no other option. If he tried anything . . . well, I would hurt him. Really badly. And with that, I gathered up my long sleeves and stood up at the speed of a tortoise.

As we walked down the corridor, I kept my fists balled. I could hear Mr. Yao's footsteps behind me, the way his feet made the lacquered floorboards creak, the sound of his mild cough; these seemed to drown out the noise from all the other parties that were going on in the *chinglou*. Fortunately, the man did not walk too close or even try to engage me in conversation.

When we reached an isolated corridor, I turned around and bowed to indicate that we had arrived. We stood at the entrance to one of the private bathrooms. But something in the man's face changed, and he glanced around warily before suddenly seizing my arm. My scream was completely lost in the large hand that pressed over my mouth and nose.

"Jing, please listen to me! I swear in the name of Guan Yin that I mean you no harm."

Wait. The man was pleading. "My name is Yao Hong, and Auntie San is my mother. You know Auntie San, don't you? The cook?"

Yes. Auntie San talked about her son a lot, but I had never met him. Pinned to the wall, I barely managed a nod. Then Mr. Yao broke into an apologetic smile that entirely changed his face. "I am truly sorry if I frightened you out of your mind, but it was necessary to put up a proper show to avoid suspicion," he said, letting me go.

I leaned back against the wall behind me and pressed my palm over my forehead. My mind was reeling and I had trouble breathing. Blood pounded in my ears.

"On the day you were brought to the *chinglou*, we had waited all night for you to show up, and only found out the next morning that you had been caught and sent to Yuegong Lou during the night . . . ," he said, careful to keep some distance between us. "My mother wanted to get you out, but she needed someone who could visit such a place without raising suspicion. I do not frequent *chinglou*, but it so happens that I have a friend, Mr. Zhang, who has a good relationship with this place." Yao Hong paused, scratching the back of his head.

Bits and pieces started to click—Yao Hong's uneasiness with the courtesans, his insistence on having me join them, and even his resemblance to the kind cook I knew.

"So . . . your friend, Mr. Zhang, knows about this?" I wasn't afraid anymore, but somehow my voice still cracked.

"Yes, he does." Yao Hong nodded. "But Zhang is an old friend. I would trust him with my own life."

In order to avoid suspicion, we agreed that I should attempt my escape at least a few days after that night, so none of these kind people would be connected to my disappearance. It wouldn't do to have Auntie San or Yao Hong blamed for my escape.

"A fortnight," I said. My chest was still pounding, but this time from excitement. Finally, my escape was becoming a reality! "In exactly two weeks, I shall attempt my escape during the night."

Yao Hong nodded. "We will be waiting for you at our house with a map and the supplies you will need for your journey. But, Jing, it will be entirely up to you to escape from this place and meet us at the rendezvous."

I nodded and hugged myself. Auntie San had not given up on me after all.

▪ ▪ ▪

The very next day, despite the fact that I was still far too young, Qia Mama announced her intention of promoting me to an apprentice. After a feast to celebrate the occasion, I was given a new name— Hua Xianzi, which meant "little flower fairy."

I couldn't even summon up a polite smile. Sometimes, I caught sight of the longing in Miao's eyes as the older girl gazed at me. How silly and ironic our circumstances were. I would gladly have given my place to her. Everyone seemed happy for me, though, and the courtesans showered me with gifts of jewelry, clothing, and makeup.

"See, I knew Hua Xianzi had it in her from the moment I set eyes on her!" Big Hair was bragging, her numerous hairpins tinkling excitedly in her *faji*.

"Oh, don't speak as though you were the only one who saw her potential, Lei Hua; we all did."

"Did you like the plum blossom hairpin I gave you, my girl?"

"This *hanfu* would look absolutely lovely on you, Xianzi! Do try it on."

Amid all the enthusiasm, however, Chang Er continued to call me Jing. Not that this bothered me in the slightest. I didn't even like that silly name. But the other courtesans had begun gossiping among themselves, saying that the *mingji* was actually worried that my promising future as a courtesan would affect her standing in the *chinglou*.

"Xianzi will surely surpass Chang Er someday," Chili was saying, sounding very sure of herself. "Our resident *mingji*'s just jealous because one day, she will no longer be the pearl in Qia Mama's palm."

I didn't like to think of Chang Er as jealous. She was as close to a perfect woman as I could imagine. I would never forget how she had attempted to come to my rescue that night, offering herself up in my place. No one in my life has ever done something like that for me, and it warmed my heart every time I thought of it.

I was also certain that if I wasn't actually going to run away soon, with the full amount I'd fetch as such a promising apprentice, my price would be able to help Mr. Guo pay off a considerable chunk of his debts. But I would never forget how they treated me and how Mrs. Guo had robbed my mother's bangle from me. And because of that, even though I loved Jun'an dearly, I did not feel the least bit sorry that his parents would never be getting even half a copper piece off me.

It served them right.

▪　▪　▪

Qia Mama made good on her word and immediately started my courtesan training. As an apprentice, I didn't have to entertain the patrons of Yuegong Lou, but I was relieved of all maidservant duties. An apprentice's only job was to learn, and a tutor had been engaged to come in each morning and teach me to read and write, and in the afternoons, I would learn things like painting, music, and dance. Within the first two days, my teachers were already showering me with praise as they reported my progress to Qia Mama.

"I've never taught a brighter child, Madam Qia," my literature teacher said. "And she takes such a great interest in learning. A pleasure to teach indeed."

"The girl's not much good in singing, but she definitely has a way with the flute," said my music instructor.

Everything else aside, I had to admit that I thoroughly enjoyed my lessons and didn't mind showing that eagerness. It would continue to mislead Qia Mama that I no longer had intentions of running away.

Even with my new standing within the *chinglou*, the entrances and windows were always locked at night, so my only way out was through the balcony of my bedroom. After my promotion to an apprentice, I had been moved to one of the rooms the courtesans shared, but the lucky thing was, although it now faced the front of the building rather than the back, our room still had a balcony, so it wouldn't affect my plans. The thing was to find a ladder of some sort long enough to bring me four levels down. The longest rope I could find within the premises was the one they used for the well in the front yard, and that wasn't even half the length I needed. Since I was still not allowed out of the *chinglou*'s premise, there was no way I could possibly get another rope, or even ask Auntie San for help.

As my deadline loomed ever closer, I slept less and less each night, racking my brain for a way of escape. Even with two days left, I had made no progress. Would I miss this chance that I had been given? I pulled the bedsheets over my head and wept. It wouldn't do to wake the others.

I twirled and chewed at the ends of my hair . . . then remembered something. I wiped away my tears and sat up. It might be my only resort.

Lighting an oil lamp, I crept out of the room. It was easy to pretend as though I needed the bathroom, which was where I was heading anyway.

The bathroom smelled heavily, as usual, of urine and vomit, and the floor made sticky sounds as I trod inside. I pinched my nose and breathed through my mouth. This wasn't the nicest place to carry out what I wanted to do, but it was the safest. Setting my lamp on the floor, I reached into my hair and removed the two ribbons that I had received from Sisi. I recalled clearly the spider's instructions before we parted ways.

Burn a ribbon and scatter its ashes into the ground, for then I shall know, and will come to your aid.

Crystalline and translucent, the ribbons seemed to sparkle in the flickering lamplight. It was a huge pity to destroy something so magical. I sighed and dangled one of them over the oil lamp. Placing the ribbon in the ceramic lid of the lamp, I watched as it caught, and when I dared a small intake of air, I found, to my delight, that the bathroom was filled with a pleasant kind of burning aroma as soothing as incense. As the ribbon slowly burned out, only ashes were left in the lid. I replaced the remaining ribbon in my hair and picked the lid up carefully. This was my last hope. But would the spider really come? Would she still remember me after such a long time? Was she even still alive?

A sudden bang startled me so much that I nearly toppled over. I turned around in horror and saw Big Hair at the door. Off work, Big Hair's hair no longer seemed so big. She had flattened her *faji* out of shape from sleeping, and now it lay squashed on top of her head, all accessories askew. On any normal day, I would've marveled at how different this made her look, but now my heart only sank as Big Hair opened her mouth and asked, "What are you doing here, Xianzi?" Then she gave a loud hiccup and almost fell as she stumbled into the bathroom.

She was drunk! If I'd had time to thank all the gods in heaven, I most certainly would have. I heaved an inward sigh and stood up. "I was just going to the bathroom, Jiejie. Do you . . . need help?"

Please, say no.

"*Ai, ma!* No, I'm fine. I just need to . . ."

With a retching sound, Big Hair rushed to the nearest wooden bucket and began vomiting into it. Hoping that she wouldn't notice the peculiar smell in the bathroom, and that she'd forget everything in the morning, I slipped out the door.

20

THE GIANT
SNOWFLAKE

The next day, I went out into the garden and scattered the ashes of the silk ribbon in the snow under a plum tree. The tree branches were covered in frost and completely bare. Would Sisi really come to my aid? Would she even get here in time? And if she did, what could she possibly do to help me? I didn't know, but I allowed myself to hope. *Jing* were magical creatures after all.

I had only one day left. Tomorrow night, I would have to escape the *chinglou* or miss my rendezvous with Yao Hong and Auntie San.

I went through my entire day without taking in much of what I was doing or anything that was happening around me. I missed the rhythm and multiple notes on my flute, forgot my steps during my dance lesson, and couldn't remember most of the poems in class. In the end, my teacher, worried that I might not be feeling well, dismissed me for the day and told me to rest.

In my room alone, listening to the noise coming from the lower floors as the *chinglou* opened up for business, I slid the wooden balcony door open and sat on the threshold, gazing up at the pink clouds against the faint lavender sky and the lightly falling snow that covered everything in its path. Snowflakes landed on the folds of my pale yellow *hanfu*, on my loose hair, and on the flute I held in my hands. The weather was supposed to be cold, yet I only felt the warmth of the tears on my face.

"Please. Please, little spider. Hear my cry . . ." My words came out in puffs of mist that quickly got lost in the wintry breeze. To warm my fingers, which were starting to numb, I lifted Baba's *dizi* to my lips and started playing. The mournful tune serenading the snowfall gave the sunset an ethereal air, and I felt better beholding such beauty. I half closed my eyes. If something so beautiful was so fleeting, why couldn't I disappear along with it . . . ?

Wait, what was that? My last note going completely out of tune, I sat up straight. There was a tiny voice in the wind.

"Jing," it said. "Jing, my kind, young friend."

I squinted into the distance. *Holy Huli Jing, that's an abnormally huge snowflake!* But as the wind carried it closer, I realized it was a tiny white balloon, and hanging from it was my little *jing* friend!

Sisi waved her forelegs at me as the wind brought it closer and closer. I held out the top layer of my skirt and she landed on the soft fabric along with a few drops of my tears. She looked up at me with all her beady eyes full of concern.

"Dear friend, why are you crying? I am here, and I will do everything in my power to help you," Sisi said, patting my hand.

I wiped my tears dry. "I suppose I am just too relieved to see you. I—I was so worried that you might not have heard . . ."

"Of course I would have. I live in the earth, and when my own silk returns to it, I always know."

"I thought you might be hibernating."

"Well, spiders do go to sleep in the winter, but we *jing* have spiritual energy—our *chi* keeps our bodies regulated," said Sisi proudly, standing up higher on her legs. "Now, what can I do for you?"

There was no time to fill Sisi in on everything that happened since we'd parted ways, and she seemed to know this. She asked no questions and merely sat motionlessly in my lap and listened. When I had finished, she turned to face me.

"Jing, you do not understand how joyful it makes me to know that I am exactly the right one to help you out of this predicament," Sisi declared and did a small leap. "I am going to spin you a silken ladder. One that is strong enough to carry your weight and long enough to reach four floors down this building. And I'll do it in one night. You will find it hidden under the snow beneath the plum tree in the garden tomorrow morning."

If I could hug my friend without potentially crushing her, I would have. "Really? Could you really?"

Sisi nodded. "It may be impossible for a regular spider, but I'm a *jing*. If I have to use up all the silk in my abdomen for you, I will do it."

I picked her up with both my hands. "Thank you so much, Sisi . . . you don't know how much this means to me."

"I do know," Sisi said, gazing up at me with all her unblinking eyes. "I know exactly what it feels like to be saved."

And at that point, I wept again.

Now I could escape! Tomorrow night, I would leave this place forever! As a thin veil of silk appeared

222 • Celeste Lim

above Sisi's abdomen, forming a round little balloon in the wind, she spoke.

"I have to get to work immediately, but I cannot stay indoors in case I am discovered. So remember, you will find the ladder underneath the plum tree tomorrow." She lifted off my palms, and the wind picked up and blew her off the balcony. I stood up and leaned out on the wooden banister, hardly feeling the bitter snow under my bare feet.

"Goodbye, Sisi! Thank you for everything!"

"Good fortune, and may you fare well, brave human child." Sisi waved her arms as she slowly descended into the garden below. And I waved until I saw her land safely and scurry under the bushes.

◾ ◾ ◾

Finally, it was the night of my escape.

Past dawn, I crawled out from under my covers. Sneaking over in turn to where Chili, Snowflake, and Big Hair were lying, I made sure that all of them were fast asleep before heading back to my own bed. I should have been sleepy as well, but my chest was throbbing with excitement. And it was hard to sleep when you wore travel garments underneath your robe.

I had on a thick woolen tunic tied in place with a sash over a matching pair of pants, which were more convenient than a *hanfu*. There was no time to tie a proper braid, so I bundled up my hair into a messy bun, securing it with a pair of chopsticks so it wouldn't get in my eyes.

I reached beneath my quilt and pulled out a light satchel. I only packed my own clothes, Baba's *dizi*, and the little grass bracelet that Jun'an had woven for me. I left out the meaningless trinkets I'd received from everyone else. Let all of those stay here and become mere memories.

I pulled at the flimsy threading that sealed my thick quilt, then reached in and felt for Sisi's silken ladder. I crept all the way across the room to the door that opened onto the balcony landing, freezing on the spot whenever I stepped on any floorboard that creaked. The wooden sliding door was my last and trickiest obstacle, for if I didn't open and close it fast enough, the awful draft would stir the others, and if I did it too quickly and made too much noise, it would wake them as well.

I tucked the ladder firmly under one arm, then wiggled and squeezed three fingers in between the door and the side beam. It didn't make any noise.

With my small frame, I would only need to move the door less than two feet to be able to slip through.

I slid the door an inch. Hardly a sound. Just a dull rustle as the door glided smoothly in its tracks. I grinned at my ingenious foresight to oil the tracks earlier that day. A sharp draft was already seeping through the crack, so I lost no time in sliding the door wider and quickly slipping through. Fortunately, there was no wind, so I managed to open and close the door behind me without too much trouble or noise.

The wooden boards on the landing were so cold it felt like I was standing on knives. I pulled on my socks and shoes, and then unraveled the ladder to tie one end of it to the wooden beams of the balcony. I tested the strength of my double knot with a few hard jerks. Sisi's silk felt firm and very strong. I secured the other end of the ladder around my waist, circling it twice around myself. When I was done, I stepped closer to the edge of the balcony and looked down.

I swallowed. It was high, but if I could climb up and down trees, I shouldn't make too huge of a fuss over four levels, especially when it was to save my own life. I let the remaining parts of the silk fall over the edge and watched as it dangled halfway down. Then I took a deep breath and hoisted myself over the beams and climbed to the other side. I tested the ladder one last time before trusting my entire weight to it and began the slow descent. A few times the wind picked up and I swung in midair, but my feet continued finding the thick knots I had made along the silk, and my hands kept me steady.

I leaped off the ladder above the last few knots, my goatskin boots making a dull slosh as they plunged shin-high into the snow. It was after I had untied my waist that I turned around and saw something that made my blood turn colder than the snow around my legs.

"Chang Er Jiejie!"

The one thing that I had completely forgotten to consider was the *mingji*'s inconsistent working hours outside of Yuegong Lou! She must've just returned from a late party and managed to catch me red-handed. Had all this been for absolutely nothing? My hands trembled as I clutched at my sleeves.

Chang Er stepped out of the shadows, lifting the paper lantern in her hand. "You're bold indeed to attempt running away, Jing."

Despite the cold, I fell to my knees and kowtowed several times into the snow. "Please, Jiejie, I beg of you! Do not take me back to Qia Mama! Oh, please—" I sobbed.

"And very wise."

Wait, what?

I lifted my head from the snow and found Chang Er standing in front of me. She kneeled to my height and gently brushed the snow from my face. "You have made a brave and very wise decision in running away," she said. "You are a very fortunate girl to not have been born into the life of a courtesan."

What exactly was happening . . . ?

Chang Er was obviously waiting for a response, but what could one say? Was there even an appropriate response in this case? A magical answer? I still couldn't tell whether I was in trouble, but her eyes . . . the warm lantern glow made them look amber and fiery, but her eyes looked like they carried all the sorrows of the world. I had to say something.

"But . . . but, Jiejie, you are such a successful *mingji*—beautiful, rich, and famous . . . and Miao—" I twisted the hem of my sleeves. "Miao looks up to you and wants to be just like you one day."

Chang Er shook her head. "Miao is a foolish girl—a girl whose future is certain to be that of a common, nameless courtesan," she whispered absently. "There is a lot more to the life of a courtesan than meets the eye, my dear child, which is why you should count your blessings that you were not meant for this." She paused for a brief moment. "Do you know why I insist on calling you Jing?"

I shook my head.

"Well, it is a beautiful name, for one thing. The word consists of three repeated characters of *ri*, which on its own means 'the sun.' Let me show you." Chang Er proceeded to write my name in the snow:

晶

"See? But as a whole, the word means 'crystal.' Now why do you think that a crystal is written with three suns in it?"

When I shook my head, she continued. "It is because crystals are beautiful things that sparkle in the sunlight, so the word shows that a crystal has a lot of sunshine in it." Chang Er took my hands in her cold ones. "Jing, don't you feel your parents' love for you in your name? It is full of blessing and not something silly and meaningless like Hua Xianzi."

A certain kind of ache spread through my chest, making me long for Huanan all the more. Chang Er continued, still holding my hands. "Forget Hua Xianzi, Jing. 'She' never should've existed in the first place."

I hesitated a few moments before asking, "What about you, Chang Er Jiejie? What is your real name?"

Another pause before she answered. "I no longer remember. I was sold to the *chinglou* as an infant."

The moon lit one half of her perfect oval face, and I saw the moisture that was welling up in her beautiful eyes. It was then that I realized what an unfortunate woman Chang Er was, for what were wealth, fame, and beauty when you had nothing else that truly mattered? She was a grown woman with her own will, and yet she did not even belong to herself.

"I . . . I'm sorry, Jiejie . . . ," I whispered. Never in my life had I felt so thankful for my name.

"Silly girl, don't be." Chang Er smiled and wiped the tears from my face. "Before you go, I'd like you to have this." She reached behind her head and carefully pulled out a hairpin from her *faji*. It had a sharp point that ended in the shape of an opened folding fan, with intricate red patterns carved onto its translucent white surface.

The ornament looked so exquisite that I immediately shook my head. "Jiejie, this is too valuable. I cannot have it."

"Nonsense; it's hardly worth a few copper pieces," Chang Er berated me. "It was one of the first gifts I bought for myself with my own money, and I know it will look stunning on a young girl like you." She inserted the ornament into my hair at an angle, tilting the fan to one side. "Take it, along with my blessings for a happy future."

"Jiejie . . ." My whole body was shaking, but not from the cold. I moved back and kowtowed heavily into the snow. "Jing has nothing of value to give you in return for such kindness, but I will remember this for as long as I shall live."

"That will be enough for me, dear child. And you'd best be going now." She stood up, promptly untying the pale blue cloak on her shoulders and wrapping it around me. "Take this as well; it is made from good material that will keep you warm during your journey," she said as she pulled the thick furry hood over my head.

The white fur that lined the edges of the cloak felt soft as it tickled my cheeks like gentle fingers. I could only mumble an almost inaudible word of thanks as I hugged her tight.

THE DIVINE TRILLER
OF WHATEVER

The smaller streets were dark, and I had to grope my way, sometimes half-blinded by shadows, until I came out onto a wider street. Here, the brightness of the moonlight guided me as I plodded through the silvery-gray snow that had accumulated higher than my ankles.

The moment I passed the gates of Xiawan, I jumped into the air. For the first time in my life, I was free! I didn't belong anywhere or to anyone, and there was no one to tell me what to do and where to go. Never had I felt so buoyant, so weightless, as though if I wasn't careful, I could float right up into the sky and become lost in the clouds.

I ran. I ran in circles, in straight lines, arms outstretched. I cartwheeled across the snow-shoveled road, walked on my hands, ran toward the moon, and I would've hollered and yelled if I didn't have to worry about getting caught. But as I stopped to catch my breath, I thought about people like Auntie San, who had given me provisions, a clear map, and had cried so much when I bade them goodbye that Yao Hong had to step in . . . Jun'an, who had been distressed for many days after I left, but when Auntie San told him about my plans to escape, had jumped for joy . . . and, of course, Chang Er.

My heart sank a little. But I gently slapped my cheeks and quickened my footsteps. *Silly Huli Jing, don't let these emotions slow you down. You're going home!*

Would my family be happy to see me? What would Baba say? Would Pan remember me? I hummed a lullaby. Pan would be turning four this year. And Wei, my dearest brother. How much had he grown since I left? Was he taller than me, perhaps?

With the orange glow from my lantern and the moonlight showing the way, I hastened down the main road, which had been cleared of snow for the carts. At Auntie San's, Yao Hong had cautioned that Yuegong Lou might start a search for me tomorrow, so it was vital that I used the time I had today to cover as much distance as I could. The map I had been given would take me to Baihe town and then

232 • Celeste Lim

back to Huanan, but to avoid a search party, Yao Hong had mapped out a smaller path that was less traveled on.

"Yuegong Lou will most certainly know you're gone by noon and come looking for you at the Guo household, even though they know for certain that you wouldn't be there," Auntie San had said as she handed me a lantern. "Their goal will not be to get you back but to kick up a fuss and demand that the Guos return the deposit they paid."

Good! I felt a fierce sort of satisfaction at the thought. Those wicked people deserved nothing better than a rotten century egg.

Although I was already feeling the exhaustion from being awake since midday the day before, I forced myself to move on. I could afford short naps when I began traveling down the smaller paths in the morning.

▪ ▪ ▪

I didn't know exactly when it was that I became lost. I supposed it started with the unsettling gnawing at the back of my mind as I tried to follow a particularly winding road that was so small it should've been considered a dirt path. Not too long before that, I had still been following the main road without much difficulty until the map told me to turn into a smaller one. Here, the trail became less visible because it was not as frequently traveled, but all I had to do was occasionally clear the snow with my feet to be able see the pathway.

After that, it had started to snow. It worried me, but I had pressed on, because I needed more distance from the main road. When I came to a signboard, I had to lift my lantern up close and brush the accumulated frost off the wooden board before I could read it. I clearly remembered checking the map before taking the path to my left, which was the one I was currently supposed to be on. It was a small one, so I had figured that after traveling a little farther down this road, I should have earned some time to rest. The sun would be rising soon, in any case.

Then the snowfall grew thicker, and that was when it started becoming difficult to follow the road. As the falling snow quickly hid the path from view, I had to start kicking snow aside as I walked, hugging the lantern to my chest to shield it from the wind. Gradually, for every few steps I took, I had to bend over and clear a foot of snow ahead of me to check that I was still on the road. I did not know exactly when I had gone off course, but before I realized it, the path underneath me had completely disappeared, and try as I might, I couldn't seem to find it again under all the snow.

The panic that seized me was immediate and so great that crying didn't even occur to me. I had only one thought: *Let me find it.*

I frantically started shoveling snow here and there with my bare hands, but instead of finding the path, I found the trees around me growing thicker and thicker, until I had to finally admit that instead of finding my way, I was only getting myself more and more lost.

I had wandered into a forest.

As though satisfied with the trouble it had caused, the blizzard died down and stopped. I sank beneath a bald maple. And although my chest hurt from panting, that was when the crying finally caught up. I didn't have to worry about search parties finding me now. I doubted anyone could.

▪ ▪ ▪

"Do not cry, my child."

That voice again—the voice in my dreams.

"Do not cry; you are not lost," it whispered, gentle as a feather. "But it's time to wake up."

"But I'm so tired."

"No, you must wake up, child. Now," the voice said more firmly.

My eyelids were partly glued shut by frozen tears. When I opened them, the sun shone in my eyes. It was probably late in the afternoon. I had overslept. I touched the extinguished lantern in between my legs. It still felt warm; the fire must've burned out not long ago.

Around me, trees and bushes grew in close quarters, and there was no distinct and continuous space in between the growths to indicate the possible existence of a path underneath the snow.

"Not lost, she says . . . ," I muttered as I stood up, brushing the snow off my cloak.

Here I was in the middle of a forest, and although it didn't look frightening at all, with the sunlight shining over the skeletal trees and reflected by the sparkling snow, I would definitely change my mind by nightfall. Who knew what else besides wild beasts lived in these forests? Ghosts? *Jing?* Bandits? I didn't want to find out. So there was really only one thing to do—find my way out before it got dark and scary.

I slung my lantern behind me and strode in the opposite direction from the sun. Baihe town was east of Xiawan, so if I headed in a straight line in that general direction, it was likely that I'd stumble upon a road leading there sooner or later.

Trudging through the forest after a blizzard was difficult and tiring. The snow was shin-high, and if I didn't lift my feet completely out of the snow when I took my next step, I could catch my foot on a branch or root and fall. But still, I hardly stopped for rest and even ate as I walked. I didn't want to spend another night here.

But it was winter, and by the hour of the rooster, it was already getting dark. As the sun drew farther away into the horizon, I started to run and stumble.

Please, just a little more time. Let me find it.

When all that was left lighting the sky were a few rays of weak light, I was panting so hard the cold air hurt my chest, and despite the chill, my palms were wet with sweat. I lit the lantern, but the fire only made everything else around me darker than it already was. And worse still, the flickering flames created shadows that lurked and wavered against the trees and bushes, and around corners. Something was always moving, but never within sight. And the sounds of the forest seemed to grow louder as well— the wind whistling, trees rustling, owls hooting . . . Everything was coming alive . . .

I fell to my knees with a sob. "Please . . ."

I pulled my hood over my head and started to cry. Please, I didn't want to spend another moment alone in this frightening place! Could anyone possibly find me now? Compared to here, even Yuegong Lou was starting to seem like a good place to return to. I wanted someone to talk to, a friend beside me. Even an animal friend like Saffron or Sisi would be wonderful.

As I curled into a tiny ball within the small circle of light from the lantern, something pressed against the side of my waist. I reached inside my cloak and pulled out Baba's *dizi*.

I gazed at the sleek instrument, fingering the warm, polished wood. Then I brought it to my lips. My notes wavered at first, broken by sniffles, but soon, I was playing a lullaby Baba had taught me as a child. I closed my eyes, shutting out all the shadows that had frightened me.

Suddenly, just at the end of a line, an even clearer tune sounded overhead. A song that almost exactly matched the one I had been playing. I gasped and looked up. Perched on one of the lower branches of the tree in front of me was a little nightingale.

Could it be? Could this nightingale possibly be Koko, Mr. Guo's pet? As I stared, the bird tilted its tiny brown head to one side and regarded me solemnly. I hardly dared lift a finger for fear of frightening it away. Then the little creature fluffed its feathers and trilled, repeating the exact same melody I had just played. After a line, it stopped and continued to gaze at me with its beady black eyes.

Careful not to make any sudden movements, I repeated the same notes in a lower pitch. As beautiful as a *dizi* sounded, no instrument could ever reach the pitch that nightingales could. But nonetheless, the little bird seemed impressed, for it did not fly away, but instead dropped to an even lower branch.

I started a different tune on my flute, then stopped. This time, the little thing fluffed its feathers and trilled at the top of its voice.

"Jingjing! Jiiiiiiing!"

There was no mistake about it this time. I let my flute drop as my hands flew to my mouth. "Koko! Oh, Koko, it is you!"

As soon as I held out my hands, the nightingale flew into them, just as he so often did back at the Guos' when I fed him every day. "You've been here in this forest all along, haven't you?" It just felt so good to have familiar company that I didn't mind whether or not he could understand or respond to me. "You didn't know how to fly south for the winter, did you? You poor thing, of course you don't. You were kept in that cage too long. But don't worry, I will take care of you," I cooed to him as I lightly stroked his head with the underside of my finger.

The bird squeezed his eyes shut and ruffled his feathers vigorously. He never much enjoyed being cuddled. I chuckled; that little gesture meant—

"Stop touching me!"

Yes, that.

Wait. Was I hearing my own thoughts?

"I said, stop the cuddling!" The bird opened his beak. "You really do know how to ruffle a bird's feathers."

I screamed. Koko flew off my palm and landed on the lantern.

"Now, is it such a big surprise that I can speak? I feel insulted." He tilted his head and ruffled his plumes huffily. "Seeing as how I learned your name ages ago, this shouldn't have come as that much of a shock."

"But . . . but—" But that was completely different!

"Yes, that's right, my girl!" Koko trilled proudly.

What's right? I hadn't even said anything yet. But Koko went on as though in his own world.

"I, the Divine Triller of Xuanji, am a nightingale who has absorbed enough *chi* to elevate into a *jing*, which grants me the ability to speak," he said, puffing up his light-colored chest.

Now I knew exactly why they called this feeling "tongue-tied."

"I'm known as a *niao jing*, like any bird that has attained a higher level of consciousness," Koko said, nodding his tiny head. "Have been for some time now, but I am a relatively weak *jing* until I am able to elevate into a proper deity. So when I was captured by Mr. Guo's servant one day, I had to hide the fact that I was one, to avoid being killed." And what was an unmistakable sigh escaped his beak. "I was held in captivity for such a long time that I was about to give up hope of ever escaping, until you came along." Koko's eyes fixed unblinkingly on me. "I could tell you are a kind girl, Jing, which was why I told the spider *jing* in our garden to seek your help. I am not sure whether she gave me away when she met you, but later on, I even 'learned' your name on purpose, hoping to give you an indication that I am no ordinary bird."

I replayed all those times I'd spent with Koko, whatever I could remember about him. So that was why he refused to repeat my name in front of Yunli.

"I liked you a lot," the bird continued. "And felt simply dreadful when I saw that my escape had caused you pain. Therefore, even after I left, I stayed close, waiting for you. Because I knew one day you'd escape."

"But . . . but how did you know I was going to do that?"

He shrugged his wings. "You may call it animal instincts, I guess. In any case, I believe you've landed yourself in a bit of a situation, am I not right?"

I nodded. "Yes. I'm on my way home to Huanan, and I got lost."

"Well now, I reckon my services may be of some help here." Koko flexed his wings and took flight, landing on a branch overhead. "Part of any *jing*'s spiritual training to attain divinity is to accumulate positive *chi* through doing good deeds. So in order to become a deity, Li Jing, I have decided to stick with you and help you. I shall be your friend, or in our current situation, your compass."

I wasn't about to argue against such a wonderful idea, but Koko went on persuading me anyway.

"The forest is filled with danger and *jing* of all kinds! Snake, tree, centipede *jing* . . ." Koko shuddered. "But worry not, for the Divine Triller of Xuanji will get you out of here in no time!"

"Wait, isn't your name Koko?"

The nightingale chirped indignantly and took flight. "That is a silly pet name your father-in-law gave me. And thankfully, not my true name. And the Divine Triller of Xuanji is only my *jing* title. Don't you know? *Jing* never reveal our true names."

"But why?"

"It poses a certain sort of danger for us."

I tilted my head. So that was why Sisi had asked for a nickname instead.

"Well, I think Koko is a nicer name than the Divine Triller of Xuanji," I said, patting his little head.

"It's the Divine Triller of Xuanji!"

Whatever.

KAIZHEN, THE
GOLDEN YOUTH

Koko was as good as his word. It was fast approaching dusk the next day when we finally left the forest and managed to cross over to the next mountain. The path we were on had grown narrower, marked only by the wheel ruts from the carts of traders who traveled frequently between Baihe and Xiawan.

I was about to suggest that we light a fire and rest for the day when we heard a sudden yell, and then a volley of barking. The noise seemed to have come from farther down the road. Someone was in trouble.

"Let's go see what it is." I ran off even though Koko yelled at me to mind my own business.

What soon met our eyes was a boy, hardly older than myself, encircled by a pack of wild dogs—five of them! The dogs seemed to have gone completely mad, barking and snapping alternately at the boy's heels. He had a dagger in his hands and was holding it out as he tried to fend the dogs off.

"*Tian, ah!* We have to help him!" I cried.

"If you ask me, we should run before the dogs decide we'd make a better meal."

Glad I didn't ask. I found a dead branch off the side of the road and set it alight with lamp oil. Carrying the burning branch, I let out a cry and advanced slowly toward the dogs, gripping the branch more tightly than was necessary.

The beasts turned and saw me with the dangerous-looking torch. They began to hesitate and whimpered as I waved the burning branch from side to side in a threatening manner.

"G-Get away! Go on . . . ! Off with you!"

At another wave of the flaming branch, the dogs abruptly turned and ran off in the other direction. I let out the breath I hadn't realized I had been holding and drove my end of the torch deep into the snow on the roadside. It wouldn't do to lose this flame, for I had little oil left for the journey.

The boy stood there in silence, staring at me but still holding on to his dagger, and it was only then that I realized I was looking at the most peculiar human I had ever seen in my life. The boy had hair that shone the same shade as the golden sun behind him, and huge, deeply set eyes that were the color of imperial jade—not light, not dark, but a rich, sparkling green.

Was he some sort of celestial sprite or deity that had descended from the heavens? He looked so otherworldly. But I shook my head.

Silly Huli Jing! Just because a person looks peculiar doesn't necessarily mean he fell from the sky!

I hurried over. "Are you hurt? If you are, I have some medicinal balm that might help." I held out a small jar, but the boy shook his head. He had suffered no injury, it seemed. He sheathed his dagger and then pointed at my forearms, indicating the scratches I had gotten while handling the branch.

"Oh, that's nothing. I'll fix it in a wink." I dabbed a bit of the ointment onto the wounds. The scratches were long, but very shallow. Not a big deal. "My name is Jing. What is yours?" There was a moment's silence, and just when I was beginning to think the boy wasn't going to answer me, he replied.

"Kaizhen."

What an unusual name. But I shouldn't be too surprised. This boy was probably a traveler from somewhere far away, which would also explain his curious appearance. Chang Er had spoken of foreign traders coming to China, especially to big cities like Dongjing, and some had the most curious features.

"These men are huge and tall like giants," Chang Er had related to the courtesans after returning from one of her trips to the imperial city. "They have fuzz on their arms as curly as dried tea leaves, and some have the most bizarre hair, as golden as this bangle on my wrist! And I once entertained a man who had eyes the color of the morning sky. I couldn't stop staring at him and nearly embarrassed myself in front of the magistrate!"

Although I had never seen such peculiar people, I probably shouldn't make a big deal of it, in case it made me look silly and ignorant. I invited Kaizhen to share our bonfire and told him that if he needed someplace to rest for the night, it made sense to stick together out in this wilderness, at least for the night, anyway. Who knew whether those dogs might return?

Koko, however, was not immediately agreeable to this idea. He did not trust the boy enough to reveal that he was a *jing*, so I introduced him as a tame nightingale pet. But this tame nightingale pet sure had a lot to say about that night's plans!

"I tell you, it's a bad idea!" Koko hissed at me when we were out of earshot.

"I don't see how it can be." I crossed my arms. "It's too dangerous for anyone to be out alone. Especially a young kid."

"There's just something about him, Jing," said Koko, hopping restlessly back and forth across the branch of an oak tree.

Hmm, Koko must've been thrown off by Kaizhen's exotic appearance. "There are many humans from foreign lands who look different than what you're used to seeing, Koko," I began, feeling quite knowledgeable and pleased with myself until another thought struck me. "Unless . . . you're thinking he might be a *jing*?" It was unlikely, but not impossible.

Koko neither nodded nor shook his head, which unsettled me even more. "There are extremely powerful *jing* out there that are able to conceal their aura and take completely human forms. And when they do, they are nearly indistinguishable from normal human beings. Even a fellow *jing* wouldn't be able to tell them apart," he said.

At that, I remembered the *baigu jing* during the Ghost Festival—the powerful White Lady who looked completely human, except for her skeleton hands. How powerful must a *jing* be to be able to appear entirely human and mingle among people undetected?

"Although from pure instincts I can feel this boy has no malevolent intentions, there's still something about him I can't quite put my feather on." Koko flapped his wings once for emphasis. "The question is, if he were a *jing* as we suspect, why is he in disguise?"

"But what if he isn't one? If you don't feel he means us any real harm, wouldn't it just be too cruel to send a helpless boy on his way like that?" My own time of solitude in the woods before I found Koko had been terrifying, and I wouldn't wish for another person to go through the same experience.

Koko sighed and shook his head. "I'm just trying to be cautious. But perhaps you are right. Maybe I'm being a little too wary."

And that was how the three of us came to spend the evening together.

The boy had nothing at all except the simple clothes he wore, a fabric pouch, and the dagger hanging from the sash at his hips, so I offered him some of our food and insisted on sharing my cloak, though he did not seem very bothered by the cold in the first place. "It's big enough for the both of us." I sat down next to him and pulled the cape over our legs.

Kaizhen didn't speak much at all and did not touch his half of the pork bun I offered him. He was gazing at me with his extraordinary eyes. I looked away, rubbing the mole on my forehead, and attempted to make conversation, since I couldn't very well expect Koko to break the ice.

I bit into my half of the bun while Koko pecked at the crust from his perch on my wrist. "So where are you headed?" It took a while for me to realize that Kaizhen wasn't going to answer my question. But the good thing was that he finally began to eat. Maybe I should try another one.

"Where are you from?"

Still no answer. Perhaps those questions came off a little too personal? I pressed my lips together and lapsed into silence. The flames from our bonfire lit up Kaizhen's already fair skin and created dancing shadows of a strange kind among the trees behind him. I could make out the flickering silhouette of what seemed like something with pointy ears . . . and—

"What about you?"

I jumped a little. Kaizhen had stopped eating and was looking at me, waiting for an answer.

"Where are you from? And where are you going?" He rephrased his questions.

There was no compelling reason to hold back information like he had, so I told, and soon I was telling him many more things. He learned about my marriage, the Guos, Jun'an, my letter, and then the *chinglou*, and never once interrupted. Before we realized, it was already late into the night. The fire had burned down a little, and Koko had tucked his tiny head under his left wing on the branch above us and fallen asleep.

"So now I'm finally going home." I lowered my voice as I leaned back against the maple-tree trunk behind us. Yes, I was going home, and at the thought, a familiar knot of anticipation formed in my stomach.

Soon. If I kept up my pace, very soon, I would be able to see them again. I'd be able to hug Baba, cuddle Zhuzhu in my arms, kiss Wei on the forehead, and finally live with my family again. Without really thinking, my hand went to my left wrist, but it was bare. "They even took my bangle from me. It was the only memento I had of my dead mother."

Kaizhen finally spoke. "Perhaps you might get it back someday."

For a moment, I had thought he was just saying it on a whim, but when I saw the seriousness in his eyes, I believed him. "Thank you." I beamed.

Suddenly, he reached over for my hands. My face grew hotter than if I'd stuck it right into a burning hearth. But Kaizhen's eyes lost their softness as they examined my fingers. The scars from Mrs. Guo's horrible *zanzhi* still looked ugly and fresh in the orange firelight. I drew my hands back and tried to sit on them. "These are permanent, I'm afraid," I laughed. "But they don't hurt anymore." Then I snuggled farther into my cloak and turned the other way. "Let's sleep; I'm tired."

Kaizhen said nothing, and I listened to him poking at the fire. Then I must have drifted off. The cold didn't bother us that night, and I slept so comfortably that it felt as though I was in my own bed back home.

▪ ▪ ▪

I had been sure that Koko intended to continue hiding the fact that he was a *jing*, which was why I was pleasantly surprised when he decided to give himself away the very next morning.

We were getting ready to go, and I had asked again where Kaizhen was headed. He pointed toward the sun. "It's much farther than Baihe, where I'm headed, but it's eastward nonetheless," he said as he put out our fire. Actually, Kaizhen might not have been that shocked if Koko hadn't hopped up behind him when he least expected and suddenly spoke in his loud, squeaky voice.

"Then why don't you come with us?"

I laughed as Kaizhen jumped and spun around, dagger in hand. When he saw that it was only Koko, his emerald gaze went from fiercely alert to puzzled and then surprised.

"You're a *jing*," he said.

As the three of us made our way down the road, I looked up at Koko flying over our heads. "So why did you reveal yourself, Koko?"

"Well," he began, flying in quick circles, which often indicated that he was in a good mood, "I figured since we'll be stuck together for a while, I can't very well continue acting dumb. Especially considering how you have such a penchant for getting into trouble."

I did not bother to argue, and turned to Kaizhen. "You don't seem as surprised as I was when I found out Koko was actually a *jing*."

"The Divine Triller of Xuanji, if you don't mind." Koko landed on my head and stomped on it. He still hadn't tired of correcting me whenever he could. "I have my own pride as a *jing* and will not degrade myself by adopting some silly pet name a human gave me. If word got out to other *jing*, I would be a laughingstock for at least a thousand years!"

"But this isn't practical at all," I argued. "Think about it. If you're staying with me, we are going to be around humans a lot . . . and if I used that peculiar title in front of others, it would surely expose your identity, would it not?"

"Fine, I allow you to use that silly name in front of humans."

I rolled my eyes. "Koko, I am not going to bother switching your name around under different circumstances for the sake of your pride." I turned back to Kaizhen. "So where were we?"

"You were asking why I didn't seem surprised to learn Koko's true identity. The truth is I've run into many *jing* on my travels. I have since learned to be wary of living beings in general, human or animal, which was why I did not reveal where I was headed until just now," he said. "And besides, the bird's eyes betray him. They belong to a creature more intelligent than one with a simple bird brain."

"True as it may be," Koko huffed, "I won't have you demeaning my lesser kinfolk."

I couldn't help the smile spreading across my face. My chest felt light and bubbly, and I walked as though there were springs attached to my feet. I had a new traveling companion, had found a lifelong friend in Koko, the Divine Triller of Whatever, and was on my way home. Could things get any better?

DAOLIN VILLAGE

Nearing evening the next day, Koko gave an exuberant tweet in the air above us.

"I see a human settlement not too far ahead."

Although the weather had been pleasantly mild after the awful storm a couple of days ago, it'd still be wonderful to make a stop at a village. "We could spend a night and stock up on food and even some oil for my lantern," I said. Although Kaizhen seemed a little uncertain about the idea, he nodded his consent.

Since joining us on our journey, he had become more comfortable with disclosing information about himself. We learned that he was thirteen, and had come from a far northwestern province. He was the son of a traveling trader who had fallen ill with a rare disease on one of their voyages, so Kaizhen had to travel on his own down to one of the major cities in the east to procure some rare herbs prescribed by their local medicine man.

"Hejian," he said.

"That's a long way away," I gasped. "I think it's almost another fortnight's journey on horse cart from Baihe town."

Kaizhen shrugged nonchalantly. "I'm used to traveling. Been on these roads quite a few times with my father."

"Oh," I nodded. "I was worried that you might be heading farther north. My father says the Jurchens invade our northern borders too often for it to be safe. Hejian is a fine place, though." Talking about other places gave me a fluttering feeling in the stomach. How wonderful it'd be to spend one's life exploring so many new and unknown places far away. As a simple farmer's daughter, the farthest I had been from my own village was only Xiawan. And Xiawan, from the stories I'd heard, was nowhere even nearly as exciting as places like Hejian, one of the biggest cities in the northeast, and the imperial city of Dongjing. Next to Kaizhen, I was like a frog who'd lived its entire life in a well.

Before long, we arrived at a village that, at first glance, did not seem much larger or different from

Huanan. The wooden sign just next to the gates told us that this was Daolin village.

"It would be wonderful if we could stay here for the night," I said. How nice to have a roof over our heads after so many days of sleeping out in the open.

"We'll need to ask permission from the village chief," said Kaizhen.

From just a brief walk around the place, we could tell that this community thrived on farming, for the village was set in a valley, and so had plenty of water needed for irrigation. But because it was winter and planting could not begin until spring, as we wandered the outskirts of the village, we saw that the large square patches of farmland were bare and covered in a thin layer of snow. Like Huanan, the agricultural community earned their keep from livestock and other work during winter.

Most of the huts closer to the outskirts were blacksmithing forges. The work made a lot of noise, but the open furnaces created so much heat that it felt pleasant walking by them. As we moved closer to the main street, huts thinned out into stalls that flanked the barely cleared road, leading to the village center. The numerous wooden stalls sold mainly food, farming tools, livestock, and warm clothing made from animal skins. Although many villagers couldn't help staring at Kaizhen's uncommon appearance, they were pleasant and polite enough not to point it out. I looked at Kaizhen out of the corner of my eye. Although he remained vigilant and careful, he didn't seem bothered by the curious stares. But there was something else. I could be wrong, but something felt slightly amiss in this place.

"Do you notice anything?" I asked in a small voice. Kaizhen turned to me. The look on his face told me that he did, but he wanted me to voice my doubts anyway. I frowned and lowered my voice even more. "The people." All the villagers, or most of those we had seen, looked gaunt and pale. Some even had huge dark circles beneath their eyes. They looked sickly and weak, some more so than others.

"That's some improvement, my girl." Koko landed on my left shoulder and chirped in my ear.

I turned to him. "Is this something we should be worried about?"

"Doesn't look as though this village is starving," said Kaizhen with a shrug. "Probably an outbreak of the common cold or something."

"I don't sense the presence of sickness or disease," said Koko, fluttering around our heads. "But you had better ask around just to be safe."

As we continued along the main street, passing villagers who bustled around purposefully with carts and loads, I allowed myself to be distracted by the calls of hawkers and the glorious smell of all the food on display around us—the familiar fragrance of deep-fried tofu, *tang hulu,* beef tripe noodles . . . and wait, there was something else—an unfamiliar aroma, but absolutely no less mouthwatering.

"What is that delightful smell?" And before Kaizhen could stop me, I drifted off to the side of the road and stopped in front of a stall that sold *chuan* skewers. "I simply must have one of these! What is it?"

The burly hawker behind the stall passed the straw fan he was holding to the elderly lady beside him and beamed at me. "You mustn't be from around here if you've never tasted *shenxian* skewers, little girl. These are made from a delicious local fruit found only in Daolin."

I paid him a copper piece for two skewers and handed one of them to Kaizhen. He nibbled absently at it, and when I finally saw him trying to catch my eye, he directed his gaze toward the hawker. His message was clear: *Ask!*

I glanced over at the man behind the stall. Perhaps due to my initial excitement, I hadn't noticed that he had the same pale, sunken features as the villagers we had seen, and his mother beside him was so skinny and brittle that she looked like a dried ginseng root.

"How do you find it?" the lady asked, sitting us down on a bench beside their stall.

I couldn't tell what fruit this was, but on the skewer, it was juicy, sweet, and savory at the same time. "These taste absolutely heavenly," I said. Then, after swallowing my last bite, I said, "Sir, ma'am, my friend and I are traveling eastward and happened to come upon your village. But we were concerned when we saw how most of the villagers seem to be in low spirits . . ."

"Low spirits?" The hawker's heavy brows came to meet in the center. "I'm afraid I do not quite understand."

"Perhaps that wasn't the best way to describe what I mean . . ." I floundered for a more appropriate phrase.

"They look sick, that's what she means," Kaizhen said with an impatient edge in his voice. I rolled my eyes. I was only trying to be tactful.

This time, the lady nodded. "Oh, I see now," she said, her missing teeth making it a little difficult to distinguish her words. "Well, most of them may appear that way, but I can assure you that there's nothing wrong. As you can see, we may be a small community, but we're not short of anything here. Food and trade is abundant, even in winter! We are a fortunate village, thanks to the blessings of the Shenxian Tree."

Kaizhen and I glanced at each other. Even Koko, though he was being very discreet about it, had stopped hopping around on my shoulder.

"I've never heard of the Shenxian Tree." I voiced everyone's question.

"You children may not have, since you're not from here," the hawker said as he went back behind his grill. "But it happened just ten years ago. As you know, the name *shenxian* means 'deity.' And back then, there had been a particularly severe drought that started in spring, so Daolin was having a difficult time with the cultivation of our fields. But no matter how much our local shaman prayed to the skies for rain, nothing came even once for many moons. There were no crops for harvest that year, and those winter moons had been the hardest that the village has ever been through . . . we were poor, starving, and dying.

"And then, one day, after the ninth and tenth deaths of children in our village, a mysterious tree suddenly appeared overnight on top of a small hill just behind our village. It was the most beautiful tree anyone had ever seen, with a thick golden-brown trunk and leaves that shone like jade under the sun. And that wasn't even the best part." Here the man paused to make a sale, but I couldn't help prodding.

"What's the best part?"

The hawker lifted a batch of his skewers off the grill with a grunt. "The best part was that on each of its golden branches grew dozens of large, shiny, pink fruits that looked like glistening gems."

"At first, we thought they were peaches, but they were this huge." The elderly lady made a round shape with her hands approximately the size of a rock melon. "The fruits were juicy, crunchy, and sweet as honey. And they can be cooked in any way, with anything, to make the most exquisite dishes. In fact, the skewers we sell are made from exactly that."

The man cleared his throat, and then continued. "The magical tree bore fruit all through the winter, and sustained the whole village throughout the entire season. It continues to bear fruit to this very day. The prayers of our shaman had been answered, and the gods had sent us the Shenxian Tree as a sacred gift to save our village from starvation. So after that, the tree was given its name, and has become an object of worship in Daolin."

I nodded. This wasn't much different from the White Lady of Xiawan and our Great Golden Huli Jing. "I suppose there's no reason to worry, then?" I turned to look at Kaizhen, making big puppy eyes. It was too late in the evening to go back out and find a place to camp. Surely one night couldn't hurt?

Kaizhen considered a moment. "I suppose. But we'll need directions to the village chief's house."

▪ ▪ ▪

The village chief, Mr. Sun Bingyu, turned out to be a jolly man in his fifties with a thick, bushy beard and mustache. Though he also had the same slightly pale look, the man seemed to be in higher spirits and better shape than the villagers we had met so far. Having no children of their own, Chief Sun and his wife genuinely seemed to adore guests, and insisted we stay for dinner.

"And if you need a place to stay for the night, it might as well be here," the chief said as he spooned in the steamy lotus root soup, not caring about the droplets of broth that dribbled down his beard. We were all seated at a round dining table just next to the kitchen hearth. I planted my hands on my lap and kept my focus on a crack in the table. The couple was so hospitable they wouldn't allow me to help with the cooking at all. I wasn't used to being served. Koko, in the meantime, had reverted to his normal disguise and was hopping about the table expectantly.

The chief's petite wife, who was now laying out steamed vegetables and a sizzling pot of braised chicken and string beans, straightened up. "Now, eat as much as you want. I don't want you being all reserved and shy over such a plain and simple dinner."

"Oh no, Mrs. Sun, this is more than we could expect," I said. "And I do not feel it is right for us to just stay and give nothing in return. I'm really good with any type of work around the house, so if—"

But the kind lady did not let me finish. "Nonsense, child. As long as you do not live in Daolin, you're a guest, and you shall be treated as such no matter who you are." She filled our ceramic bowls with fragrant white rice. I had to swallow to keep myself from drooling on the table. Rice was truly a godsend after days of living on hard, icy *mantou* buns. Although the food was less lavish than what I had had at the Guos' or the *chinglou*, it was enough to make me give up arguing and pick up my chopsticks.

Satisfied to see us starting on the table of food, Mrs. Sun sat down and continued. "You really should let the chief take you around our village tomorrow. He'll tell you where to get the things you'll need for your travels."

I looked up from my already half-empty bowl. "Could we perhaps visit the Shenxian Tree as well? I would dearly love to see it."

The grown-ups paused, and just as I was beginning to think they were about to say no, the chief's wife said, "Of course you can. It—It really is quite something to behold."

She sounded less enthusiastic about the magical tree than the hawker and old lady had been, but why? Wasn't it common courtesy for travelers to pay homage to a sacred being once they stepped into its territory?

▫   ▫   ▫

"So what do you think about this magic tree?"

Lying on my straw mat, I turned onto my stomach and asked the others, folding my arms under my chin. It was late in the evening, and the couple had already retired to their room, which was also the only room in the small hut. But they had laid out thick straw mats and goatskin rugs for us right next to the warm hearth with its dull embers. Kaizhen was sitting cross-legged on his mat, polishing the blade of his dagger with a piece of cloth dabbed in oil under the flickering light of the lamp that stood between our mats.

"I don't know," he admitted after some time, setting his blade aside. "The closest thing to a magic fruit tree I've heard of are the peach trees of immortality that belong to the goddess Xi Wangmu, the Queen Mother of the West."

"But that's impossible," Koko said. "Those peach trees grow in the orchard of the Queen Mother's celestial palace on Mount Kunlun, which is far beyond the human realm."

"If that's so, do you suppose the Shenxian Tree is a gift to the village from Xi Wangmu, then?" I asked. "Didn't they say the fruits looked like giant peaches?" I'd heard of a magic tree somewhere before . . .

Koko hopped over to the lamp. "Well, we'll find out tomorrow." He put out the flames with a flap of his wings, leaving the room lit only by the silvery moonlight that streamed in through the cracks of the windows.

Listening to the blustery wind outside, I tried to stay awake a little longer, enjoying the sounds of the wind, Kaizhen's rhythmic breathing, and the soothing smell of incense coming from the small altar just by the door.

• 24 •

THE SHENXIAN TREE

I was the first to wake the next day. This was rare, for as early as I usually got up in the mornings, either Kaizhen or Koko was always earlier. But that day, when I opened my eyes, Koko had his small head tucked under his right wing as he perched on the back of a chair, and Kaizhen's eyes were still closed. Those wisps of golden hair looked like ripples on a lake during sunset. And I had never seen such skin, fairer than the finest porcelain; lashes that fanned out like the feathers of a golden siskin; and even the pronounced ridge of his nose . . .

"Are you done staring?"

I gasped and jerked back as Kaizhen opened his eyes. My cheeks felt so hot they stung. A girl who so brazenly allowed her gaze to linger on a man either

268 ▪ Celeste Lim

had no shame or too much nerve. So which one was I? What would Kaizhen think of me now?

He was looking at me without a word. I wished he'd say something, but even worse than his silence was the vague hint of amusement playing at the corners of his lips. "I'm sorry. Just that it's time to wake up." I got to my feet and then tripped on my rug. The couple was stirring in their bedroom, and I should help prepare breakfast, and then we'd visit the magic Shenxian Tree and I could put my embarrassment behind me.

Soon, after a simple breakfast of dough fritters, preserved egg congee, and soy milk, the chief led us through the square toward the back of the village.

"We shall go around to the village shops so that you can procure whatever you need for your travels," said Chief Sun. "But if you should like to stay longer, you're more than welcome as well." The man slapped a beefy hand on Kaizhen's shoulders, sending him reeling. "My wife does so love it whenever we have guests to stay, especially ones so young and beautiful." The couple obviously had a soft spot for children. It was a huge pity they did not have any of their own.

As they did in Huanan, the villagers of Daolin rose early. Though the sun had barely risen, the streets were already filled with people—some running errands on foot with sacks over their shoulders, others with handcarts, slowly trundling along the main street with their wares. Everyone stopped to greet the village chief, and it was easy to see that the burly man was a respected and beloved leader. Truly, other than the fact that people had dark eye bags and tended to be on the scrawny side, this was a perfectly pleasant village.

"I don't understand why you're so worked up over a tree," Koko said softly as he landed on my shoulder.

I shrugged. "I keep getting the feeling I've heard of a similar magical being, but I can't seem to recall exactly what. But I'll probably remember once I see it," I said. "Besides, it's common courtesy for travelers to pay homage to local deities whenever we pass through their territories. It will give our journey blessing."

"Sure it will," Kaizhen muttered.

As soon as we walked out of the village, I saw, standing on the peak of a small hill and surrounded by a low line of wooden fences, the most magnificent thing. The Shenxian Tree was exactly as the villagers had described—thick golden trunk and branches, sparkling green leaves, and on each branch hung the most tempting pink fruit: fat and ripe, just waiting to be plucked and eaten. I couldn't take my eyes off it.

"It's beautiful, isn't it?" There was an unreadable expression on Chief Sun's face as he opened a small gate in the fence to let us in. A vertical board next to the tree showed the words:

"Its name is indeed fitting, don't you think?" I said. Kaizhen, who stood beside me with his hands in his pockets, was gazing up at the tree, which towered more than twenty feet above us. He seemed a little silent this morning. Was he perhaps mad at me from earlier?

I was just about to nudge him when Chief Sun spoke. "Here, try one." He reached for a fruit that hung on the lowest branch.

The fruit was not as heavy as I'd expected, and the surface of its pink skin was as glossy as a persimmon's. It was such a perfect heart shape that I almost couldn't bring myself to eat it. I glanced up at Chief Sun, and when he nodded, I took a whiff of the tantalizingly sweet smell, then bit into it.

It tasted just as good as the old lady had described, or even better—like cool, watered-down honey—and its flesh had a soft fibrous texture. I handed it to Kaizhen. "It's amazing! Try it." But he only took a polite bite from the fruit, saying he didn't much fancy anything overly sweet. Koko, however, wouldn't even taste it.

Why were they acting so weird? I'd understand if Kaizhen was mad at me and refused to eat, but Koko loved fruits!

The chief suggested that we pack a few *shenxian* fruits for our journey, and we thanked him for his kindness. Later on, he gave us directions to certain shops in order to get the things we needed before leaving for his daily village patrol. As we wandered along the main street, I could hold back no more.

"You two are behaving very peculiarly today," I said. "Kaizhen, are you mad at me? And, Koko, I really thought you would've liked the *shenxian* fruit, but you wouldn't even try it."

It was only then that Koko finally spoke.

"That tree is a *jing.*"

I stopped in my tracks. "A *jing*?"

Koko nodded. "You may not have noticed, but being a *jing* myself, I can sense it. The *chi* or aura that the Shenxian Tree emanates belongs to that of a *jing*, not a deity."

Kaizhen folded his arms. "I'm not surprised, but what puzzles me is, what is it doing here?"

I thought for a moment. "Maybe like the Great Golden Huli Jing back in my village, it's just a tutelary spirit that's protecting its territory?"

Kaizhen rolled his eyes.

Koko jumped up and down on my shoulder like he did whenever he was frustrated. "But the *chi* from this one is heavy and negative."

"Which means," Kaizhen continued grimly, "it's on its way to a demon, not a deity. Only *jing* that absorb positive *chi* through doing good deeds can elevate into deities." Kaizhen cast a look at the villagers around them. "That might explain the sickly people. Its fruits are probably poisoning them in some way."

At that, I looked around at the villagers of Daolin. Almost everyone was wearing that pale, gaunt look as though it was a trend.

I punched my palm. "Now I remember!" I led them aside, where we could have more privacy.

We sat down on a patch of grass next to a half-frozen pond.

"I've heard before the tale of a man-eating demon tree called the Renmian Tree," I said. "Its name means 'the Tree with a Human Face.'"

"Now that you've mentioned it, I remember listening to the story from my cage when you told it to Jun'an," said Koko. "You said that it is weak, but is also one of the most cunning of *jing*."

"Yes, and if my guess is right . . . if this really is a Renmian Tree," I continued, "it might be 'farming' the entire village of Daolin as its spiritual food. In that folktale, the Renmian Tree bears tasty fruits in order to tempt humans to eat them, and through this, it is able to absorb their *chi*. Little by little, the humans in the village will grow weaker and weaker until they are depleted of life force. And when the whole village is wiped out, the Renmian Tree will uproot itself and travel in search of another." I shuddered. "It is an evil being, the Renmian Tree."

"Well, it's become quite obvious, hasn't it?" said Kaizhen. "I'd bet all my tails this village has been living under the evil influence of the Renmian Tree this entire time."

"But you have no tail," I couldn't help pointing out.

Kaizhen made an impatient sound. "It's just an expression."

I fished out one of the *shenxian* fruits from my bag and studied it. "So that's why you refused to eat it, Koko," I murmured, then turned to Kaizhen. "Did you know about this, too?"

The boy shrugged. "I just never liked sweet things."

"But I ate a whole fruit; do you think it'd do anything to me?"

Koko shook his head. "Not if it's only one, I believe. The villagers of Daolin have been eating this for years. I'd reckon it's supposed to be a slow death."

"Although I'm almost certain we're quite close to the truth, how are we going to be absolutely sure the Shenxian Tree is an evil *jing* as we suspect?" I asked, stroking my chin like a professional *yamen* detective.

But Kaizhen was looking at me as though I had tofu for brains. "Why do you need to be absolutely sure? Don't tell me you plan to stick around and find out," he said. "Now that we know something suspicious is afoot, it is in our best interest to leave as soon as possible."

I gasped. "Don't tell me you mean to leave an entire village of people to their deaths?"

Kaizhen crossed his arms. "It's none of our business," he said matter-of-factly, then turned to Koko. "Surely you don't approve of this madness she's suggesting?" Koko shrugged his little shoulders. He knew how stubborn I could be, but Kaizhen wasn't finished. "Besides, even if things do turn out as well as we hope, this is still too dangerous for a couple of children and a little bird *jing*."

"But by the time we reveal the Renmian Tree for what it really is, we'll have the entire village on our side," I argued. My conscience simply wouldn't allow me to turn my back on people who have shown us nothing but kindness. Now that I finally had the freedom to make my own decisions, I would stick with them and make them count, no matter how much I hated disagreeing with Kaizhen. After all, he was only worried about our safety.

I gave his sleeve a beseeching tug. "Please, Kaizhen; could you live with yourself if you had knowingly walked out on a dying village without even trying to help?"

Kaizhen rolled his eyes again to tell me that he most certainly could, but seemed to relent nonetheless. "And how do you plan to reveal the tree's identity?"

I played with the ends of my ribbon, trying to recall the details of the lore. "Because the Renmian

Tree feeds on humans, it would actually bleed human blood when hurt. In the folktale, a brave warrior shaman plunged a sword into the tree's trunk and drew blood."

"So we're going to stick something in it and see if it bleeds," Kaizhen concluded, making it sound as though I had suggested we give the Renmian Tree a kiss. I pretended not to catch on.

"Yes, but we can't do it in the morning. The tree is sacred to the villagers, and we don't want to offend them by doing anything that might seem disrespectful." I dropped my voice to a whisper. "I think it's best if we stay another day and do it tonight."

Kaizhen's eyes narrowed. "I really don't like this idea of yours. But if we have to do this, you must promise me to leave everything to the villagers once we've done our part." He laid down his condition, and I nodded so hard it made me dizzy.

▪ ▪ ▪

Chief Sun and his wife were more than happy to have us stay for another night. In fact, the chief's wife was so thrilled that she spent the entire late afternoon in the kitchen preparing a feast.

"I heard from my husband how much you enjoyed the *shenxian* fruit, Jing. So I figured I'd cook some for tonight," she said, laying out a plate of the fruit, diced and fried with minced pork. "I find that it goes really well with meat." Then she turned to Kaizhen. "I know you don't fancy anything too sweet, my boy, so I've cooked it with my special homemade sauce. It creates this tangy flavor that's simply enchanting."

To be honest, the dish smelled absolutely mouth-watering, but I felt differently toward the question-able fruit now. Somehow, it didn't seem as appetizing as it had that morning. Perhaps I could just stick to the side dishes of chicken soup, onion bread, and garlic-fried bamboo shoots for the night. But Kaizhen was politely thanking Mrs. Sun for her efforts and picking up his chopsticks without any hesitation, and I realized that there would be a lot of explaining to do if the kind couple noticed that I had suddenly changed my mind about the fruit in just under a day. So I followed Kaizhen's example and promptly helped myself to the main dish.

It ought to have been wonderful. But to me, it now had a sinister taste. The sweetness of the fruit had somehow developed a sharpness to it that left a peculiar aftertaste in my mouth. Therefore, with every spoonful of the dish, I shoveled in mouthfuls of rice to cover up its taste. Kaizhen, on the other hand, seemed not the least bit perturbed, and ate as though the food did not bother him at all. He even praised Mrs. Sun's cooking when she had asked him whether the dish was to his liking.

That night, right after we had sneaked out of the house to carry out our plan, I threw away all the fruits in the monsoon drain outside the village.

THE RENMIAN TREE

"Remember that our plan is to alert the villagers the moment we verify that it's the Renmian Tree," Koko reminded me again. "Absolutely no sticking around."

"All right, I know," I muttered, trying to keep up with Kaizhen and at the same time maintain my balance on the uneven pathway in the dark. I knew Koko was just worried for our safety, but if I had bothered to count, this was probably no less than the fifth time he was repeating this.

We slunk along the sides of the main road in the village, keeping as much to the shadows as possible. We had stolen out of the chief's house only well after midnight, taking our belongings with us. I pulled Chang Er's cloak tighter around my neck.

How could Kaizhen withstand this weather with so little on?

It was dark, and even darker in the shadows, but the moon provided just enough light for us to make out obstacles in our way. I had a lantern in my hands, but we agreed to light it only at a safe distance, in case anyone should see us. After climbing over the back fences of the village, I lit the lantern before we headed up the hill toward the tree. From a distance, the Shenxian Tree still looked ethereal, even during the night. The moon cast its silvery beam upon it, making it look like a sparkling diamond tree. When we came close enough, I turned to Kaizhen.

"I'll do it." I removed from my hair the fan-shaped hairpin that Chang Er had given me. Kaizhen seemed about to protest, but I had already pressed the handle of the lantern into his hand. This was my idea, so I was going to do this.

He muttered something and held out his dagger. "Use this."

I smiled and took it from him, replacing my hairpin. The flames from our lantern cast a garish orange light upon the tree, and at that moment, somehow, it didn't look so beautiful anymore. I held up the dagger, and with a grunt, stabbed with all my might.

Almost as soon as the blade pierced the surface of the trunk, a shrill, unearthly scream cut through the night. Startled half out of my wits, I jumped back at the same time that Koko gave a warning cry, and when the dagger was wrenched out of the golden bark, dark, rich red blood started oozing from the open wound.

I should've been able to hear the entire village awakening, coming out of their homes and rushing to the back of the village. I should've been able to hear the shouts, the sounds of metal clanging, and rapid footsteps as villagers dashed up the hill toward us, but I didn't, because right before us, the once beautiful Shenxian Tree was shuddering violently, and a horrible, grotesque face was beginning to surface on its trunk.

A pair of eyeballs crawling with veins rolled into the craters that had formed on the bark. A huge slit appeared beneath the eyes, and opened to reveal rows of teeth that looked eerily human. I could only stare, transfixed, at the deformed face on the trunk that was contorted in rage.

This was the true form of the Renmian Tree.

The burly hawker we had met the day before was the first to recover. "Chief Sun, what is happening to the Shenxian Tree?"

It was clear that none of the villagers had ever seen the *jing* in its true form. But before the chief could even respond, the eyeballs of the tree rolled in their sockets and fixed on one person.

"Give me the girl, and I shall spare your village!" the Renmian Tree screeched at the village chief, its leaves rustling fiercely as it shook its branches.

Immediately, the hands belonging to the skewer hawker landed firmly on my shoulders. I froze. Were these hands here to shield me from harm, or to keep me from running away? Chief Sun looked completely dumbstruck, and from how firmly he was gripping his spade and the way his eyes darted between me, the villagers, and then the tree, it was obvious he was torn.

Torn? I wanted to scream. Were they going to sacrifice me after all? To give me away, just like how the Guos, the *baomu*, and my family did? How could they! But just as I was about to begin struggling, the chief spoke.

"No . . ."

His trembling hands, which were gripping the wooden handle of the spade, were turning white from the force.

"No?" the Renmian Tree echoed through its bared teeth. "Do you realize what you are saying to me, beloved chief?"

But it seemed Chief Sun did not need another confirmation.

"Enough! You shall not have the girl!" He cast his spade roughly upon the ground and pointed an accusing finger at the tree. "You promised never to demand another human sacrifice and to continue bearing fruit for the village!"

"Yes, but that was more than ten years ago," the tree drawled. "Surely, after all these years of helping your little community prosper, I'm long overdue for my second serving?"

Second serving? A murmur rippled across the crowd as people whispered and shifted disconcertedly.

"What?" the hawker behind me asked. "Chief Sun, what is this?"

"Yes, what is the Shenxian Tree speaking of? What second serving?"

"The chief knows something . . ."

Then came the screechy voice of the tree. "Yes, your chief has been hiding something from you all this time. Ask him; ask him what he's done."

Chief Sun was about to say something when a scream erupted from the back of the crowd.

"No!"

Everyone turned around to see the chief's wife stumbling through the people, and when she reached her husband, she clung to his arms, tears soaking his sleeves. "No, Bingyu, don't tell them! Don't bring back the past. I have lived each day trying to forget; don't bring it back, please . . ." But the resolve in the tired lines upon her husband's face was clear, and Mrs. Sun could do nothing other than break into hysterical sobs. As though for support, the chief held her close as he lifted his gaze and addressed the entire crowd.

"A few days before the Shenxian Tree first appeared on this hilltop, it had revealed itself to me in the forests where I had been hunting alone. At that time, the village was suffering the worst of the drought . . . there had been no food for almost a fortnight. The tree fed me its fruits and claimed to have been sent by the gods in heaven to save our village from this calamity, which was to last for another whole year. I—I knew there was no way that the village could outlast the drought, so I fell to my knees at its roots and thanked it for coming to save us . . ." Chief Sun swallowed something that seemed to have stuck in his throat. "And this was when the Shenxian Tree said that its help had to come with a price."

Mrs. Sun, who had been reduced to hiccups, let out a howl. "Bingyu, please!" she beseeched him, hardly noticing his trembling arm around her.

A dull pain was spreading across my chest, for I had forgotten to breathe. What could the price be? What sort of sacrifice could cause such pain and sorrow for a man and woman? I glanced over at Kaizhen, who had his arms pinned behind his back by another villager. He was glowering at the chief, his lips pressed into a hard line.

Chief Sun's jaw tightened as he spoke again. "I'm sure everyone still remembers our children. My boy Po, and little Miyu."

The crowd murmured again.

"Yes, of course, died from illness . . . all the children were weak from starving."

"They were so young."

"Yes, only six and three. So tragic . . ."

"But what do Po and Miyu have to do with this, Chief?" someone asked.

There was a pause, and when the chief spoke again, only a crack in his voice betrayed his emotions. "The tree allowed me three days to consider its deal. And in the end, for the sake of the village, I drew a pact with the Shenxian Tree . . . that in exchange for the sacrifice of my two children, it would ensure the survival of Daolin for all time."

The crowd gasped. My hands flew to my mouth.

What did the chief mean? What had he done? Surely he didn't . . .

"But . . . but that's impossible, Chief!" exclaimed the farmer who had been holding Kaizhen, so shocked that he did not realize he had let go. "We buried Po and Miyu in the village cemetery! I lowered their caskets into the ground myself!"

The chief looked away. "The caskets were empty, weighed down with sand. My, my children were—"

"Buried alive under the roots of this tree!" Mrs. Sun screamed as she wrung her hair. "I dug the hole with my own two hands." And the woman gazed at her hands with such hatred, as though seeing the blood of her children on them. "Po . . . he suddenly woke up from his induced sleep and found himself in the pit. But he just lay there, too weak to crawl out. I remember his gaze when he opened his one unburied eye and looked up at me . . . looked up at his own baba and mama. Shoveling. Shoveling soil into his face, all over him, burying him alive!"

Time seemed to have stopped as we listened to this horrific story. Chief Sun and his wife couldn't really have sacrificed their own children. Didn't they love them? How could any parent give up their own child in such a manner? My head started to throb.

How similar we were. Our fates.

We've all been sacrificed for the benefit of others. And in my mind, I saw the faces of Mrs. Guo, Aunt Mei, and even my own father.

But on the other hand, how much grief and guilt this couple had had to bear since then. Yes, Po's and Miyu's fates were sad and undeserved, but did the chief and his wife really have it better? The children were dead, and had perhaps even now been reincarnated into a better life. But their parents still had to live on, and live each day in the painful knowledge of having done such a horrible deed. Sometimes, it seemed, it could be harder for the ones giving up a loved one than the ones being given up.

Perhaps—maybe—that was how Baba felt as well?

"I'm sorry to say that you have been deceived, Chief," said Kaizhen. "A benevolent *jing* would never ask for a human sacrifice."

"Yes!" My voice cracked as I cried. This wicked tree was the cause of all this hurt and sorrow. Well, I wasn't going to let it thrive on people's grief any longer. I would reveal to the chief and his village the demon that it was. "This is a demon, an evil *jing* that you have been worshipping, Chief Sun! Not a deity at all! It's called the Renmian Tree, and it's going to kill the entire village!"

But my revelation only caused some to gasp in astonishment and a few others to raise their eyebrows.

"But that's not true, little girl," the skewer hawker said. "We lived on its fruits and survived the drought for a year. Without it, the entire village would've perished."

"Yes, but don't you understand? It's a trick!" I stomped my feet. They had to understand, they had to! "The Renmian Tree is an incredibly cunning *jing* that absorbs the *chi* of humans by tempting them with its life-absorbing fruits! Haven't you noticed your deteriorating health, all of you, despite having survived the drought? Don't you see what your village has become?"

"A larder of spiritual food for the Renmian Tree," Kaizhen answered for them. "And it's not going to stop until it has sucked the entire community dry of *chi*, and then it will move on to find another village as gullible as yours."

"It's a slow death, but a certain one!" My heart skipped a few beats when the tree finally let out a deep shuddering laugh and spoke.

"Insignificant children . . . do you think it does any good now to reveal the truth to this dying village? It has grown so weak that it will perish whenever I wish it to! Daolin was doomed to die the moment its foolish chief invited me, a Renmian Tree, into his village to become a so-called tutelary spirit."

The tree rolled its eyes back in their sockets as it laughed. This was my chance! I grabbed two lanterns from among the villagers and hurled them at the tree with all my might.

The Renmian Tree must not have expected this at all, for the moment the lanterns crashed into its branches, it let out an earsplitting screech and started to thrash wildly. The fire had caught immediately and its leaves were going up in wild, hungry flames.

"Burn, you evil tree!" I grabbed the urn of lantern oil we had bought and splashed it at the tree. The flames went even higher.

The earth beneath us began to shake as the tree yanked its gigantic roots up from the ground. When the tree stood at its full height, with one side of its leaves on fire, it began to stomp about wildly, thrashing all the time, and that was when everyone started to panic, scream, and run. Then the Renmian Tree suddenly lashed out with one of its branches and seized my right ankle.

"Jing!" Kaizhen yelled as he tried to grab my hands. I screamed and tried to reach out, but we were too late. In a whir of movement, I was dangling upside down from a dangerous height.

"You!" the tree shrieked, shaking me like ragdoll. "Even if I should die, you shall accompany me in death!"

I was going to die. Was everything over? Then I heard a familiar screech and lifted my gaze.

"Koko!" My brave little friend was flying toward me. "Koko, eyes! Aim for the eyes!" I reached upward toward my ankle and, with Kaizhen's dagger, began to hack at the branch that gripped me.

Koko didn't need to be told twice. He zipped straight through the branches of the tree like an arrow and struck the tree directly in its left eye. The tree let out another piercing shriek, blood immediately spurting from its wound, and with a single careless swipe of its branches, it hit Koko.

I cried out as my little friend was knocked almost twenty feet away, and at the same time, the grip around my ankle loosened. I fell to the ground, landing heavily on the side of my head and right shoulder.

My vision blurred, and I could only just make out Kaizhen far away, running toward me, yelling. The

Renmian Tree looked as though it was about to lift its roots and grind me into mush.

My head spun. I couldn't move. I was going to die.

Then there was a raging, thunderous howl. I squinted, and thought I saw, in a blinding burst of emerald flames, Kaizhen transforming into a gigantic five-tailed fox, bright golden as the sun. He dashed across the hill and pounced upon the thrashing tree.

"*Huli jing!*" someone wailed as though the end of the world was near.

Was it my *huli jing*? I squinted harder and my head throbbed even more in protest.

Perhaps I was already dead, and it had come to take me away.

Dimly, I could make out the *jing*, wrestling fiercely with each other; the tree lashed out at the fox, its burning branches swiping. Was the fox hurt? I had to save it. I wanted to help, but my head spun every time I moved a muscle.

Then the fox leaped back and breathed a jet of green fire at the tree.

The tree went up in dancing emerald flames, the smoke from its inferno rising high up into the sky. The fox was coming toward me. It was looking at me with its green eyes. Was this our Great Golden

Huli Jing? It picked me up. My head spun from the pain in my shoulder, but I didn't even have the strength to moan.

I lay on its back. The fur was warm, soft and prickly at the same time. We were flying. I saw clouds around us and felt the wind in my face.

Was I dead?

Maybe. Maybe he was taking me home, to where my spirit belonged. When I woke up, I would be with Mama.

I smiled and slept.

■ 26 ■

THE SIBLING OATH

I stirred to the oddly familiar sound of a rooster's crow. I was in a room.

A small wooden room. With no windows.

Why did the mistress lock me up? What did I do wrong again?

I sat bolt upright. No. I was already free from the Guos, free from the *chinglou*—I ran away. I was on my way home with Koko and Kaizhen. And then there was the village that had been cursed by the evil tree *jing*. Was I still in Daolin? What had happened to the tree?

Wait. There was a fox, wasn't there? I fell, and a fox saved me.

My right shoulder throbbed from a large purple bruise where I had fallen. My head still hurt, too. But I needed to find out if everyone was all right.

The moment I threw off my cape, I realized I had been sleeping on a bed.

A straw bed.

And not just any straw bed. It was mine—my own bed that I used to share with Wei.

Somehow, I was home.

My head spun even more. And I had to lie back down. How exactly did I get here? Surely I'd dreamed the part where the fox took me away? Where were Koko and Kaizhen? I pushed myself back up, and my hand touched something smooth and cold on the bed. I looked down.

Glossy, cold, and black as the night.

It was my mother's jade bangle—the one that was taken from me, the one I thought I had lost forever. But instead of answering questions, the little jewelry raised even more.

▫ ▫ ▫

I ran out from the house and looked up into the sky. From how high the sun was, I knew it was around midday. There was no one in the house, so I pulled on my goatskin boots. As it was in Daolin, winter was a resting period for families in Huanan who farmed for a living, and mine usually went around the village and even down to Baihe town for odd jobs. Most of the time, Baba worked at a black-smith's forge, where he would also fix his farming tools, while the rest of us stayed home, taking up needlework and weaving, pickling food for sale, and caring for the livestock.

Where should I go first? To find Baba? Or my little brothers?

I pulled on my cloak and rounded the bend that led to the backyard. And then I saw Grandmama, cleaning out the coops, with a child I didn't know, a child about Jun'an's age when we first met . . .

I opened my mouth, but only air came out. For so long I had dreamed of coming home, of seeing my beloved family again. And on countless nights, I had imagined what I would say if I ever saw them again. Where were all those words now? Lost in my wheezes. Lost in my tears. Just, lost.

I walked closer.

The boy heard me, perhaps, and turned around. His eyes opened as wide as copper coins. "Holy Huli Jing! Grandmama, is that Jie?"

"Jing!" Grandmama gasped.

Pan ran over and almost tackled me to the ground. He remembered.

He remembered me.

He remembered his *jiejie*.

With a sob, I hugged him back. Oh, how much my little Zhuzhu had grown. He was turning four soon, so different from how he had looked in my arms as a baby.

Grandmama ambled over with her walking stick. I exhaled when I saw the smile on her face. She was happy to see me after all.

Pan prattled on and on. "Finally you came home! I missed you, Jie! How long are you staying?"

A pair of warm hands landed on my shoulders. "Help me into the house, child," said Grandmama as she took my arm.

"Can I go get Baba? Please, please?" Pan pleaded and ran off after Grandmama nodded her consent.

Grandmama sat in her wicker chair as I made her a cup of steaming rice tea. I wiped at my wet eyes. I missed doing this, missed the way she smiled as she sipped the fragrant tea, and also her approving nod whenever I got the temperature just right. Grandmama had lost even more hair. Her wrists looked thinner, and her hands shook a little as she brought the rim of the cup to her shriveled lips. If it had been the old Jing, she would not have noticed such things. All she'd be doing was waiting impatiently for Grandmama to finish her tea and wondering why it always took her so long. But now, I could stand here forever, watching her enjoy the tea I'd made.

Grandmama looked up and seemed to study me closely, squinting. "Dear child, how you've grown," she murmured, as though to herself. Then she reached out her coarse hands and took mine. "How has the Guo family been treating you?"

Something welled up in my chest and got stuck in my throat. Was it time to confess everything? To tell my family all that had happened? That I had, in fact, run away? But I was saved from having to answer my own question, and Grandmama's, when Baba's and Pan's hasty footsteps reached our front door. I turned to see my baba, panting from the run and sweating profusely despite the bitter frost.

"*Tian, ah!* Son," Grandmama exclaimed. "Running like that in this weather? Anyone would've thought you haven't seen Jing in a hundred years. Be sensible and do get dry—"

But before Grandmama could finish, Baba, completely ignoring the nagging, had reached over and pulled me into a firm embrace. He did not have to say anything, for at that moment, I began to cry. And I couldn't stop.

"Baba . . . Baba . . ."

How could I have believed that Baba was a self-ish man? That he had felt good giving me up for those five silver pieces? Look at the way he ran all the way home from work; look at how Baba was hugging me now. Was this the behavior of a man who did not love his daughter?

My tears soaked through my father's sleeves as I bawled to my heart's content. I cried, and screamed, and cried. But Baba kept his arms around me, hugging me tighter and tighter. Look at how much my baba missed me. Look at how painfully and fiercely he missed me. I had been wrong. I was wanted. This was my family.

Finally, I could stop hating.

I had come home.

When Baba released me from his hug, I winced from the pain in my shoulder. He noticed immediately.

"What is wrong, Jing? Are you hurt?"

"I . . . fell down a tree." I avoided Baba's eyes. It was technically the truth; Baba didn't have to know it was a Renmian Tree. It wouldn't do to have him worry about my adventures.

"Let your grandmother have a look at it. I'll get the healing balm," said Baba, and he was about to rush off when Grandmama stopped him.

"For Buddha's sake, Tao, please get dry. You'll catch a terrible cold. Let Pan retrieve the balm."

As Pan and Baba disappeared from the room and Grandmama pulled down the side of my lapel to reveal my right shoulder, I felt like crying again, not from the pain in my wound, but from seeing how Baba fussed over me as anxiously as he used to fuss over Mama.

"Such a terrible bruise . . ." Grandmama shook her head as she took the ointment from Pan. "I never liked it when you climbed trees; what if you broke an arm or a leg?"

I smiled. This was practically nothing compared to the other kinds of pain I knew.

"Ma, how is Jing? Is she hurt anywhere else?" Baba soon came back in with a rag draped over his head. I couldn't bear to see him worrying anymore.

"No, Baba. I feel fine. I only fell on my shoulder, and it's nothing."

As Grandmama gently massaged the soothing balm into my shoulder, I looked around. "Where's everyone else?" I hadn't seen Wei or Aunt Mei anywhere.

"Gege gone; Aunt Mei went to Baihe today!" said Pan.

"Oh, so Wei tagged along, then?" I couldn't wait to see the look on his face when he came home.

Maybe I could hide somewhere and give him a good scare.

There was a long pause, and something turned inside my stomach as the grown-ups exchanged glances. Baba turned away, an unreadable look on his face. It was Grandmama who spoke.

"Wei left for a weeklong field trip with the schoolmaster."

Oh . . . but it didn't matter. I smiled. "I'll get to see him when he gets back anyway."

"Jing," Baba began, but stopped when Aunt Mei came in through the front door, saw me, and dropped the cage of cackling geese she had been carrying.

▪ ▪ ▪

On my journey home, I had imagined a hundred and one scenarios that could entail upon my unexpected return, but none of them could've prepared me for Aunt Mei's reaction when she learned the true reason I returned.

"You ran . . . away?" Her eyes looked as though they could burn me to a crisp.

"I had to, Aunt Mei." I backed away instinctively. "They sold me to a *chinglou*!"

Surely she knew what kind of place that was? But her face contorted into an angry grimace in the flickering light of the oil lamp. "And so you dared to show your face, foolishly thinking that you still have a home here to return to? Don't you know that a daughter who is married is like water that has been splashed out of a bucket?"

It wasn't a question. It was a plain statement.

I understood now. I no longer had a home here. I didn't belong and neither was I welcome. I screamed as Aunt Mei delivered a painful twist to my left ear.

"Now, you listen, and you listen closely! From the instant you were wedded into the Guo family, you belonged to them and they are entitled to do anything they want with you. Whether they treat you like a daughter or a slave is their prerogative! Do you understand?" With every sentence, she gave my ear a rough jerk. "You have no one but yourself to blame for the kind of misfortune you have. If you had prayed to the Golden Huli Jing more fervently for a good marriage, maybe this wouldn't have happened. I will personally escort you back to your in-laws tomorrow."

"No! I won't go back!" I cried. I would rather die.

I was genuinely surprised when Pan ran over and clung to me. "No, Aunt Mei! I want Jiejie to stay. I don't want her gone like Gege!"

I buried my face in his hair. And then, even Baba spoke. "Jie, I don't see why this has to be done. Jing could very well come home and stay. I won't let her return to Xiawan and be treated in such a way."

But Aunt Mei turned and flared at Baba. "Stop siding with her! Do you realize the amount of trouble she'll be getting our family into?" When Baba did not seem swayed, Aunt Mei pointed a quivering finger at him. "So if Wei runs away and comes back knocking at our door, you're going to stand by and let that happen, too? Tao, don't be stupid! What is done cannot be undone, at least not in this fashion. If you—"

My arms loosened around Pan. What did she say? Wasn't Wei out on a field trip?

"Aunt Mei, where is Wei . . . ?"

"You speak only when you are spoken to, child!" she snapped, but I reached out and held her wrist in my hand.

"I want to know what happened to Wei."

"Why, you . . ." Aunt Mei tried to shake my hand off, but my grip was firm.

"Tell me!" I screamed. "What have you done to my brother!"

"Jing! What has become of you?" Baba got in between me and Aunt Mei and held my shoulders. "Please, calm down and we'll tell you everything."

My whole body was trembling, and my next words came out a whisper. I could hardly bear to hear myself say it. "You sold him, didn't you?"

Pause.

"It's not like that—"

"Didn't you?" I screamed. *It's not like that?* Really? He'd used the exact same words when he tried to explain marrying me off to a living hell. And it wasn't like that? Was it really? "What have you done . . . oh, Baba, what have you done?" I let out a sob as I fell to my knees. How could they do to Wei what they'd done to me? How could they put my little brother through the same thing I went through? My sacrifice should have been enough! Why wasn't I worth more than five stupid silvers!

"Jing, we had no other choice." Grandmama finally spoke. "Pan fell very ill the year he turned three, and we did not have enough money for the rare medicinal herbs that he needed to take for six months. The only way was for Wei to be adopted into another family. Wei was the one who offered to go, Jing," Grandmama continued. "The Huang family runs a prominent blacksmithing business but has no sons to bear the family name. They had been very taken with Wei when Baba brought him along during his winter job."

"Jing, I didn't know what else to do . . ." Baba was pleading with me. "Without Wei, Pan would have surely died. He did it for Pan."

I looked down at Pan, who was holding my hand and gazing back at me.

I let go. Lies . . . None of them were telling the truth! How could Wei have offered to be given up? "I shall never forgive what you've done!" I yelled at everyone and ran into the room Wei and I used to share. I slammed my first door.

I had long ago learned not to feel sorry for myself no matter what happened, but I hadn't taught myself not to feel sorry for the ones I loved. My poor Wei. Where was he now? What was he doing? What if his new family didn't truly love him? What if they hurt him? What if they had a *zanzhi*? He would be so lonely and so scared . . .

"Why are you so stupid, Wei!" I clawed at the flattened straws on our bed as I sobbed. My hands swiped at something amid the straw and it flew across the room.

A book.

A simple one with a few rice-paper pages bound together with string. The same kind that Wei used when he went to school . . .

I picked it up and opened it. I recognized my brother's handwriting immediately—his wobbly lines and careless strokes. I traced them slowly with my finger. There were lines being repeated across a few pages, obviously part of an assignment. I didn't know most of the words, but I had learned enough from my short time at the *chinglou* to recognize the simple ones, which was why I abruptly stopped a few pages in.

I saw my name. And Pan's.

There was a character that meant death. And then another that meant sorrow. I didn't understand the rest.

This page wasn't an assignment. And I needed to know what it said.

I hugged Wei's book. I would pay a visit to the shrine tomorrow. Shenpopo or Lian could help me read this.

BABA'S TEARS

I got up before sunrise, just as the sky was turning a lighter shade of navy. I kneeled in front of Mama's mortuary tablet and touched my head to the ground thrice.

It's good to see you again, Mama.

Soon after leaving the house, I passed by our patch of farmland, now bare and covered in snow. I slowed down when our bull came into view, tied to a peach tree on the side of the dirt path, exactly where Pan had told me he'd be. My little brother had named him Mou Mou. When I approached the bulky frame, Mou Mou lifted his head and gazed at me with his dark brown eyes.

Hissing gently, I reached out and touched the long, wrinkly snout. It was slightly wet and had a stale sort of smell. Mou Mou snorted and half closed his eyes. I wasn't sure how I felt, watching this sedate creature lying here without a care in the world. This creature that was bought from the bride price that I had fetched from the Guos. This creature that had, in a few ways, replaced me within my own family. It belonged here even more than I did.

I laughed. My chest constricted so tightly it started to hurt. I let my hands drop to my sides. It was really no use mulling over this, trying to figure out how I was supposed to feel about some bull I had been traded for.

I continued my way toward the shrine, and soon passed by the still quiet village square that would be bustling with activity within the hour. Nothing much had changed. One wouldn't be able to tell the difference between this morning and another morning more than a year ago. It reminded me of a poem I had learned while in Yuegong Lou, written by Li Qingzhao, one of the greatest poets of our dynasty:

> *Everything around me remains unchanged,*
> *but not the people; everything is done,*

> *And yet, tears flow before I can*
> *utter a word of my bitterness.*

Only the dirt path leading to the village square was cleared of snow, and I walked along it, listening to the sounds my shoes made brushing against the sandy dirt. The wooden stalls that flanked the sides of the main street were empty, and I could still identify to whom each one belonged: Peng, the florist; Lu Shang's mother, Da Yeye, who sold the tastiest meat buns; Hun's butcher stall . . .

I made almost an entire round of the village before arriving at a flight of steps that would take me up to the shrine. The logs that lay on top of each other were visible against the whiteness of the snow.

I took care to avoid ice on the wood. Wei and I used to dash up and down these steps. Back then, we didn't care whether we might fall, and even if we did, we'd have just laughed at each other.

Soon, I was at the rickety front gate. The huge brass gong stood on the side where it always had, its center faded from the number of times it had been rung. I picked up the mallet and gently struck the center once, pausing for a moment to listen to the reverberating chime that made me think of ripples spreading out in a pond.

When I entered the main hall, someone was already waiting beside the altar.

"Yue Shenpo." I almost forgot to bow to the sha-maness, who walked up and cupped my cheeks. Was it my imagination, or did Shenpopo's hands feel coarser than they had the last time they'd touched me?

"Silly girl. You no longer live here, but you can still call me Shenpopo, just like all the other children who grew up here," the old lady said with the same smile that always reached her eyes. "My, my . . . you're a young lady now."

And it was only then that I noticed I was no lon-ger shorter than the shamaness, but almost a foot taller. This brought back more than just memories and reminded me of someone else, too.

"Where is Lian?" I glanced around for my best friend. She would've turned fourteen this year. Would Lian still be taller than I was?

"She is due for her shrine maiden initiation next year," said Yue Shenpo. "I have sent her on a pilgrim-age to the goddess Guan Yin's temple on Changbai Mountain to receive her blessings. Her journey will probably take one moon cycle."

Then I wouldn't get to see her . . .

Oh, stop it, you crybaby. You should be happy for her. And besides, she's not the only friend you have. What about Kaizhen and Koko?

I had been so distracted with homecoming that I hadn't even thought about my missing friends. "Shenpopo, have you seen a fair-haired boy around the village by any chance?"

Shenpopo's thin eyebrows came together. "No, I haven't seen any new faces around. Who is this fair-haired boy you speak of? Your husband?"

"No, I came home to visit; he's just a friend who traveled with me." My cheeks grew hot, and I fumbled for Wei's book in my waistband. "Um, Shenpopo, could you please help me read something?"

Shenpopo nodded and took it from me, studying the page I had turned to. I twirled and tugged at the ends of my ribbon. Then she began.

They live in Xiawan.

If I become the son of the Huang family, I can see Jie again. I will find her, and I will get to keep our promise.

Pan's condition is getting worse. Shenpopo said he wouldn't survive the week if his fever is not treated. There is nothing else we can do. It's either me or Pan, and I don't want Pan to die like Mama did. Dying hurts too much. Everyone would cry. I don't want everyone to cry. I'm sure Jie would have done the same thing. She loves Pan so much. Jie would have been proud of me.

I sank to my knees. "Oh, Wei . . ." I curled into a ball on the ground and wept. So part of the reason he left was because of me. He had wanted to leave . . .

Could it have been him? That one time when I had thought I heard my little brother on the streets . . . could it have been him? All this time, he had been in Xiawan . . . How could fate be so cruel?

I cried and pounded the floor till my fists were numb. "Oh, Wei . . . why do you have to be so brave . . . ?"

Shenpopo kneeled and wrapped me in her arms. "In that way, he is like his sister."

It was only a whisper, but I heard it like the ring of a gong.

▪ ▪ ▪

In the afternoon, I made my way over to the blacksmith's forge with Baba's lunch. I had learned to cook well under Auntie San's guidance, and today was the first time I cooked for my family.

When I arrived at the forge, I found Baba working hard in the backyard. He stood just next to the blazing hearth, hammering an ax into shape. The moment he turned his blackened face around and saw me, he immediately put his hammer down and dipped the ax into the cooling tank. It made a sharp, drawn-out hiss.

"Jing."

It was all he could say. He looked so surprised and happy that I wasn't still completely mad at him. My heart ached.

"I . . . I brought lunch. I made it myself."

I looked down and tried not to cry. Why did he have to look so happy? It was just lunch; why did he have to look as though I was giving him the world?

I held out the lunchbox, filled with food he liked, and that was when Baba's face shifted from a big smile to a big frown.

He grabbed my hands and pulled them toward him, his eyes widening at the ugly scars on my fingers. I tried to tug my hands back, but Baba held on to them firmly.

"What is this?" he asked. "How did you get this? Did the *chinglou* do this to you?"

After a pause, I shook my head and gazed at him. "It was Mrs. Guo."

There was a long silence. Baba stroked my fingers so gently, as though afraid that he might still hurt them if he wasn't careful enough—as though they were his wounds. The moment Baba's tears landed on the back of my hands, he fell to his knees in front of me.

"Baba!" So shocked I almost couldn't speak, I tried to pull him up. "Baba, what are you doing?"

"B-Baba is sorry, Jing . . . Sorry for what I have allowed to happen to you and Wei." Before I could stop him, Baba touched his forehead to the ground in a deep kowtow. "Forgive your baba for being a weak and useless man . . ."

I began to cry and pulled at Baba's arm, but he wouldn't budge. "Baba, you mustn't! There is gold beneath a man's knees. You mustn't kneel to your own daughter; it is not right." To see Baba ridden with such guilt that he would stoop to kowtowing to his own daughter broke my heart.

I hugged him. "You mustn't blame yourself, Baba, because I don't, not anymore. And Wei doesn't, either." I took out the book and recited Wei's words. "He wrote this before he left. He wanted to leave, he wanted to save Pan as much as any of us, and he wanted to come to Xiawan." Here, I paused. "So he could be with me."

Baba looked up. "He doesn't even know where you lived. Did he find you?"

I shook my head, and a single tear wet my cheek. "There must be a dozen Guo families in Xiawan, and the city is too big. Fate wasn't on our side."

Baba put his forehead in his hands. "Your mama wouldn't rest in peace should she know of the horrors I have put her children through."

"My mama would be smiling beneath the Nine Springs if she knew of the people we have become through our hardship." Baba had done no wrong. Wei was right. Any of us would have done the same thing for Pan.

Before I could wipe away my baba's tears, he had pulled me into another hug. "Oh, Jing . . . my brave, wonderful daughter."

When we finally broke apart, I held up the lunchbox. "Here, Baba, eat up before it turns cold."

Baba gazed for a long time at his food, as though it were gold pieces rather than simple rice, peanut and tofu broth, and fried vegetables. "It's . . . really great to have you back, Jing," he said, gently rubbing the side of my cheek before picking up his chopsticks.

It might have been winter, but my heart felt as though it was blooming like an ocean of flowers in spring. One mustn't forget that parents who asked for forgiveness from children were as rare as children who talked back to parents. Which was why, right there, sitting next to my baba as he ate the lunch I prepared, I felt sure that, at that moment, I had to be the happiest girl in the whole world.

▪ ▪ ▪

We were sent to bed early that evening. Pan fell asleep after my second story about the time I met the White Lady Baigu, but it was still too early for me, so when I heard hushed voices coming through the door, I crept toward it. The flickering lamplight streamed through the crack under the door. The number of different voices told me that Baba, Aunt Mei, and Grandmama were all there.

Pan's loud snores disrupted my eavesdropping, but after pushing the door open just a smidgen, I could hear better, and even see a part of Baba's back. I could just barely see the side of Aunt Mei's face, but not Grandmama's. Baba had his head down, as though studying something on the table. Then Grandmama spoke.

"What you are looking at, my son, is a letter of divorce. The village teacher read it to us earlier today."

My heart missed a beat. Did this mean that I could now stay here? How wonderful to be finally free of the Guos forever.

But Grandmama did not sound happy. "The letter states that the reason for divorce is that the Guo family would not tolerate having a runaway as a daughter-in-law."

Aunt Mei snorted and crossed her arms. "Who would? I daresay that no family in their right minds would ever accept such a disgraceful daughter-in-law! With this divorce letter"—Aunt Mei jabbed forcefully at the paper—"your daughter has as good as wiped out all her future prospects of finding a husband."

"Enough, Mei." Grandmama took the letter before Aunt Mei could ruin it. "Your cutting remarks do little to help at this point."

I bit my lower lip.

Had I no right to run away? No right, even, to save my own life? I was now a reject of society. I clenched my fists and bit down harder on my lip.

But did Baba see me as one? Did it matter that everyone else did if Baba didn't?

I took a deep breath. *That's right, Jing. Why should you care for the words of someone who does not care about you?* What I truly wanted to know was my baba's thoughts. I clasped my hands together and held my breath as Grandmama continued.

"Therefore, in compensation for an undesirable bride, it says that the Guo family has the right to demand from the Li family . . ." Grandmama paused here, as though exhausted. "A return of the bride price—the *pinjin* that they paid for her."

At this, Aunt Mei flared up again. "It's five silver pieces, Tao!" she hissed at Baba. "How are we ever going to have enough to scrape through this winter? You tell me that! And all because of her, our family now has an extra mouth that we shouldn't have the responsibility to feed in the first place!"

"Jie!" Baba stood up, casting the piece of paper to the ground. "I won't have you speak in such a manner! Jing is my daughter and always will be. If I have to give an arm and a leg to raise her, I will. The only reason I even agreed to her marriage in the first place was because I had managed to convince myself that she would be going off to live a better life. But now that I know what the Guos are like, I am not the least bit sorry that Jing has been divorced. By the gods, even if they had wanted her back, I wouldn't have allowed it! Selling my daughter to a *chinglou*? I have a good mind to go all the way down to Xiawan and show the Guo family the back of my shovel!"

"*Tian, ah*, son, I understand your anger, but do keep calm, you'll wake the children." Grandmama tugged at Baba's sleeves, then continued in a low voice. "I'm sure that after the *chinglou* found out about Jing's escape, they would've refused to pay the Guos any money for her, which would be the main reason they are making this ridiculous demand. But do not fret, we'll think of a way somehow . . ."

When Aunt Mei looked as though she was about to say something again, Baba shot her a look so piercing that she shut up immediately.

I crawled back under my rug. No one wanted a dishonorable girl who had the nerve to run away from those to whom she belonged. No one but my baba.

My wonderful, loving baba.

But as much as I loathed admitting it, Aunt Mei was right. By running away and coming back, I did get my family into trouble—in more trouble than they could, or deserved to, handle.

Then it became clear what I must do.

▫ ▫ ▫

When I was certain that the entire house was asleep, I crept out of the bedroom. Lighting the lamp at the center of the table, I smoothed out a blank piece of paper. And then, on it, I left a drawing that I made with one of Wei's ash sticks.

I drew a big square shape, and then over it, a triangle. Under the roof, I drew four faces—one for Baba, one for Pan, another for Grandmama, and the last one with a sour look for Aunt Mei. Outside the house, looking in at the other four, was another face—a happy, smiling face of a girl.

I rubbed the bangle on my wrist. It used to remind me of Mama, but now, looking at it, I realized that it reminded me of Kaizhen as well. Had he not said before that the bangle might return to me someday?

I twisted it off my wrist, kissed it, and placed it on my drawing.

HOME OF THE SPIRIT

An old Chinese saying goes, "As good news never goes beyond the gate, bad news spreads like wildfire."

By morning, almost the entire village would have heard of the misfortune and disgrace that had befallen the Li family. Therefore, as I trudged through the silvery moonlit snow, I grew more certain that I had made the right decision.

If I could not undo the consequences of running away from the *chinglou* and the shame and financial burden it brought upon my family, the least I could do was save Baba from having to feed and care for that extra mouth.

Instead, I would find my friends. I could help Kaizhen find the medicine for his sick father. I would help Koko accumulate good deeds so that he could elevate from a *jing* to a deity. Eventually, when the uproar over my escape died down, I would go back to Xiawan and find Wei.

But will you ever return here?

I stopped on the dirt road and looked back at my home from a distance. The gates that led into Huanan village flapped rigidly in the wind, but other than that, all was still in the night. From my backpack, I fished out Baba's bamboo *dizi*.

I will come back, someday.

Then I lifted the instrument to my lips and played. This was goodbye.

I had only just finished the last line when a harmonizing twitter rang through the air. That sound! I lifted my eyes and saw Koko, my little feathered friend, zooming toward me at top speed.

"Jing!" Koko flew into my arms.

"Oh, Koko, I have been worried about you!"

"And I've searched for you for days," said Koko. "The boy told me I'd find you in Huanan village."

"Kaizhen! Where is he?"

"We went our separate ways. He has continued on his journey to Hejian."

"Oh . . ." My heart sank. Why had Kaizhen left without even stopping to say goodbye? Perhaps he didn't care as much as I had thought.

"So how have you been, my girl?" Koko asked. "What happened after Daolin?"

I scratched the back of my head. "I don't know exactly . . . I fell from the tree, so I might have passed out during the incident. It sounds completely impossible, but I woke up the very next day in my own bed in Huanan. I even dreamed that Kaizhen transformed into the Great Golden Huli Jing, defeated the Renmian Tree, and flew me all the way into the sky! It was all very strange," I said. "But what happened to you?"

Koko chuckled. "What a silly dream! The boy told me that the village chief had dispatched someone to send you home after the incident, as a way to thank you for saving their village. The boy found me and nursed me back to health. By the time I came round, he had already been on the road for a day." Koko hopped onto my shoulders. "When I grew strong enough to fly, he told me to watch over you before we parted ways."

"Did he say anything else?"

Koko shook his head. "If you're worried about the tree, I assume it must've quickly burned to its death, because the boy said the fire eventually grew so great that everyone had to run." He paused, then asked, "So why are you out here? Where are you going?"

I looked away.

Yes. Where did I belong, now that Huanan was no longer home?

I sniffed. *Silly Huli Jing, no more crying.*

Wait. The Huli Jing shrine.

The Great Golden Huli Jing.

Shenpopo.

I tried to remember something the shamaness told me once before:

If we seek the home where our spirit belongs, we will always find refuge, for its doors will always be open even when all others are closed.

My spirit's home—the place I still had yet to find. Where was it, this magical place where I belonged? It wasn't difficult to arrive at a decision. "I have to go to the shrine," I said. "There I can consult the oracle of the Great Golden Huli Jing, and maybe receive guidance on where I should go, what I should do."

Koko nodded. "Then let us go."

My hand absently went to my wrist, where Mama's bangle had been. It would hopefully help Baba with his financial burden this winter.

Of all the times I had had to be given up for others, this time was different. This time, I made the decision. And I was going to be happy with it. I wouldn't let another tear fall.

I did not really notice how far we had come until I had climbed the eighty-ninth step of the shrine.

"This it?" Koko asked, landing on my shoulder. I nodded and, without thinking, reached for the mallet that hung beside the gong's frame. But I stopped before hitting the gong. Ringing it might wake Shenpopo up. And if the Great Golden Huli Jing could miss my prayers just because I didn't ring the gong, it wouldn't be all that great now, would it? I replaced the mallet and pushed the gates open.

The front yard of the shrine was dark; without my lantern, I would surely have tripped on the uneven cobbled path. In the prayer hall, a big red candle burned on either side of the Huli Jing statue on the worship altar. But instead of taking a set of incense as usual, I took a cylindrical bamboo tube that stood next to the incense holder. The tube, only the size of a bottle of wine, was open on one end and held a hundred flat *qian* sticks that were used in a form of fortune-telling called the *Qiu Qian*. Upon the *qian* sticks were numbered inscriptions that contained the deity's answer to the question asked and could be deciphered with the help of a Chinese fortune-telling almanac.

As I kneeled with the *qian* tube in hand, Koko flew up into the rafters so he wouldn't distract me. The flames from the candles cast flickering shadows upon the statue, making it look as though it might be moving. Gazing up at it, I remembered the time when I had thought I saw the statue grin at me while I had been praying.

It must've been the shadows doing the very same trick. I sighed. It was also the same day I had brought my first offering to the guardian. Now that day seemed like so many lifetimes ago. The girl who had kneeled on this very mat and prayed to win a tree-climbing match might have been a completely different person.

It even felt like another life, for that girl had had a home, and knew clearly, without a doubt, where she belonged.

I shook my head. What was I waiting for? Hadn't I come here to seek answers?

I closed my eyes.

Great Golden Huli Jing, I suppose it is our ribbon of Yuan *that has led me back here once again . . . I have come to seek your divine guidance, as I have nowhere else to go, nowhere that I belong. Please, show me the path upon which I am to walk.*

As I repeated my request over and over in my mind like a mantra, I began to shake the cylinder, tipping it at an angle away from myself. The little *qian* sticks made a pleasant clattering sound as they were shaken back and forth in the tube. Gradually, one stick slowly moved up and away from the rest, and when it left the tube altogether, it fell onto the floor with a little tap. I now had my answer from the guardian.

"Thank you, Great Golden—"

I dropped the entire tube of sticks.

The Huli Jing statue had blinked its eyes! Both of them!

The loud noise brought rapid footsteps to the hall. Then Shenpopo was standing at the door, panting. She squinted at me. "Jing? Is that you, my child?"

"Yes, Shenpopo, it is," I replied, my hand still on my chest. "I—I'm sorry to have startled you out of bed. It's just that . . ."

Wait. Was it even a good idea to tell her what I'd just seen?

"Oh . . . well, no need to be sorry, love," said Shenpopo, quickly recovering from the surprise. She walked over and sat down on the prayer mat beside me, smoothing out the folds of her simple white robe. "What I'm concerned about is—what brings you back to this place at such an hour?"

I sat up straighter. And then I told Shenpopo everything.

"So now I do not know where to go." I twirled my sash around my fingers. "It was only when I remembered your words to me that I came. When I think of how big the world is, and yet there isn't a place where I belong . . ."

Don't cry, silly Jing. You made that choice, remember?

Shenpopo braided and rebraided my hair. "And you think that perhaps this place will give you a sense of belonging because of your *yuan* with the Great Golden Huli Jing?"

"Well . . . not really, I suppose." If even my own home did not make me feel like I belonged, how could I expect to feel more at home anywhere else? It didn't make sense . . . And all of a sudden, I felt strangely alone—alone, but not lonely. I was independent, a separate and distinct entity from everything and everyone around me. I had felt the same way when I left Xiawan's gates, as though I did not belong anywhere, or to anyone . . . and yet, somehow, I wasn't sad at all. I was peaceful, because

I finally understood that I belonged to only one thing—myself.

"Shenpopo . . ." My hands were shaking. "Maybe all along, I have been searching for the wrong thing. I've always thought I needed to find a place that would make me feel like I belonged—the home of my spirit, as you had put it. But I think I've realized that a true sense of belonging should come from within myself. From here." I placed a hand over my heart. "So that no matter where I am, no matter where I go, nothing and no one can make me feel different."

It was as though a heavy sack of rice had been lifted off my chest. So this was what Sisi, my little spider friend, had meant about carrying one's home with oneself. This was why Sisi never felt sad wherever she went, because home was in her heart.

She belonged to herself.

Just as I belonged to myself.

Shenpopo placed a hand on my shoulder and lifted my chin. "You're a bright girl, Jing, just like your name. And you are absolutely right, for just as one cannot put a grain of rice back into its husk, what is done cannot be undone. But out of this grain of rice, one could make nourishing food." Shenpopo placed a wrinkled hand on my forehead.

"Ultimately, it is what we make of what is done to us that counts. You have been through unspeakable horrors, and yet you've managed to bloom like a lily, untainted from the mire."

Then she glanced down at all the *qian* sticks, scattered across the floor where I had dropped them. "I see that you had been intending to consult the Huli Jing through *Qiu Qian*. Let's see what the oracle says, shall we?"

I glanced down at the floor as well. My first *qian* stick was indistinguishable from the rest now. "But . . . I dropped the entire *qian* tube by accident. I can no longer tell which stick is mine."

"Do not fret; we could always consult the oracle again," said Shenpopo, gathering up the *qian* sticks and then pressing the full *qian* tube back into my hands. "Here, do the *Qiu Qian* one more time."

I started to shake the *qian* tube, closing my eyes, but this time, I changed my prayer: *Great Golden Huli Jing, I have found my purpose. Let me stay at the shrine to serve you. I shall learn to be a great shaman and healer so that no child will have to suffer from horrid illnesses like my baby brother had.*

When I finally heard a light thud aside from the constant clacking made by the other *qian* sticks, I opened my eyes. Shenpopo picked up the one on the

330 ▪ *Celeste Lim*

ground and gazed at the little inscriptions on it. "It doesn't look too good, but we'll only know for sure after we've consulted the manual. Come along."

With my heart in my throat, I got up and followed Shenpopo to her desk, where the shamaness brought out a thick red book and started flipping through the pages.

"Hmm . . . oh . . ."

I wished Shenpopo would hurry up. I felt as though my seat was burning my bottom. The crease that was deepening in between Shenpopo's gray eyebrows did not ease the tightness in my stomach at all, and I jumped when she finally spoke.

"What will you do if the oracle says no?"

My mouth hung open, but no words came out. Shenpopo had a point. What if the oracle didn't agree that this was where I should be? But I wanted to stay.

But do you want it enough?

I fidgeted with my sash. Yes, and somehow, I had to convince Shenpopo to take me in. "I . . . I want to stay here, Shenpopo."

"And you're insisting, even if the results of the oracle advises otherwise?"

I nodded. "I want to make this decision for myself and not because of the oracle. But only if you will have me, of course," I added, dipping my chin. I didn't have to listen to the oracle, but I did respect Shenpopo's wishes. If she couldn't take me in, then I would travel the world with Koko and find Kaizhen, which was equally tempting.

Shenpopo's face broke into a smile. "You will make a fine apprentice." She wrapped my cold hands in her warm ones. "Remember, in order to be spiritual mediums and not lose ourselves, we must realize that although the fates of humans are up to the gods, the decisions in life are still up to us. Strength of character is never with those who blindly follow. You need to be able to make your own choices and walk your own path."

Feeling Shenpopo's hands firmly enveloping mine, the overwrought feeling in my stomach unwound. Something new was about to unfold in my life—a different chapter, a road I picked for myself. And it was then that I remembered the promise I had made in my prayer to the Great Golden Huli Jing while I was trapped in the *chinglou.*

If I come home, I will forever devote myself to you.

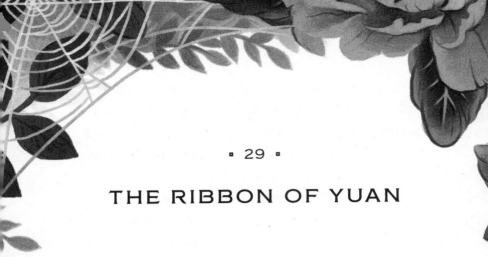

- 29 -

THE RIBBON OF YUAN

As I had anticipated, there was great commotion down at the village the next day. Baba was looking for me. And sure enough, from the gates of the shrine, Shenpopo and I soon saw Baba and Aunt Mei running up the log steps, Baba taking two at a time and Aunt Mei looking more sullen than usual.

"Yue Shenpo! Have you seen—" Baba was panting in between his words, and then stopped short when he spotted me at the gate. "Jing!"

I had never seen my baba look so happy as he dashed up the last few steps and hugged me.

"Jing, you're here! We were so worried when we found your note! Why did you run away? You don't have to worry about going back to Xiawan anymore. The Guos won't be giving you any more trouble; Baba won't let them."

"No, Baba. I'm not going home." I shook my head, trying my hardest not to cry. "I know I've been divorced. I overheard you and Aunt Mei and Grandmama talking about it. They demanded a return of the five silver pieces. I know our family has barely enough to get by in winter, but I cannot undo what I've done, and I'm ashamed to admit that I do not regret running away from the *chinglou*. But I do feel sorry for the hardship that I have brought upon the family . . . For such a dishonorable daughter, I cannot make Baba suffer all the consequences of my actions. At least you will have one less to care for—"

Before I could finish, Baba reached over and pulled me into a hug. His quivering voice broke my heart.

"Why? Jing, don't think like that. Don't talk like that! You're my daughter, and I already said that I'd do everything I could to raise you—I'd give an arm and a leg; I'd sell that bull we have."

This was the hardest thing I had ever done—insisting on goodbyes was far more difficult than just running away. I broke our embrace and looked up. Baba eyes were red, but mine were, too. "Baba, I really want to be here. I'm not leaving because I'm scared or confused. I know exactly what I want."

334 • *Celeste Lim*

Baba looked at me as though he could not understand what else I could possibly want more than being with my family. "What do you want?"

"I want to become a shamaness, like Shenpopo."

At my words, Aunt Mei could no longer remain silent. "Don't be silly, child! You have some nerve going around begging others to take you in. Stop making trouble for Yue Shenpo! Don't you think you've already caused enough trouble for your own family? Have you no shame?"

I looked at my aunt. With everything that had been going on, I had almost forgotten that she was there. But strangely, her words no longer hurt or frightened me. This surprised me at first, but then I understood why.

From the day I decided to take charge of my own life, I will no longer be influenced by you and your words. I didn't run away because I was scared of you, Aunt Mei, I did it because I love Baba.

I smiled to myself, even as Aunt Mei continued with torrents of harsh words.

"Your baba has already said that you could come home; what more do you want? You ungrateful little—"

"Mei, if you won't stop talking to Jing like that, go home!" Baba bellowed.

Pride swelled in my chest. My baba was standing up for me, again. At length, Shenpopo walked up and placed a hand on Baba's arm.

"I would be happy to have Jing as an apprentice, Mr. Li, for you have raised a fine daughter, one who would make a great shamaness in the future. You should be proud."

Baba had such a look of wistfulness in his eyes that it must have pained him to speak his next words. "Are you certain that this is what you want?"

One could travel the entire land of Song and never find a father who loved his children enough to acknowledge their will rather than bending them to his own. I had the best baba in the world.

I nodded. "Baba, I have learned that my true home is in here." I pressed my hand to my chest. "My heart tells me where I belong."

Baba's shoulders sagged. "And what does it say?"

"My heart lies in my desire to help others," I said. "Baba, the ribbon of Yuan ties me to the shrine, to the Great Golden Huli Jing. I want to be a shamaness and master the art of healing so that no child in our village will have to suffer like Pan did . . ."

With a kind of half sob, Baba pulled me back into his arms. Somehow, I knew now that he would let me have my way. His shoulders were shuddering, and I stroked his back the way Mama used to whenever I was upset. Koko flapped his wings in an encouraging way on one of the branches of the barren trees around us, reminding me of the earliest days in spring when sprouts and blossoms would start popping up on every branch and twig, like how my heart was feeling now.

"Baba, remember that time in spring when we were coming to the shrine and you told me about my name?" I asked. Baba nodded, still hugging me. "Shenpopo had told me on the same day that names will carve a person's destiny. And, well, perhaps mine did. My name is Jing, and maybe this is where I should be. And . . . it's not as though I'm living very far away. We'll get to see each other all the time, won't we?"

Finally, Baba loosened his embrace and looked me squarely in the eye.

"Come back for dinner often," he said. Then, as though remembering something, he reached into his sleeve and produced Mama's bangle. He gently slid my left hand through it and held my hand tight. "And keep this so that Mama can watch over you. Black jade can ward off evil. It will be useful to Huanan's future shamaness."

The smile on his face spread all the way to my own lips.

And from somewhere among the trees, Koko started a song that sounded hauntingly similar to the songs Baba used to play on his *dizi*.

▪ ▪ ▪

Later that same day, as I was sweeping snow from the stone path in the front yard of the shrine, someone else came running up the steps.

"Lu Shang?"

I almost dropped the broom I was holding. My childhood nemesis! Lu Shang was the last person I'd expected to see. What business could he have here?

"You're really back, Huli Jing!" Lu Shang exclaimed as he reached the top of the steps. Then abruptly, he dropped his gaze all the way down to his feet. "I didn't mean to call you that; I just forgot. I guess I'm still too used to—"

"It's all right," I interrupted, no longer holding back my smile. "What brings you here?"

It seemed such a long time ago since Lu Shang had last made fun of me. To be honest, I rather missed our bantering. But somehow, things felt too different now to pick up exactly where we had left off. After all this time, Lu Shang had lost the baby fat around his chin and developed the chiseled features of grown men. His face that had always been filthy from playing in dirt was now dusky and clean-shaven.

"I heard that you've returned, and came to see for myself," he said, still not quite looking into my eyes. "Honestly never thought we'd see you again."

I played with my bangle. "Neither did I."

"Your baba said that Shenpopo has taken you as an apprentice."

"Yes, so I suppose I won't be going anywhere else."

There was a moment of silence. Then it was Shang who spoke.

"I'm glad you're back."

And the curious blush on his face reminded me of the delightful plum blossom buds that we would soon get to see when all this whiteness gave way to color.

· WEAVING
THE CRYSTAL RIBBON ·

"I don't want this to be a history lesson."

This was one of the first things I decided before I began Jing's story. But history on its own has inspired so much of this novel that it is worth a quick note.

Though the characters, incidents, and certain places in the story are purely fictional, the story is set in AD 1102, during the Northern Song dynasty in the Taiyuan province of Medieval China; and much of the detail in the story, such as the practice of *tongyang xi*, traditional rituals, and the invention of paper money, are historically accurate.

Jing's story begins in the second year of Emperor Huizong's reign, one of the last emperors to rule before the Jurchens from the Jin dynasty up north invaded and claimed the northern regions, which included the Taiyuan province where the fictional Huanan village and Xiawan are supposedly located. They also conquered major cities like Hejian, and later even the capital of Kaifeng (then known as

Dongjing), forcing the Song forces to withdraw south to Lin'an. This historical event, later coined "The Jingkang Incident," marked the beginning of the Southern Song dynasty.

Although the magical elements in the story are fictional, that isn't to say that the people in those days didn't believe in such magical creatures and deities; some of the Chinese beliefs, practices, and rituals mentioned in the novel still exist, and certain characters, such as the *huli jing*, spider *jing*, and *baigu jing*, are drawn from classical Chinese literature and compilations such as the *Shanhai Jing*, *Journey to the West*, *Soushen Ji*, and *Liaozhai Zhiyi*.

What I especially hope to bring to attention is the tradition of the *tongyang xi*. Although the Chinese Communist Party (CCP) banned this after its establishment, it is still practiced in rural areas, generally among poorer communities. My *ama* (grandmother) used to tell us many such horror stories, including one about how our great-grandmother bravely fled China during the great famine and came to settle in Malaysia.

At the time I heard this, similar tales appeared in the Chinese books I read and the shows we watched on TV—all stories about how maidens endured and persevered through horrors and injustices, in the end finding balance and contentment. There was, however, none about them breaking free. Which is why I so needed to write about a girl who did.

· ACKNOWLEDGMENTS ·

Before I sat down to think about my acknowledgments, I had wanted to make it oh so witty, funny, and lighthearted. But when I finally made a complete list of these amazing and lovely people I wanted to thank, I only felt like crying. I owe them too, too much.

First, Enid Blyton, thank you for writing books that shaped me into the curious and adventurous person I am today. Without your books, I wouldn't love books.

I owe a ton of thanks to my agent and fairy godmother, Rosemary Stimola, who saw and believed this book in its infancy, and also to Allison Remcheck, for her amazing edits before it was submitted.

A huge thank-you to my Scholastic family, especially my mentor/editor, Andrea Davis Pinkney; my copy editor, Jessica White, who had an encyclopedic mind that spotted all my inconsistencies; Carol Ly for the mind-blowing cover design; and artist Olivia Chin Mueller for the inspiringly accurate cover art. I couldn't in all my life have imagined anything better.

Thank you to all my professors and friends at Manhattanville College and The New School, who were endlessly supportive of me and my writing. I'd like to give a shout-out to Professor Phyllis Shalant, whose class inspired the very first chapters of this book; Professor Jeff Bens, who saw the book through its first draft; and Professor Caron A. Levis, my helpful and inspiring thesis advisor. Also thanks to my beta readers—Cheryl, Aly, and especially Xiao Ming, for telling me apples didn't exist in China back then! And a very special thanks goes to the people who read the very first and worst book I wrote more than ten years ago. Thank you, Ning, Yeeng, and Yen Ping, for telling me that it was good.

Finally, a thank-you to Mum and Dad, without whom this whole dream wouldn't be possible in the first place. Thank you for finally letting me walk my own path. And, Darius, you *sikjik*, for bullying me into mentioning you even though you did nothing, so I'll be an annoying sister and embarrass you here.

And just so I could end on a light note—thanks, Em, for being the sunshine you are.

· ABOUT THE AUTHOR ·

Celeste Lim was born and raised in Malaysia, where she spent the early years of her life envious of the children she read about in English storybooks. Something special happened when she learned to draw from the golden threads of her own heritage, weaving *The Crystal Ribbon*, a story that was inspired by her great-grandmother and a culture that she had once ignored.

A graduate of the MFA in Writing for Children and Young Adults program at The New School, Celeste lives in Queens with her Pomeranian, Hamlet. *The Crystal Ribbon* is her first novel.